THE TARGET

SPECIAL EDITION

LENA HENDRIX

LENA HENDRIX, LLC

Copy editing by James Gallagher, Evident Ink

Proofreading by Laetitia Treseng, Little Tweaks

Cover by Sommer Stein, Perfect Pear Creative Covers

To the Gemmas of the world—you may be broken, battered & scarred, but you are beautiful.

LET'S CONNECT!

When you sign up for my newsletter, you'll stay up to date with new releases, book news, giveaways, and new book recommendations! I promise not to spam you and only email when I have something fun & exciting to share!

Also, When you sign up, you'll also get a FREE copy of Choosing You (a very steamy Chikalu Falls novella)!

Sign up at my website at www.lenahendrix.com

ABOUT THIS BOOK

All I wanted was a break from my small-town life. **Not to be stuck driving across the country with my older brother's gorgeous, infuriating best friend.** Charming, cocky federal agent Scott Dunn is back in my life. And I hate him.

Four years ago, Scotty was the center of every one of my fantasies. He was funny, kind, **and eleven years older than me**—a protector. But one ill-timed confession and he vanished from my life without so much as a goodbye.

Now I've been called to testify against the criminals who kidnapped me, and the gorgeous, infuriating man I tried so hard to forget has been assigned to protect me. I want answers, and he refuses to give them.

But as much as he claims to hate me too, I see the way his eyes linger on my skin. How his hands itch to reach out. He understands me in a way I've never let another man get close enough to know. My scars, physical and emotional, are a constant reminder of the girl I used to be.

A girl I try to forget.

As we travel across the country, the tension and simmering heat become unbearable. He's pushing me outside my comfort zone, while I'm desperately searching for control—until I realize **Scott is more than willing to give it to me.**

Once this is over, I know he'll disappear again. But for now, **he's surrendering his control, and I'm going to take it.**

"I STILL CAN'T BELIEVE you're leaving." I lay across Kate's bed and pouted up at my best friend as she folded a shirt and stuffed it into her already-too-full suitcase. Her wavy brown hair was pulled into a low side ponytail with an enormous emerald silk scrunchie only she could pull off.

I looked at the ends of my own pale blonde strands. As a rebellious, unsupervised teen, I'd dyed it coal black. It was getting longer now that it wasn't so overprocessed, and it was *finally* getting to a length below my shoulders after I'd hacked it to a short, blunt bob in a bathroom mirror four years ago.

"Is Trey still blowing up your phone?" I smirked at Kate. She'd been casually dating a guy from our biology class. When she'd made the decision to leave after college graduation, that had included cutting ties with the poor guy.

"We're parting as friends." She flashed her teeth in an uncomfortable smile. "I think."

"Such a heartbreaker," I teased. "At least in Michigan you'll have your pick of guys. Sexy berry farmer? Yes, please!"

Kate came from a small town in Western Michigan and had told me all about the acres and acres of blueberry farms and the beaches tucked into the coastal dunes of Lake Michigan. It sounded like a dream.

"Fat chance. I'm moving from one small town to another. Only this time everyone already knows me and remembers my very unfortunate phase with bangs."

"Maybe you'll just become an old maid." I laughed at my own joke. Kate was stunning, with thick brunette hair and emerald eyes. I suspected she was the main reason we rarely had to buy our own drinks at the Tabula Rasa, the local bar in Tipp, Montana.

"Hey, kettle. It's me, pot." Kate shot me a smirk as she turned and continued packing the last of her clothes into the suitcase. She tapped a finger against her lip and looked up. "When was the last time you let someone in your pants? Hmm . . . oh, that's right. *Forever*."

I made a face at her. Sometimes having a best friend who knew all about you was a real pain in the ass. She wasn't wrong though. It had been almost a year since I'd dated anyone, and the three sad outings the guy had taken me on had fizzled fast. There was just something unappealing about the immature, flighty guys my age, and they seemed to do *nothing* for me. I was quickly becoming bitter at only twenty-three.

The ruggedly handsome face of Scott Dunn flashed through my mind, and I hated myself for it. I hated that he was still the standard I seemed to set for any man who came after him. Truth was, no one ever came close. When I'd first come to Tipp, Scott had been a US marshal assigned to protect my brother and me—witnesses under federal protection because of the life and choices my two older brothers had made. With an absent mother, I'd been thrust into the fray. Scott had been charming and kind and there for me when I was still healing.

He had been everything.

Until he wasn't.

I chastised myself for even allowing myself to think of him as anything other than who he was—a liar and a coward. Refusing to let him sour my last few minutes with my best friend, I refocused on Kate and how much I was going to miss her.

"Don't forget your granny panties," I teased as she swiped a pair of underwear off the bed. Kate paused midfold and stuck her tongue between her teeth, balled up the underwear, and tossed them in my face.

I laughed, snagging the pair midair and tossing them back to her. I rolled to my back, and a deep sigh whooshed out of me. "I'm just going to miss you so damn much."

I willed the tears away as I focused on a small water spot on her apartment ceiling.

Kate moved the suitcase to the floor and settled on the bed beside me, our shoulders touching. "It's just Michigan, not the other side of the world."

"Are you nervous?" I asked.

Kate shrugged and stared at the ceiling. Kate and I had recently graduated from the small local college a few towns over. May was coming to a close, and soon summer and all its possibilities would stretch out before us.

At first I had used the community college as a way to get out of the daily demands of working on a cattle ranch—a cattle ranch that wasn't *really* a cattle ranch. It was all part of the facade.

The lie.

When I was nineteen, my older brother Evan and I had moved to Redemption Ranch in the middle of nowhere to hide in witness protection. To become completely different people.

I met Kate in class my first semester, and we became inseparable. She was one of the few people who knew about my double life. She never asked questions, but after one too many times of her eyes trailing down my neck and arm, taking in the road map of my scars, I'd finally let her in. She knew everything there was to know about me, and there was a measure of comfort in that.

Now, four short years later, she was leaving me behind.

"I bet your brothers are thrilled you're coming home." I clasped her hand and tucked it under my chin.

"Now that Pop is gone, and my brothers are . . ." Kate rolled her eyes.

I'd heard a thousand stories about her older brothers. Despite the fact she was the baby of the family, she took care of them, having grown up with her aunt after her mom died and her dad got sick.

She looked down at her pile of clothes. "Aunt Tootie could use the help." A small laugh bubbled out from her. "I still can't believe I'm moving in with my elderly aunt. I'm such a loser."

"You are not a loser. You're taking care of your family, like you always do. You've got your whole life to figure out what's next." I couldn't help but feel a tiny pang of jealousy. While I was still under protection, my options were limited. Technically speaking, I was free to do whatever I wanted, but with two slightly overbearing brothers, my options felt stifled. Besides, tugging at the back of my mind was always the threat of someone from my old life finding me. It happened four years ago, and the nagging thought that it could happen again was daunting.

I was safe in Tipp, a town where everyone knew that

Laurel Canyon Ranch wasn't just a working cattle ranch but a cover for witness protection. The whole town looked out for one another, and you got a no-questions-asked second chance in Tipp. That was something I tried desperately to not take for granted.

"Come visit me soon." Kate bumped my shoulder, and her serious mossy-green eyes pinned me in place.

"I will," I lied. "Maybe Sophie and I will make the trip."

Humor danced in her voice as she tried to suppress a laugh. "Just make sure she's the one driving."

I rolled to my side and propped my head on my hand. "What's that supposed to mean? I'm a fantastic driver."

Kate barked the laugh she'd been holding in. "Bullshit. Tell that to the construction sign!"

"Oh my god." I rolled my eyes. "That was *one* time!"

A fit of laughter consumed us both. I laughed so hard I nearly peed my pants thinking about that trip. I rarely left Tipp, but two years ago my friends had convinced me to drive a few hours to an outdoor music festival in Bozeman.

I was driving, and we were laughing and chatting, flying down the interstate. We all needed to pee, so I pulled off the highway onto the ramp for a rest stop. The next thing I knew, a ROAD CLOSED sign came out of *nowhere*. Of course the sign was directly in my path, and there was nothing I could do but blast through it. Wood splintered. The three of us screamed as everything moved in slow motion.

As I steered the car to the shoulder, the *whoop-whoop* of a police cruiser came up behind us. Sophie and Kate could not stop laughing.

When the officer strode up to check on us, my pulse was hammering. I speared them with a glare. I tried to tell the police officer that it was a mistake—that we hadn't known the upcoming rest stop was closed for construction. I explained where we were headed and that I hadn't seen the sign until it was too late.

He studied the three of us quietly, and when he walked back to his cruiser, I was certain I was getting arrested. I was *not* looking forward to explaining that one to Ma Brown, the woman who ran Redemption Ranch with an iron fist. She was generous and kind, but she didn't tolerate bullshit. I was also not looking forward to explaining to my brothers that I'd gotten into yet another little fender bender.

Instead of slapping handcuffs on me and throwing me in the back of his cruiser, the officer brought back a rag and wiped the orange paint that had been transferred from the construction barricade to the windshield. This, of course, sent the two idiots next to me into a fresh fit of giggles.

Relieved I wasn't getting arrested, the sympathetic officer suggested someone else take the wheel, and I had gladly sat in the back seat for the remainder of our trip.

It was one of my favorite memories.

Kate hugged me close, and we both let the fond memory settle between us. We sat quietly for a long while, and I fought tears the whole time, reluctant to leave her embrace.

If my life were my own, if I truly had a say, I probably would go visit Kate. In fact, I knew I would. But that wasn't my life. I would constantly be looking over my shoulder or have Evan and Parker hounding me via text to check in. My brothers could worry and hover unlike anyone I'd ever seen.

Finally I broke the silence between Kate and me. "I think you're right though. I need something . . . *else*. An adventure, maybe." I added quietly, "I feel stuck."

"Well, I am the proud, new owner of a giant, old-ass farmhouse. So there's a room for you whenever you're ready."

We hugged again, and I squeezed her an extra second

before letting my arms fall. I left Kate to finish packing. It was too hard to see her drive away and leave me behind, so I was sure to make my exit before she pulled out.

When I stopped my old truck at the intersection at the edge of town, I paused. Left would take me down the winding country road toward Redemption Ranch, where my small, safe cottage was waiting for me. Right could take me down an entirely different path. I could drive away and start a whole new life—if I wanted to.

With a sigh, I turned left and headed home.

2

GEMMA

SOPH

Kate, you still haven't sent us pictures of the house!

> A gigantic farmhouse is better than a cramped one-bedroom cabin, I can promise you that.

SOPH

Try living with your parents.

KATE

I'll send pics tonight! Pretty sure this place is haunted. Was hoping it was a sexy ghost. No dice.

I SMILED DOWN at the text from Kate. She was a nut. It had been two weeks since she'd driven out of Tipp and headed home. I missed her every day, but the text thread with her, Sophie, and me was enough to ease the lonely ache that had weaseled its way into my chest.

With a quick turn of the wheel, I redirected my truck and barreled down the long gravel driveway. My friend Effie and her fiancé, Josh, were celebrating their adopted son's tenth birthday today, and I had promised to arrive early and help her before the guests arrived. As the brakes of my truck squealed to a stop, I knocked right into the large, decorative rocks that lined the long drive.

"Shit." I scurried out of the truck and used my boot to push the stones back into place. I glanced around, relieved no one had seen me misjudge the distance and how close I was to accidentally plowing right through the decorative edging.

After only two knocks, Effie ripped the door open, the wind causing her natural auburn hair to swirl around her shoulders. Though her eyes were wild, Effie was stunning. Hollywood stunning. Literally.

She was a former Hollywood starlet who'd landed in Tipp in search of a place to lie low and solve the mystery about the father she never knew. In the midst of all that, she'd fallen hard for the town's golden boy and never left.

"Finally!" She grabbed my wrist and pulled me into the foyer and into a hug. "Thank you so much for coming. I'm not ready!"

I glanced over her shoulder at Josh, who smiled down at her and shrugged at me.

"How can I help?"

Effie finally released me. "I need to finish hanging the decorations, but I could use some help getting all the food set up in the kitchen."

"On it, boss." I squeezed her hand and made my way back to their kitchen.

As I passed Josh, he bumped my shoulder. "Thanks, kiddo."

I stifled an eye roll and gave him a flat smile instead. *Kiddo*. I was twenty-three years old and would forever be a child in their eyes. It was infuriating, but deep down I knew he meant no harm.

The kitchen was a wide, open concept that flowed directly into the living room, where Malcolm and a friend were engrossed in a video game.

"Happy birthday, Malcolm!"

His dark head of black curls turned in my direction. His wide smile beamed at me. "Thanks, Gemma! Go—get him. No—"

I laughed as his attention was pulled back to whatever space game he and his friend were playing.

I rounded the large center island. Josh and Effie had a gorgeous home. My palms smoothed over the rich, cool white quartz. Years ago Josh had built his home with his brother and left no luxurious detail behind. Their place was so different from my cramped little cottage, and the island was huge and uncluttered. A grand bay window above the sink opened up to their yard, which stretched on and on until it hit the edge of a small forest. Their home was tucked away. Secluded. Safe.

Envy tugged at me as I pulled open the refrigerator door. Inside it was filled with salads and dips. Appetizer trays and charcuterie. I glanced over my shoulder to see something was already in the oven warming, so I set to work on pulling the serving dishes from the fridge and arranging them on the island.

When I saw the Post-it Note stuck to the top with a drawing of where each item should go, I shook my head and laughed. Effie really wanted everything to be perfect for her kid. Nearby, Effie and Josh were bantering about the place-ment of decorations. Affection and love filled their house, and I ignored the uncomfortable twist that thinking of my own childhood inevitably brought. Most birthdays were forgotten or spent with one of my mother's many faceless companions.

Josh wandered back to the living room, and he and Malcolm chatted as I did my best to follow Effie's drawing. Finally satisfied, I carefully pulled the large sheet cake from the back of the fridge and balanced it on my forearms. The cake was massive, and I didn't have a clue where to put it.

A little panicked, I set it down next to the large chrome sink and popped my head into the living room. "Hey, where does Effie want the cake?"

"Hell if I know." He shrugged and smiled. "She'll rearrange it twenty times before she's happy with it. On the island, maybe?"

I gave him a quick salute before ducking back into the kitchen to stare at the gigantic cake that was definitely *not* going to fit on the island. I carefully considered my options and decided to overrule Effie's very specific drawing, then completely rearranged the food on the island. I set appetizers and little bites in careful arrangements in the center, opting to put the salad and main dishes along the back counter with the plates and silverware. People could snack on the appetizers and when it was time for dinner, make an efficient line around the island for the food.

My palms found my hips, and I nodded in satisfaction. Down the hallway I could hear Evan arrive with my sister-in-law, Val, and their almost four-year-old son, Mateo. In a flash, Mateo zipped down the hall and straight onto Malcolm. The boys groaned dramatically as Malcolm slid off the couch and wrestled my little nephew.

Laughing, I dried my hands on a towel and heard my oldest brother Parker's voice boom down the hallway. He and his wife, Sienna, were living in Bozeman, and I was surprised to hear him. My steps were swift through the corridor as I found my family jammed into the foyer, exchanging hugs and talking over each other.

I squeezed in, giving a brief hug to Evan and Val before Parker tugged me into a firm embrace.

"Hey, Gem." His voice was deep and rough and *so* Parker.

I stifled a laugh. "Hey. It's good to see you." His daughter Molly was balanced on his hip, and I kissed her soft, chubby cheek.

"I didn't realize you'd be in town," Effie said to Sienna. "This is a fantastic surprise!"

Sienna's smile went wider. "That's the best part. We're coming back for good! I have one last semester, and after graduation we're moving home."

My heart soared as Parker grinned down at his wife. They'd moved to Bozeman so Sienna could go to school to be a nurse. Parker and I had a complicated relationship, but over the years, he'd proved to me he wasn't the stoic, angry man I thought he was. He'd made difficult choices, and one of those choices included doing his best to exclude me from the very criminal activities he and Evan had gotten tangled up in.

I absently tugged at the collar of my shirt, pulling it in to make sure my scars were covered. Everyone knew they were there, but I knew that to my brothers, my scars were painful reminders of how their choices had disfigured me and changed our lives forever.

Parker's eyes flicked to my hand and away from my face, and I knew he'd caught the movement. I took a deep breath and clenched my jaw once before smiling widely at the group.

Parker and Sienna were missed, and their returning to Tipp meant that our ragtag family was back together again.

So, of course, that meant I would stay.

THE AFTERNOON SUN was sagging behind the trees as Josh grilled on the back patio. The party had grown to include more people from town and the ranch, along with some of Malcolm's friends. He and his buddies ran around the yard while my brothers stood, staring down at the grill like sentries.

I sat in the small semicircle of women, dividing my attention between little Molly and Mateo as Sienna gushed about her and Parker's move back to Tipp. They'd be house shopping soon. Starting a brand-new adventure. I was happy for her, and for me, that they were coming back. A weird nagging feeling—*Was it jealousy?*—wouldn't leave me alone as she spoke of their grand debate regarding buying something quaint or building something new. Tipp had become my home, but I couldn't help wanting something more.

Escape.

After dinner and presents, the crowd had dwindled down to our inner circle.

"Can we eat some of Miss Irma's pie?" Malcolm's eyes were full of hope as Effie considered his request.

"You ate, like, four hot dogs, plus cake and ice cream. Aren't you stuffed?"

Malcolm's grin widened as he ran a hand down his trim stomach. "My dessert stomach is still hungry."

I laughed and Effie rolled her eyes. "There's more ice cream in the fridge, but please don't make a mess." She shook her head as Malcolm ran off in search of pie and ice cream. "That kid, I swear. He's a bottomless pit."

Only moments later, Malcolm returned, looking glum. Apparently the tub of vanilla ice cream had been left on the counter and was a melty, drippy mess. It got cleaned up quickly, but we all knew Irma's famous apple pie wasn't the same without a scoop or two of vanilla bean ice cream.

"What do you say we head to town for a scoop?" Josh suggested.

Malcolm's eyes went wide, and a grin spread across his face. It was his birthday and a Friday night, so Josh didn't mind going all out for him.

Effie looked between Josh and Malcolm and shrugged. "Let's do it." She twirled her finger in the air to round up the troops.

"I can drive," I offered.

"No!" my family shouted in unison. I rolled my eyes and walked back toward the kitchen.

Un-freaking-believable.

The moms rounded up their kids, while I did the last of the dishes. Everyone was getting ready to head out when Josh opened the door and my heart stopped. Time froze as I stared down the long hallway at the front door.

Standing on the porch with his hand raised, about to knock, was Scott Dunn.

My hands trembled, and the serving platter I was drying clattered onto the kitchen island with a *crack*.

Scott's eyes flew to mine. He stood in worn-in denim and a simple white T-shirt. The sleeves were tight around his biceps, the defined line between his shoulder and triceps on full display. The smooth cotton stretched across his hard chest.

He looked good. Damn good, and I hated him even more for it.

Four years.

Four years and he still had the ability to suck the air from the room. I forced my feet to carry me past the gawking, confused faces of my family as I sailed toward the door.

"Scott," Josh said as I hurried past the two men, gulping the outside air as I tried to breathe. "Come on in. We're about to head to town for some ice cream, but . . ."

"Thanks. Sorry to interrupt. I actually need to talk with Gemma."

The way his mouth moved over my name sent a bolt of electricity up my spine, and I bristled.

"Gem. I need to talk to you." The authority in his tone did nothing to calm the warmth pooling in my stomach. In my loneliest moments, I'd imagined what his voice sounded like. I had wondered if I had forgotten the deep timbre or the way his vowels rolled into one another. Turns out my memory was pretty fucking good, because his deep tone was exactly as I remembered.

Gathering my courage, I willed my voice not to crack. With my back still to him, I turned my head. I wouldn't dare give him the satisfaction of seeing me falter. "I have *nothing* to say to you."

I cranked open the driver's-side door and turned to look over Scott's shoulder. Parker and Evan were standing, fists clenched. I barely shook my head to let them know to stand down, and they understood.

"Gemma." Scott's voice had softened, but the way his hazel eyes bore into me, I had to look away.

He took one tentative step toward me, and in one sentence the whole world fell away. "You've been called."

3

SCOTT

I HAD EXPECTED Gemma's fury. Hoped for it, really. Lord knows I deserved it after the way I up and left four years ago without so much as a goodbye, let alone the explanation she deserved. What I hadn't prepared myself for was the impact of seeing Gemma again.

A day had passed, but I could still feel the hit—square in the chest. The blast of it speared through me, burning straight back to my spine. Her crystal-blue eyes were the same shade as I recalled nearly every night since leaving Montana. I imagined every fleck of silver and the way she could emote with a flick of her eyebrow.

Gemma and her brother Evan had entered witness protection at Redemption Ranch around the same time I had requested a transfer back to Montana. My hometown wasn't far, and over the years of US marshal work, I'd grown tired of not having a place to call my own. I'd craved roots.

Back then, Gemma was recovering from her injuries. She was scared and angry. Adrift. I saw her in the months when she was at her lowest. But she put in the work and embraced her new life at only nineteen. More than a decade older than her, I knew better than to allow myself to think of her as more than a witness I was assigned to protect. Not a siren enchanting me.

But what my head had told me didn't matter. I was drawn to her.

Because you're a prick and you know it.

I swiped a hand over my face. Back then, Gemma had been a kid on the brink of adulthood. She'd had an entire new life ahead of her. A second chance.

But she was all woman now, standing in Ma Brown's office at the main lodge of Redemption Ranch in full-on meltdown mode as the setting sun streamed through the office window and settled over her tensed shoulders. Her brothers, Evan and Parker, stood with their arms crossed over their chests. Fury filled the small office. I couldn't blame them. It was the day after I accidentally crashed a little kid's birthday party and blew up Gemma's life.

Man. That really was shit timing.

"This is a part of the deal. You knew that when you came here." Ma Brown looked over the glasses perched on her nose. Her voice was sympathetic, but facts were facts. Being in witness protection meant that when the US attorney called for your testimony, you provided it.

"I'll go." Evan straightened from the wall and took a step toward Ma.

"They don't want you, Ace." Ma had always had a soft spot for Evan. "It's a miracle anyone found the men responsible, but with them finally in custody, the attorney general isn't letting this one go."

Ma's eyes flicked to me but refocused on Evan. Parker stood still, leaning against the wall and radiating murderous energy.

Parker's eyes never left the floor. "She already gave a statement for the grand jury. We all did."

"Billy Massaro has been indicted," she continued. "Denied bail. This is happening. He refused a plea bargain and is opting to go in front of a jury. My guess is he thinks his hold on the city is tight enough that he can scare a few jurors into a *not guilty* verdict."

"Jesus fucking Christ." Parker was seething, likely because the very men he'd associated with were crawling out of the sewers to wreak havoc on his new life.

Ma held up her hand and Parker stilled. "We will not let that happen. Massaro is at the top, and they're pushing for maximum sentencing, which means Gemma's testimony and victim impact statement are the *only* option."

Ma's eyes softened as she looked at Gemma. "Once you do this, it's over. You'll be free to live a life of *your* choosing, without worry that someone is looking for you."

Gemma tipped her face to the ceiling. Tears threatened the edge of her lower lashes, but she refused to let them fall. I allowed my eyes to travel down the long column of her neck before I diverted my attention away. Parker nailed me with a glare, and the muscles in his jaw worked.

Fuck.

Gemma lifted her head, and I didn't miss the slight tremble in her chin. "We knew this day might come. I'll do what they're asking."

Ma flattened her lips into a firm line and offered a proud nod.

"When do I leave?" Gemma's eyes were glued to the floor.

Ma sighed. "The attorney general will outline the stipulations of your testimony. We'll have more answers then."

Resigned to the fact that Gemma would be providing

her testimony and there wasn't anything they could do about it, the trio filed out of Ma's cramped office. Evan shook my hand as he exited and gave me a solemn nod.

I released a breath and rounded one of the office chairs and plopped down into it. "Well, that went better than expected."

Ma shook her head at me. "It's a shame that poor girl will have to relive her darkest days. The defense attorney will try to rip her to shreds, no doubt. But once it's done, it's done."

I pressed my mouth in a firm line and nodded. I'd been a part of dozens of cases with federal witnesses, and testifying was never easy.

Or safe. Once it became common knowledge that Gemma was speaking out against some of the most dangerous men in the country, she'd become a target. A very lucrative one.

"You remember the deal, right?"

Ma's cool expression gave nothing away. "I'm aware."

"Good." I nodded once and sailed out of her office toward Gemma's cottage.

Where she goes, I go.

IRRITATION ROLLED off me when I realized Gemma wasn't home. Or at Evan's place. Or the boutique in town she loved so much.

It's like the woman wants to get herself killed.

I didn't give a shit if it made me dramatic, but she was in witness protection for a reason. It helped that the entire town of Tipp, Montana, was in on the gambit. At least I knew she had the rest of the town keeping an eye out for people who lingered too long or started asking too many questions.

It was then that it hit me. The most likely place for the residents of Tipp to be on a Saturday night.

When I opened the heavy wooden door to the Rasa, the familiar sounds and smells of our local townie bar nearly pushed me back. The music was good, the beer was cold, and the hospitality was . . . nonexistent. If you weren't one of us, the best you could hope for was the bartender Al's cold shoulder. Most outsiders didn't last five minutes before they got frustrated and headed to a different dive out of town.

It didn't matter I'd been gone four years. As soon as I walked in, I was recognized—inundated with handshakes and friendly slaps on the back.

I spotted Gemma immediately. My eyes narrowed on her as she twirled on the dance floor. Her champagne hair floated around her shoulders, and her hands rose up as though she was lost in the song. She'd always been drawn to music, and I was drawn to her.

It was a problem.

I tamped down the tingle that started in my gut. I had no right to think of her that way.

My heavy feet carried me through the crowd toward the high-top tables at the edge of the dance floor. Evan was perched on a stool with his wife, Val, centered between his knees as they laughed with the group.

After he spotted me, he raised both hands and hollered above the crowd. "Hey! Look who it is! Old Man Dunn's come out to play!"

"Fuck off." With a smile, I flipped him the bird and joined the group at the table. Out of the corner of my eye, I saw Gemma pause before she wrapped an arm around the girl she was next to and left the wood floor.

"Surprised to see you out," I said to Evan and Val. "Kind of an emotional few days."

Val nodded. She was working as an agent now too, and she knew how pivotal it was when a witness was finally called to testify.

Evan seemed less convinced. "She can video record her statement and be done with it. Over in a week." He tipped his beer back and drained it.

My stomach felt hollow. That wasn't at all how this was going to go.

Another familiar face I'd worked with as an agent on the ranch shook my hand. "You're off duty, right?" he asked. "Let's get you a shot. Welcome you back to Tipp in style."

"Ah, come on." Evan barked a laugh. "You know Scotty only ever has two beers. Wouldn't want him to get too wild, right?" Evan bumped my shoulder, and I lifted the corner of my mouth with a nod.

Truth was, I didn't like the man I became when hard alcohol entered the mix. It made it too easy to blur the lines between right and wrong. The hot lance of a painful memory shot through me. My gaze immediately tracked to Gemma, who was posted up at the back bar.

"I'm good," I affirmed. "I'll just get a Coors at the bar."

With a tap on the tabletop, I moved through the crowd straight toward the most intoxicating, and infuriating, woman in the room.

I steeled myself against my inevitable reaction whenever Gemma was near. I moved slowly through the crowd, but my eyes never left her. Her hair was longer now, still her natural pale blonde, but it hung in loose waves just below her shoulders.

I noticed that despite the sticky air in the bar, Gemma's shirt collar rode high on her neck. Her long sleeves were pulled down to her wrists. While most women wore strappy tank tops and low-cut shirts, Gemma kept herself covered. I had a good idea of the scars she hid. Last I'd seen flashes of them, they were red and angry—cutting across her collarbone and snaking all the way down to her wrists.

That woman is a warrior, whether she knows it or not.

Her shoulders and arms were toned beneath her shirt-sleeves, and her waist tapered before flaring out to the curves of her hips.

She was more muscular than I'd recalled, and a little jolt of pride ran through me at the thought of her getting stronger. Able to defend herself.

Gemma's hearty laugh pierced through the crowd. She smiled at the man standing next to her, and heat stirred low in my stomach. I remembered a time when she would look at me like that and we'd share a laugh. Before I realized I had let our innocent flirting go too far. I wanted to punch that guy in the mouth for no other reason than pure, unre-strained jealousy.

But I wouldn't lose control.

I couldn't.

"Ahem." I cleared my throat in the most painfully obvious way possible and ground my teeth together at my own stupidity.

Gemma slowly turned, her long lashes swooping down as she looked me over. Rather than acknowledge my exis-tence, she doubled down her attention on the man signaling for another round.

"Gemma." My voice was gravelly and harsh, making her flinch.

She recovered quickly and only raised an eyebrow at me.

"I need a word," I ground out, wanting to get this over with before I did something stupid, like grab her by the back of the neck and kiss the fuck out of her. I didn't need to feel her lips on mine. I recalled with stunning clarity their softness as she pressed them against my mouth. Instead, I chose a gruff, indifferent approach.

She rolled her eyes and shot a look to her friend. "Soph, I'll be right back. Keep Marcus company, and we'll have another dance." She winked at him and promised, "Next song."

The girl nodded, and Gemma strode off toward the back of the bar down the long hallway that led to the bathrooms. Marcus's eyes tracked her movements, and when his gaze lowered to her ass, I set him right with a hard stare.

Nostrils flared, fists clenched, I was sure I looked like a complete psychopath, but I didn't give a shit. His head reared back slightly, and he swapped his attention to Gemma's friend.

Smart man.

Annoyance filled me as I followed the path Gemma cut through the crowd. I wanted to go back to the carefree banter Gem and I used to have. Back to the days when I was on duty and she couldn't sleep, so we'd spend hours playing gin rummy and talking about nothing.

Even then it had been hard to keep my attraction in check, but I'd known in my soul that Gemma was healing. She needed a friend, not some old dude mooning over her.

Down the darkened hallway, the music faded. Gemma planted her feet wide, leaned against the wall, and crossed her arms over her chest.

"What is it?" Her indignant tone sent my hackles up, and I took a breath through my nose to calm my irritation.

Mistake.

Her scent was earthy and floral, like the juniper trees I'd grown up around and the wildflowers in the meadow behind my mother's house. It filled my lungs and seeped into my blood.

"Gemma, I—"

"Don't call me that."

"What? Your name?" I shot back.

"If you're here—if you're back, and it's your *job* to protect me, then don't talk to me like we're friends." Gemma pointed one long finger in my direction. As her arm reached out, I could see that the jagged scars on the inside of her wrist had faded to a pale pinkish-white. "We are not friends."

I set my jaw. I took one step closer and lowered my voice so only she could hear. "Fine. I'm letting you know that I am here to do my job, and I plan to do it. *Ms. Walker.*"

I'd added a little extra sarcasm to her name to emphasize my point before turning and stomping away from her.

Not one to back down from a fight, it was only four strides before Gemma was pushing past me on the way over to the table with her brother, her shoulder intentionally hitting me as she went by. A growl rumbled in my throat.

Back at the table, I intentionally stood where I didn't have a direct line of sight to the woman who was determined to drive me fucking nuts.

"Get your ass over here." Evan clamped a hand down on my shoulder and pulled me into a hug. "It's been too long, man."

"I hate it has to be under these circumstances, but that's how it goes."

The group nodded and hummed in agreement. Evan tipped back his beer. "You're doing your job. She's in good hands here."

He'd always been a good guy. One of my best friends, and despite his past, we'd managed to have a friendship that was easy and natural. He was the only person from the ranch I had kept in touch with in the past four years. Every few months he'd call the number to the burner phone I'd given him and check in. Every single time I wanted to ask about Gemma, but couldn't.

As Evan and I shot the shit like old times, a sense of *rightness* settled over me. I'd missed the banter and cama-raderie of the friends who lived and worked at Redemption Ranch. There was no place like it.

While I couldn't divulge the details, I filled them in on life on the road tracking and hauling in federal fugitives.

"I give you credit," Val said. "I'm spoiled here at the ranch. I couldn't imagine living motel to motel." She shud-dered dramatically as Evan pulled her closer and planted a kiss on her head.

"That's because you have me to come home to," he joked. I stifled the pang of envy at their affectionate and playful relationship. "Plus, we all know Scotty is a workaholic."

The group scoffed in agreement.

Damn right I am. For good reason too.

For the past four years, I had lived a nomadic, high-risk lifestyle that demanded control and precision. It was exhausting, but worth it.

"Can I get you another round?" The server started piling empty bottles and glasses on her black tray.

My eyes sliced to Gemma, who was on the outskirts of the group. She was actively ignoring me, but her drink was empty, while her friend's was nearly full. I imagined they'd stay for a while longer, dance, and have fun on a Saturday night.

"Nah, we're wrapping up. I think we're all ready to go." Evan told the server and nodded at Gemma.

She went to speak—to argue with him—but instead snapped her mouth shut and let her gaze drop to the table.

A round of handshakes later, the table was nearly cleared out. As Gemma moved to walk away, I sidestepped to block her path. The smooth texture of her shirtsleeve brushed my forearm, and I wished it was her skin I was feeling on mine.

"Good night, *Ms. Walker.*"

Her icy eyes captivated me. "Agent Dunn."

For another round, I stayed at the high-top, scowling at my beer bottle. I hated the way Gemma made me feel, even after the four-year sabbatical I'd forced upon myself. One look and she still made me believe I could stop running. Like I didn't have to have the next seven moves figured out.

I'd given myself four years to forget her, and it was a damn shame, but I knew for the rest of my life, there was no getting over that girl.

4

GEMMA

"AH, FUCK." I set my coffee mug down on the café table with a snap and wiped at my lip.

"Mm-hmm. That's what I thought." My friend Johnny Porter sat across from me with a smug smile as we enjoyed our weekly Monday morning coffee date. The furry sleeves of his black sweater were clearly out of place in June, but I couldn't help but smile at his quirky sense of high-end fashion. At least I wasn't the only person who wore long sleeves in June.

"What?"

He raised a thick, dark eyebrow. "Nothing. All I said was that Scott Dunn certainly made an impression Saturday night. That man turned into quite the snack."

I shrugged, attempting to sound indifferent. "I saw him, I guess."

Johnny pressed his lips into a thin line and tried to hide his smile as he nodded. "Everyone who came into the boutique was talking about how good he looked, and you're telling me you didn't notice?"

I had had four years to grow and cultivate my anger into

neat little rows. That he left without saying goodbye. That I was vulnerable and he humiliated me. That he always figured out my strategy at cards. *Cheating bastard.*

That I couldn't seem to find it in myself to *actually* despise him. That alone was enough to hate him on principle.

I shot Johnny a bland look when he was clearly calling me out on my bullshit. "I—well . . ." I sighed. "Fine. He looked good, okay?"

"Ha!" he laughed and slapped a hand on the table. His silver rings clattered against the wooden top. "I knew it!"

I tossed a napkin in his direction. "You're so annoying."

He pursed his lips at me. "You love me."

I smiled. It was true and he knew it.

Johnny and I had become fast friends, and our friendship had only deepened over the years. He owned the Rebellious Rose, a high-end luxury boutique that should have been completely out of place in our small mountain town. Instead, Johnny masterfully made fashion and skin care accessible to the women in Tipp and its surrounding counties. He could match comfort and function with style. He was also known for being able to procure unbelievably gorgeous lingerie from his aunt in Chikalu Falls. Between the two of them, I suspected every woman in three counties had at least one pair of knock-'em-dead sexy underwear.

I hated myself for the fact that I would love nothing more than to see Scotty's face if I showed up in something lacy and strappy. Then again, that would also mean my scars would be on full display.

I absently tugged my collar closer to my chest.

Across from me, Johnny's eyes went wide. "Incoming."

I held his stare, refusing to look over my shoulder. I could sense Scott before he even made it to the table. The scent of his clean, woodsy aftershave washed over my shoulder, and I willed myself not to suck it into my nose and sigh.

Scott walked up and smoothly turned the open chair beside me and straddled it. He braced his arms on the back of the chair like he had no intention of leaving.

"Hi." He reached out a hand to Johnny. "I'm Scott. We've met, but it's been a long time."

"I remember." Johnny beamed at him and shook his hand.

I glared in Johnny's direction.

Traitor.

"Ms. Walker." A tingle buzzed through me from my scalp to my toes.

"Do you need something? I'm on a date." I gestured toward Johnny, who nearly choked and shot coffee out of his mouth, as he had been midsip. I glared at him again.

Scott laughed. The short, deep rumble made the skin on my forearms prickle and my nipples pebble beneath my shirt.

"So you're following me now? Is that a thing?" I crossed my arms to hide the fact that my body was insanely attracted to his brand of controlled authority.

"Just doing my job."

"Since when is your job stalking and generally annoying?"

His jaw ticced once, and I swallowed past the little thrill it gave me to get under his skin. He unfolded himself from the chair and shook Johnny's hand again. "Johnny." Then he tipped his head to me. "Ms. Walker."

As he walked away, I unabashedly watched how his firm ass moved beneath the denim of his jeans. He couldn't see me, so I figured a little harmless ogling didn't hurt anyone. When my eyes moved back to Johnny, he was staring at me with his arms crossed.

"What?" I sipped my coffee to distract myself from the intensity of his accusing look.

"Kinda bitchy. Don't you think?"

"Who, him? Absolutely." That at least got a smile out of Johnny. "Come on. You know what he did to me. Just because he looks hot as fuck doesn't mean I should forgive him entirely."

Johnny shrugged and looked over his shoulder to watch through the window as Scott crossed the street and walked down the sidewalk. "You're stronger than me, though, girl." He fanned himself as we both stared out the window. "Damn."

∾

SOPH

Spill, Gem. Everyone at the gym was talking about another run-in with Scott Dunn. Why is this the first I'm hearing of this?!

KATE

Oh boy.

SOPH

I saw the way he looked at you at the Rasa.

KATE

Do tell . . .

SOPH

Our girl is holding out on us. He walked into the Rasa like he owned the place and THEN apparently interrupted her coffee with Johnny at Brewed Awakening.

Tell me that's not something.

> It's a small town. It's nothing. He's an asshole.

SOPH

A supremely hot asshole.

> Still. An. Asshole.

KATE

We hate him on principle, remember?

AVOIDING Scott for the rest of the week entirely was nearly impossible, as he'd made it his personal mission to be my shadow. Mostly he left me alone after I'd brushed him off at the coffee shop, but he was always lurking on the fringe. I kept to my normal schedule of running in the morning, then guzzling coffee before heading to work at the retirement home.

I'd earned an associate's degree in general studies from the community college, which just meant I had no clue what I wanted to do with my life. I'd continued taking classes until, one by one, my closest friends finished their degrees, moved on, or decided to move back home, like Kate.

"Is it Monday already?" Ms. Hannah was one of my favorite residents.

I smoothed a hand down her blanket, tucking it in tightly, just as she preferred. "No, Ms. Hannah. I picked up an extra shift this week. It's Sunday—late afternoon."

"Oh, that's nice, dear. Will I see you tomorrow?" The crepey skin around her eyes deepened as she smiled at me.

"You bet. I'm still waiting to hear what happened after John took Clara Mae to the dance."

Ms. Hannah's green eyes narrowed to slits, and I stifled a laugh. "She got what was comin' to her."

God, I loved old people. Some were crabby. Others were sweet, but they all told the best stories. I could live a thousand lifetimes through the stories they told. Mostly I think they liked having someone sit and listen to them reminisce about prom night or trouble they got into or the friendships they cherished. Most of my friends thought it was sad, but having grown up with a detached mother and fending for myself for the majority of my childhood, it was an escape to get lost in their stories for a few hours. I was surrounded by the grandparents I never had. I never even minded when I'd hear the same story for the fifth time.

"I can't wait. I'll see you tomorrow."

"Goodbye, dear. And don't forget what I told you. That mustard color is horrible with your complexion. You're a summer and should wear a plum or raspberry."

I pulled the yellow hem of my vintage, long-sleeved T-shirt and frowned. I'd say the only downside was I found the elderly just as opinionated as the rest of the people in my life. Damn, could they give their unsolicited opinions.

I only smiled and nodded as I said my goodbyes to her and the rest of the staff as I walked to my truck. I caught my reflection in the mirror and couldn't help but see Ms. Hannah's point about my shirt.

I can't order a drink or pick out an outfit without someone chiming in on what they think is best for me.

I cranked the car door open and settled into the worn-in comfort of my truck. With a deep sigh, I closed my eyes.

Just breathe.

The drive back to Redemption went quickly, and I was

relieved to make it another day without a speeding ticket. At this point, I think the local sheriffs knew my truck, and I wasn't worth their time anymore.

After stopping home to clean up and change out of my *horrible* mustard shirt, I decided to enjoy a short hike and then walk to the main lodge for Sunday supper.

The air was sticky, and I looped the sleeves of my shirt around my waist, wearing only a black tank top. On the walk, I could enjoy the breeze on my skin before slipping it back on and buttoning it up to hide my scars. Gravel crunched under my feet as I enjoyed the sounds and smells of life on a cattle ranch. Everything there was open, wild, and free.

Everything I wished I could be.

My skin prickled before I heard the steps behind me and froze. My heart thunked, and I jumped but turned to find Scott walking toward me. I instinctively untied my shirt and held it to my chest.

His steely multihued eyes moved over me. My stomach rolled, as my scars were on full display for him. He'd seen them before, but I was always careful to keep them hidden. My appearance made people uncomfortable, and I hated that fact. I slipped my arms into the sleeves and pulled the shirt closed in front of me.

I thought he might pass me, but he stopped short and stared at me. "Ms. Walker."

My spine straightened. "Agent Dunn. Stalking again, I see."

"It's Sunday. Family dinner. Ma would have my ass if I missed it."

I wanted to smile. Ma Brown hosted family dinner every Sunday. It was an open invitation and a chance for agents, workers, and witnesses alike to kick back and enjoy a home-cooked meal. It shouldn't have worked, but somehow Ma had turned a group of outcasts and misfits into a family.

I loved family dinner, but Scott being back put me on edge. *Just another person to tell me what to do.*

"It's too hot for that shirt." He nodded toward the long-sleeved shirt I was still clutching closed. I held my stare, unwilling to let him boss me around. His eyes held mine, and warmth built. He wasn't wrong, but I was too stubborn to let him know that. I knew it wasn't just the June air that had sweat clinging to my skin. Standing this close to Scott Dunn was like orbiting the sun.

Do not swoon. Don't do it. Do. Not.

After a beat, he shoved a water bottle into my hand. "Drink this." Before I could decline, he stomped away, his boots crunching the gravel as his long strides carried him toward the lodge.

How had he gone from one of my closest friends to such an overbearing asshole? He'd always been focused. In control. But back then it was fun to see him relax around me —cut loose and let go of a little of the rigidity that came with being a federal agent. Back then he was just my friend Scotty.

Granted, my much older friend, whom I harbored a significant crush on . . . but still. We were *friends.*

I slowed my pace to watch him as he walked away. I hated what he had done to me, but I despised the prickly grouch he seemed to have turned into even more. Plus, he had somehow managed to get only hotter in the four years since I'd seen him. A tiny part of me had hoped that his muscles had gotten soft or he'd started balding. At least then maybe my attraction to him might have wavered.

Nope.

Scott Dunn was all strong muscles and masculine

energy. Even the tiny gray hairs that brushed across his temples had heat pooling between my legs.

I clearly have serious daddy issues.

Once I reached the lodge, the delicious smell of dinner had my stomach grumbling. I smiled at the sounds of my found family's conversations tumbling over each other. From what I could hear, my brothers and their families were there, along with some of the agents and cattlemen on the ranch.

Lost in my thoughts of Scott, the walk had taken a while longer than I'd intended. Everyone greeted me and was loading up their plates from the family-style setup on the large kitchen island. I plated my dinner and stopped short in the dining room.

Ma had a large oak table that was big enough to fit everyone, though we were crammed elbow to elbow.

I set my jaw and forced a smile when I found my seat—directly across from Agent Dunn.

STOP STARING AT HER.

I dropped my eyes to my plate. What the hell was wrong with me that I couldn't stop staring at Gemma? Couldn't help but insert myself in her life and find ways to "accidentally on purpose" run into her in town despite the fact agents typically remained on the fringe.

She was right. I am a stalker.

"No more suit and tie." Evan's voice broke through my thoughts, and I chided myself for obsessing over his little sister. He slapped a hand on my back. "It's back to ball-busting ranch work tomorrow."

I shrugged his hand off and shot him a grin. "I can still mend a fence faster than you, asshole."

Ma cleared her throat, and my eyes flew to see her mouth in a firm line and one eyebrow raised at my curse.

I cleared my throat to stifle the laugh. "Sorry, Ma."

She smiled and winked at me, satisfied that I was properly chastised. My own mother was never as motherly as Ma Brown. Sure, she was a tough lady, but she cared deeply about the people she welcomed into her home and onto her land. Gemma used to joke that Ma liked to collect old, broken things and make them right again. In a way, it was the most accurate description possible for Special Agent Dorthea Brown.

She'd created a sense of family in the most unlikely of places.

While my father and his wife were likely on another cruise, the rest of my family was only about a forty-minute drive away. My brothers and stepsister had never left Montana. Maggie would have my ass if she knew I was back home and didn't call. I made a mental note to set aside some time to give her a call or maybe even invite her out to lunch at my brother Hayes's place—Pronghorn Brewery.

Despite having family in the area, the brothers I'd met while working and protecting Redemption Ranch had meant just as much. Evan Walker and I had shared an instant connection with trust, camaraderie, and occasional lighthearted ribbing. I bet he would feel significantly less friendly if he knew what had happened between Gemma and me.

I sneaked a glance in her direction. She was actively avoiding looking across the table at me. That much was painfully obvious. Desire coursed through me as I took in her stunning face and the way she laughed—genuine and often.

I wished I could admit that coming back to the ranch and seeing Gemma was different. That time had changed us both. I wanted to be able to say that she was older and that appreciating the graceful way she carried herself was new.

It wasn't.

I'd always had an undeniable attraction to her.

Four long years of life on the road, tracking down and

bringing in federal fugitives—two in particular—hadn't changed the overwhelming sense of rightness I felt when she was near me.

It was completely fucked-up, and I loathed my lack of self-control.

It didn't matter that at one point Gemma had seen me in a way nobody had before—or since.

It was wrong.

Still, I couldn't stay away. Someone else could have easily taken over the assignment of protecting Gemma for her testimony, but that wasn't the deal I'd made with Ma.

Gemma was my responsibility no matter how difficult being near her became or how much I wished things could be different. Being around her was like poking a tender bruise. It raised my hackles and put me on edge.

When it came down to it, Gemma would be in significant danger during the pretrial proceedings and subsequent court appearance. Being called to testify was a major risk. She would require near twenty-four-hour protection once she left Redemption. Gemma was a witness. Nothing more.

I just had to keep reminding myself of that fact.

THOUGH I'D SURVIVED SITTING across from Gemma at family dinner, it wasn't without effort. Between Gemma's pretending I was invisible and the sidelong glances her brother kept giving me, my nerves were shot.

Every time someone brought us both into a conversation and she continued to actively ignore me, I felt the tether of my control slipping.

Spending my Monday morning obsessing over a woman I could never have was the last thing I needed. There was no shortage of work to be done on the ranch—firewood to be cut, fences to be mended, cattle to be brought to pasture.

"You all right?" Evan's large frame hung partially out the window of a beat-up old farm truck as he rolled to a stop near me.

"Fine. Why?"

"Well, you're beating that fence post like it owes you money, for one thing."

I loosened my grip on the mallet. "Just making sure it's secure before fixing the wire."

Evan pushed the gearshift into park and climbed out. "Sure. Need some help? I saw last week this spot looked weak, so I loaded up with an extra roll of wire."

I glanced down the row of fence. "Figured I'll fix what I can before the herd gets brought over."

Evan moved to help mend the fence. Our routine came back to us—holding and hammering in a post or straightening it out and then wrapping and securing the barbed wire to hold it in place. We worked in companionable silence, and I let the repetitive, physical labor ease my mind.

Evan stopped to hand me a water. "Do you miss it?"

I knew he meant the ranch. My home. "I miss being outside. Seeing the mountains and nothing but open sky."

Evan nodded but stayed silent. He'd grown up in Chicago but had come to love Montana nearly as much as I had.

I was born-and-bred Montanan, and the rugged plains that changed to forests and mountains were as much a part of me as the sweat on my back or the calluses on my hands.

Being an agent for Ma Brown meant the best of both worlds—a sense of rightness and justice while still being able to be a part of the land I loved.

"It's good to have you home."

I drained the rest of my water and tossed the plastic bottle in the back of the truck bed. Evan was a good man. Sure, he had a dark and dangerous past, but he was a good man nonetheless. I wasn't sure he'd feel the same about me if he knew how often his little sister was the star of my private thoughts. I couldn't count the number of times her name was on my lips while my dick was in my hands.

Evan was one of my closest friends, and fantasizing about his little sister wasn't just inappropriate; it was a real dick move.

We were also going to butt heads once he found out that Gemma wasn't going to be able to testify remotely, as he'd assumed. While oftentimes federal witnesses could provide their testimony through streaming or a taped interview, high-profile federal cases were different. The attorney general could force Gemma to testify in person as a stipulation of her status on witness protection. There was very little even Ma Brown could do to change that.

Keeping Gemma safe was the sole reason I'd returned to Montana. I'd found a way to ensure her safety, and as a sick penance for the mistakes I'd made four years ago, her life was in my hands.

6

GEMMA

"NO. ABSOLUTELY FUCKING NOT," Parker's voice boomed in the confines of Ma's small office.

I stared at the floor as the blood whooshed in my ears and muffled the commotion around me.

Evan and Parker were shoulder to shoulder, locked in a standoff with Ma as they argued over each other regarding *my life*. Nothing felt real. Everything was off kilter. The life I'd built here was being overshadowed by the life I'd tried desperately to forget.

I looked up to find Scott staring at me. Having the audacity to look concerned.

Anger bubbled up inside me. I took one step toward him and jabbed an accusatory finger in the air between us. "You did this. Suddenly you show your face around here after *four years* and my entire life is upended!"

He didn't deny it, and it stoked the flames of my anger only higher.

"Gem, I—" Scott took a half step forward before Ma cut him off.

"The attorney general has made a decision. This has

nothing to do with Agent Dunn. You will travel to Chicago, provide your testimony, and give a witness impact statement. I know it's hard, honey, but it must be done. Then you're free."

I couldn't let the weight of her words settle over me. The hiding, the denying my past, it could all be over once I did the most difficult thing I'd ever been asked to do—face the men my brothers had worked with and tell everyone of the horrible things I'd seen. The things they'd done *to me* when I had seen and overheard too much.

My face was hot and my stomach roiled. I took a step back and sank into one of the chairs in Ma's office. The conversation swirled around me as everyone in the room talked about "the plan." Making arrangements and decisions around me, not once asking for my opinion or consent. Their words were muffled as the roar of my thoughts overtook me. Finally, my mind snagged on the word *airplane* and my head whipped up.

"No." Scott was firm and agitated. A tingle tickled my neck at his gruff tone. "Gemma doesn't fly."

I sucked in a breath.

How does he remember that?

I knew I'd shared with him my irrational fear of flying over countless nights of playing gin rummy at the kitchen island. I imagined hundreds of hours had been spent talking while we tallied up our wins in a little notebook. I'd once let my foolish heart imagine what it would be like when that notebook was full of tallies. A lifetime of moments with Scotty Dunn.

Idiot.

"The plan is simple. Gemma is a potential target, so she will be guarded around the clock. Together we'll make our way to Chicago by car. Gemma will be safe. I promise you both." Scott looked between my overprotective brothers, and I watched in horror as they relented to his outrageous plan.

I hated that I secretly loved how Scott stood up for me. But he had broken my heart, and one kind gesture wasn't enough to piece it back together.

No. I had done that work myself. In his absence, I had stitched together the broken heart of a young girl and come out of it a woman who wouldn't let it happen again.

"I don't have a say in any of this?" My voice was small, but it grew as I stood from the chair.

My brothers looked at me with surprise.

Ma folded her arms over her chest, but I caught the slight uptick on the corner of her mouth. "Did you have something to add?"

I swallowed hard. Standing up for myself, taking control of my life, was not something that fit right. Like the wool sweater everyone loved but that you found scratchy and hot every time you wore it.

I steadied my breath and did my best to not let my voice crack over my words. "If we are driving all the way to Chicago, fine. But we're taking my truck." I looked directly at Scott. "And I'm driving."

A smirk lifted on Scott's stupid, gorgeous face as I stormed out of Ma's office—and slammed the door for good measure.

I ran as fast as my legs could carry me across the gravel road and down the long path to my cottage. It wasn't until I crashed through the door and sank to the kitchen floor that I burst into tears.

KATE

I hate this for you.

SOPH

My face looks like a punching bag. I couldn't stop crying.

I'll be fine. I promise.

KATE

What can we do?

Pray for patience so I don't go to jail for punching a federal agent in the face.

SOPH

Please don't go to jail. I'd have to commit a crime and go with you. I'm too cute for that.

I'm not making any promises. I'll text when I'm on the road. Love you.

THE DAYS TICKED BY, anxiously waiting for the attorney general to make a decision about not if, but *when* I was to report to Chicago. It took less than a week, and my life had been completely upended.

Again.

I had said a tearful goodbye to Ms. Hannah and promised her that I would be back to hear how things had finally worked out with her husband, John. Sophie had come over to help me clean, but it was largely unhelpful because she would think about me leaving and burst into tears.

My refrigerator had been cleaned out, and Val had promised she'd open the windows on nicer days so I wouldn't come home to a musty house. That was it. My entire life was temporarily put on hold.

I closed the door behind me but didn't bother with the lock. No one at the ranch would mess with my home before I came back.

If I come back.

Intrusive thoughts had been nagging me all week as I prepared to leave for Chicago to testify against some of the most powerful men in the city. Both Ma Brown and the assistant to the US attorney I'd spoken with on the phone reiterated the danger I could be in while we traveled. I was putting my life at risk in order to live a life at all. To finally be able to let the past go.

When I closed the door, I looked up to see Evan leaning against my waiting truck. I had made sure to say the rest of my goodbyes yesterday. I didn't think I could handle everyone all at once, but Evan was special. I stepped off the porch and into my brother's arms. Evan had saved me when our mother had died. He and Parker had been taken away from our mother by the state when they were children. When she'd had me years later, she'd never bothered to tell them about me. Once she'd died, Evan found out who I was, and that was it. He stepped up to be the big brother I so desperately needed.

It's for his peace of mind too. No more looking over our shoulders.

I squeezed him, and tears stung the back of my eyelids.

"You're a fighter. I knew it when you were sixteen, and I know it now. There's nothing you can't handle."

"I'm scared."

"I know. But Scotty will be with you the whole way. He's the best and knows I'll break his legs if something happens to you."

A laugh escaped me. Evan was ridiculous and overprotective, but he probably meant it. I didn't even want to think about what he'd do if he found out Scott and I had flirted with the line of friendship more than once.

"You're going to be fine," Evan reassured. "This job is his life."

I looked down and away, fighting the anger that bubbled any time I thought too long about Scott and his precious job. "Yeah, I noticed."

As if we'd summoned him from thin air, Scott walked up with a duffel bag slung over his shoulder and a garment bag in the other hand. It was probably a suit that he'd need to wear in court.

Can you even imagine how good he looks in a suit?

My throat had gone dry, and I couldn't convince myself it didn't have to do with the sexy way his white T-shirt stretched across his chest.

I buried my face into Evan's chest and gave him one last squeeze before I stepped back from his hug.

He dipped his chin at me. "Give 'em hell, Gem."

I smiled my bravest smile at him and walked toward the driver's side of my beat-down pickup truck. Scott tossed the duffel in the back seat and carefully hung the suit in the cab of the truck before walking up to my brother.

"I'm trusting you with her life, man. Don't fuck this up." Evan shook Scott's hand and pulled him into a hug.

"I'd give my own for her." A shot of adrenaline raced through me at his words. I knew it was his *literal* job to protect me with my life, but hearing those words tumble from his mouth was intoxicating.

Before I panicked and changed my mind, I climbed into the driver's seat and waited. Moments later, Scott settled in next to me. His earthy woodsmoke scent filled the cab, and I immediately lowered my window to get some fresh air.

One last wave to Evan and I pulled down the gravel path toward the lodge and left him standing in front of my cottage. I clenched my teeth and didn't dare look at Scott.

Do not cry in front of him.

He stayed silent, letting me have my moment. The truck bounced as I pulled past the main lodge. I nearly slammed the brakes but only slowed and stared. Lining the road that led out of the ranch was my family.

Ma and Robbie Brown.

Val and Parker and Sienna.

Josh and his fiancée, Effie.

Staffers and ranch hands.

Even Ray, the resident grump, stood at the edge of the road.

All with their hands across their hearts.

Silent but with love and support in their eyes.

As I slowly drove by, I choked back tears.

"They're with you. All of them." Scott didn't look at me, and I couldn't look at him without being completely overwhelmed by that moment. I had grown up a lonely, scared little girl and had found my family and a home in Montana.

And I drove away.

WATCHING the entire staff of Redemption Ranch, Gemma's whole world, line the driveway as we drove away was brutal. Gemma's chin wobbled as she fought the emotions that undoubtedly rose inside her.

Hell, I even had to clear my throat and swipe a drop of moisture from the corner of my eye. I'd never seen anything like it. Gemma was so loved.

Brave, even if she didn't see it.

She swiped at her eyes and reached past my knee to dig out a napkin from the glove box.

"We can pull over. I can drive."

"I'm fine."

She wasn't, but I wasn't about to argue with her. She needed this moment, so instead of insisting, I shut the hell up.

We had a long trip ahead of us. What should have been a three-hour flight out of Bozeman would now take over twenty. While flying would have given Gemma more time with her family, the longer trip would also give her time to prepare for her upcoming testimony. Lorene Shipman, the

US attorney, and her team had sent a thick packet of questions, directives, and information to help her be more prepared for what was to come.

Agents had been sent ahead of us, mapping out our route and securing lodging that would be off the beaten path and secure. I received daily updates, asked questions, pushed back. No mission had ever been more important than this. Part of me hated that I wasn't the one who was ensuring the scouted locations were safe, but that would mean someone else would be sitting in the cab of Gemma's truck, and that wasn't fucking happening.

Though her hands were planted at ten and two, she drove like a bat out of hell. The old shocks on the truck and the rusty springs in the seat had us both bouncing around the cab. More than once I had to grab the bar on the ceiling to steady myself.

"Slow down." Last thing I needed was worrying about her wrecking this damn truck.

She shot me a sideways glance. "Am I driving or are you?"

I shook my head.

Difficult.

"I'd like to get there in one piece, preferably. Besides, we have to set pace. The agents have to clear the stops and locations *before* we get there. Isn't much use for them if we show up before they can do their jobs."

She rolled her eyes toward the ceiling but eased up on the gas. I scrubbed a hand at the base of my neck, then up over the short crop of my hair.

This is going to be a long-ass trip.

Gemma had been a mess when we'd left Redemption in the rearview, but she'd managed to regain control of her emotions. I knew she must be having a hard time, but she hid it well. It killed me that she acted like everything was fine and not like we were driving across the country for her to face one of the biggest threats of her life.

I studied her profile. So much about her was familiar, yet she'd changed in the four years I'd been gone. Her hair was longer. She was a lot more guarded, especially with me. I fucking hated that I could no longer read her.

"Is there snot on my face?" She was clearly annoyed at my attention, but her eyes stayed fixed on the long stretch of road ahead of her.

"Nope." *Just thinking about how gorgeous you still are.*

She swiped the napkin under her nose anyway, and I let my gaze fall to the window beside me. When was the last time I had been the passenger in a vehicle? Probably never —especially with women. I'd been trained from birth to be the gentleman. Offer to drive. Take control.

While I loved taking care of a woman, the perspective from the passenger seat of Gemma's truck was shifting into a new appeal. Her toned arms were set. Her eyes locked on the road. She was finally not driving like she wanted to run us off the road and was settled into the worn leather of her seat.

To be honest, I was exhausted from having control over every aspect of my life. In my line of work, one slip and it was someone's life at stake. I watched the mountains loom over the Montana landscape and let myself get lost in my own head. The fatigue, mental and physical, from my job is likely why I hadn't looked twice at a woman in years. Secrets and power sound appealing to women at first, but they quickly learn that it also means stretches of time away, *actual* secrets, zero permanence. Even when I had forced myself to talk with someone at a bar, my body had lacked any interest in taking it further.

For a while, I worried my dick was broken, but I reminded myself I had no issues getting rock-hard in the middle of the night. I shifted in my seat, away from Gemma, because she sure as shit was the star in the majority—if not all—of those nightly fantasies.

She haunted me.

"Tell me the plan again." She wasn't asking, and my lip curled in a small smile.

"Short stretches of travel. We need to give the team time to scout everything ahead of us. The US attorney will meet with you at a neutral site—likely a local attorney's office in the city—to prep your testimony and get any additional information they may need. They made their request to the witness security inspector a few days ago. Court date is in about a week."

Too long. Yet, somehow, not long enough to be trapped in the world's most uncomfortable truck with her.

Gemma stayed silent.

"I can drive if you're getting tired."

The last thing I needed was her pissed at me, especially with her shooting me daggers and likely to run us off a cliff because she was still hurt and angry. Though I deserved it. Most days I was more than pissed at myself for how I had let it all go down.

"I'm fine." The tension stretched between us. "Thank you." The softness in her voice caught me off guard.

I couldn't dislodge the gravel from my throat. "Yeah."

I leaned back in my seat and let the world fly past me with Gemma at the helm.

∽

BY LATE AFTERNOON, we'd reached the first checkpoint. The wild forests and mountains of Montana had given way to savage plains. Miles of flatland stretched as far as you could see. A small—but not too small—town was safest, easier to blend in as tourists passing through and not draw undue attention to ourselves.

Familiar with the area, I also knew that this weekend the small town was hosting its annual Wild Bronc Festival. Not practical by any means, it was Ma's idea to forgo a straight shot to Chicago and proceed at a slower pace for Gemma. She'd claimed the extra days would give Gemma the time she needed to prepare her for the emotional toll testifying would undoubtedly bring. Ma had a valid point, and there was a secret, sick part of me that liked knowing Gemma would be spending those extra days with me at her side.

We pulled into town, and I gave Gemma directions to the motel. Her eyes scanned the row of mom-and-pop shops, and a soft smile eased across her lips.

"It's kind of crowded for a small town." We circled the main stretch of town twice before finding a parking space within walking distance of the small motel.

"There's a big event this weekend. The Wild Bronc Fest." I exited the truck and began pulling our bags from the back seat.

"Wild Bronc Fest?" A low, tinkling laughter floated across the bed of the truck. "That is so Montana."

I flashed her a smile. "We do like to stay on brand."

A hit of desire coursed through me. I bent to pretend that I was lacing my boots, but I was actually checking to ensure my service weapon was secure at my ankle. My main gun was tucked behind my waistband, and I was placated knowing I had us covered. I steadied my breath to regain my balance.

Pissed-off Gemma I could handle. I deserved that. Playful Gemma was dangerous. I needed to stay focused.

In control.

GEMMA

EFFIE

Hey, Gem! Group chat so you know we're thinking of you (and so the boys can check in on you).

VAL

Miss you already.

SIENNA

Sending a big hug!

<SIENNA CHANGED the name of the group>
Redemption Syndicate

MA

I do not approve of that group name.

VAL

Ha ha. That's perfect.

CRABBY RAY

Who is this?

EVAN

You got this, kiddo. Be strong.

CRABBY RAY

Is this a spam thing?

EFFIE

Dad, it's us. Not spam.

CRABBY RAY

Siri, take me off of this chat.

EFFIE

I'll help this afternoon, Dad.

PARKER

If you need anything at all, you let me know. I know a guy.

MA

Oh good grief, I'm leaving this chat . . . plausible deniability.

<Ma Brown left chat>

VAL

Show them you're a badass.

EFFIE

Love yoooou!

SIENNA

You're a superstar! We're cheering for you!

I COULD HEAR the low hum of a television through the thin walls of the motel. After checking in, Scott did his own security sweep of my room, and once he was satisfied, he unbolted the doors that connected our two rooms.

"Leave these unlocked."

I didn't respond to his demand but only clicked the door

closed. In truth, I felt safer knowing Scott was just beyond the door. I wanted my space from him and all the feelings he seemed to dredge up, but, really, I was scared.

I looked around the small, tidy motel room. Everything was decorated in traditional western decor—old sepia photographs of sweeping plains and bucking horses. The comforter on the queen-size bed was brown-and-beige chevron. I plopped down on the bed, sprawling across it, and stared at the ceiling. My back was tired from the long car ride, but I was restless. After a few minutes of silent boredom, I walked back toward the door. I let my fingers run through the tassels of the woven yarn art that hung on the wall separating Scott and me.

Moving quietly, I placed my ear against the smooth surface. The voices on the television were indistinct, and I couldn't hear any other movement. Fear trickled through me that perhaps Scott had gone somewhere and left me alone.

"Gemma." The demanding knock at my ear and his voice had me jumping back and stifling a scream.

With a wild heart, I yanked open the door. His short hair was damp, and he'd taken off his shirt to reveal a crisp white tank beneath. My eyes immediately fell to the ink that peeked out from the tops of his shoulders. Tattoos were spread from his pecs, up over his shoulders, and, I assumed, down his back.

I had no idea straitlaced Scotty Dunn had any tattoos, and my lower stomach clenched at this delicious new information.

"What?" My voice was strangled, but I managed to control my breathing.

I looked beyond him into his room to see his shoes were

placed perfectly next to his duffel bag. Nothing seemed out of place, and even the bed was still unrumpled.

"You need to eat." His jaw was set. *Why is he always so indifferent around me? He was the one who'd fucked up, not me.*

Annoyance had me planting a hand on my hip. "And?"

God, how I hated him. Maybe hate was too strong of a word. Based on the way my core went slick when his eyes found mine, *foreplay* was more like it.

He tilted his head at me. "And what do you want?"

Tired from sitting in the truck for half a day and annoyed at the clipped tone he was using with me, I pushed back. Lifting a brow, I folded my arms under my breasts. "I want to check out the Wild Bronc Festival."

His eyes roamed over me, snagging on my chest before quickly flicking away. He turned his back to me but glanced over his shoulder. "Be ready in five minutes."

I hadn't actually thought Scott would let me go to the Wild Bronc Festival when I'd suggested it. Really, I was just being a brat. But a small-town festival that I'd never even heard of? Sign. Me. Up.

A zip of excitement danced through me as I slipped my feet into a pair of sneakers and fluffed my hair. I checked my shirt and buttoned a few more high buttons to ensure I was covered before walking back to the open door between our rooms.

I stepped over the threshold just in time to watch Scott slip on a long-sleeved Henley and pull the sleeves up his forearms. Butterflies erupted in my stomach at the sight of his strong, veiny wrists.

This was really happening. I was about to go out in a small town with Scott by my side.

"You really don't care that we're going?" I asked.

He glanced at me but continued fastening his watch. "No."

My eyes tracked his every movement. "And if I would have said I wanted to order Chinese takeout and watch reruns of *Law and Order*?"

He looked at me then. "Then that's what we would do."

Heat spread fast and tingling across my chest. The freedom of choice was intoxicating as doubts crept into my mind. "What about the crowd? Is this a bad idea? I thought we were in danger."

A slow smirk crossed his face, and my heart nearly stopped. "You've got me."

Every sinful fantasy I'd ever had about Scotty Dunn roared to life, and it was a miracle I was able to stifle the squeal that nearly pushed past my lips. I pressed them in a thin line as he moved toward the door and I followed.

Rather than pushing the issue, I let Scott drive the few miles out of town to the fairgrounds. The sun was fading, but twinkle lights were strewn across the barns and outbuildings. It wasn't nearly as large as the Cedar County Seaside Circus—a ridiculous and ironically named county-wide fair near Tipp. The Wild Bronc Festival was much more quaint and held that special small-town charm only rural places could manage.

We parked in the sea of pickup trucks, and Scott made his way to the passenger side before I could climb out. We wove through the trucks and cars parked in the grass toward the entrance of the festival. When his hand found the small of my back, I stumbled, and his large palm gripped my hip.

God, how I wanted to shift my body closer to his, tucking myself into his side. Instead, I ignored the fact that the pad of his middle finger was touching the sliver of skin between my shirt and the top of my jeans.

Friendly faces greeted us as we filtered through the crowd. Upbeat country music played in the distance, a vaguely familiar beat and laughter randomly echoed above the mass of people. I risked a look up at Scott. His eyes were trained on the people in front of us, always scanning.

I lowered my chin, tilted my head toward him, and whispered, "Are you sure this is okay?"

He only nodded. "We're not alone. Enjoy yourself."

I looked through the clusters of people to see if I could pick out any other agents, but it was impossible. I tugged the collar of my shirt and inadvertently snagged Scott's attention.

"You don't have to hide here. No one knows who you are here. Only me."

No one knows who you are here. Only me.

His weighty words echoed through my mind. I wasn't poor, scarred Gemma. Not sweet, little sister Gemma. Not even that pretty girl with the unfortunate upbringing who probably has mobsters after her.

I was just . . . me. Whoever she was.

For the first time in a while, I exhaled, letting some of the tension evaporate between us. I looked up at Scott again to see that he'd relaxed as well.

"You look old," I teased.

He looked down at me, and his nostril flared once. "I am old."

With a hip check, I bumped into him. A small food truck was parked on the edge of the crowd. "Then go buy me some nachos, old man. Extra jalapeños too."

His jaw ticced, but I could tell he was trying not to smile. "Yes, Ms. Walker."

Fuck. I loved when he called me that.

Bossing around Scotty Dunn was quickly becoming a new favorite pastime. For so long, he'd had control of my thoughts and had inspired ridiculous fantasies of us falling in love and starting a life together despite our age gap and circumstances.

I was such a hopeless idiot.

Anyone with half a brain could see that there was no controlling a man like Scott. But a wicked part of me reveled in the challenge. To flip the script and have him yearn for *me* for once.

I found a picnic table near where the music was playing and waited while Scott fetched my nachos. When he returned, he took the space directly across from me, balancing a tray with my nachos along with a hot dog for him and two drinks.

After he slid the plastic tray toward me, I narrowed my eyes at him. "I am going to eat these in the most unladylike way possible. That's not my fault. It's how nachos are made to be enjoyed." I pointed my finger in his direction as he smirked. "You shut your mouth about it."

"Yes, ma'am." Scott smiled as he bit his hot dog nearly in half, and I smiled back at him. When he turned his attention to the live band, I piled the pickled jalapeños onto a chip overloaded with cheese and stuffed it into my mouth.

His soft laugh caught my attention. "Damn. You weren't kidding."

I balled up my napkin and threw it at him, trying to cover my mouth and laugh without choking. "I told you!" I mumbled around the food. When I finally got my laughter under control and swallowed the food down, he was still smiling at me. When he reached out his hand, I stiffened.

A thumb brushed across my lower lip. "Missed some."

Instead of swiping the cheese from his thumb, he sucked it into his mouth. I couldn't stop staring as a wet sliver of his tongue darted out, and his lips closed around his thumb. My thighs pressed together, and my own mouth dropped open.

Heat snaked up my neck, and I diverted my attention away from the man I was *supposed* to be pissed at. He was still the asshole who'd shattered my heart without so much as an apology—let alone an explanation—but sitting under the string of twinkle lights at a picnic table in the middle of nowhere, my perspective began to shift.

There was something different about Scott. Something more. I couldn't name it, and I damn sure couldn't understand it, but it was there.

He felt it too. I was sure of it.

Scott cleared his throat and stood abruptly. He balled the foil into his hand and swiped the napkins from the table. "Stay here."

I watched him stalk toward a garbage can but didn't miss the appreciative looks and attention his swagger drew. My stomach tightened.

Seriously. How fun was it to be with the sexiest man in the room?

Scott may be totally off-limits, but there was no denying the fact that for the time being, we were stuck with each other.

For the next few hours, I allowed myself to be lost in the experience of the Wild Bronc Festival. I laughed as I failed spectacularly at carnival games while Scott stood nearby, shaking his head at my pitiful attempts to use a stick with a ring tied to the end of a string to set a bottle upright.

When I insisted that he try to ring the bell on a game

called High Striker, he shot me an annoyed look but stepped up to the line anyway. He gripped the long handle of the mallet. He squeezed and twisted his hands, adjusting his grip before he took a wide stance. My eyes ate up every inch of his muscular back. The expanse of his back tapered down to a trim waist. His strong legs spread wide, and I realized I had never truly appreciated how thick his thighs were.

The image of me straddling those thighs, bouncing up and down while I rode his cock, flashed in my mind. I looked away and tried not to let him see the flush of color that spread down my cheeks and across my neck.

Scott shot me one last look over his shoulder before he gripped the mallet, lifted it high, and swung it down on the thick rubber base. The weight shot up faster than my eye could track it, and a loud clang rang out above the crowd.

Cheers erupted behind me as I jumped and clapped. The excitement of the crowd was palpable. Scott shot me a smirk and pointed right at me before handing the heavy mallet back to the carnival worker. My heart thunked. He walked toward me and nodded at the greetings and congratulations from the other spectators.

A laugh bubbled up, and after the carnival worker handed him a stuffed pink piglet, Scott headed straight toward me with a genuine smile and a glint in his eye.

I looked down at the floppy polyester piglet. "Is that for me?"

His face twisted. "No way. This is *my* prize."

My mouth popped open in feigned shock. "And here I thought you were a gentleman."

He laughed and turned back toward the small stage where the band was playing. Tucked into the crook of his arm, the little piglet's wobbly head bounced with his every footstep.

"You look ridiculous with that thing," I teased.

He only looked down at me through his thick lashes and back at the piglet in his arm. "You're just jealous."

I laughed and felt lighter, freer, than I could ever remember. Scott left his prize pig with me at a picnic table while he excused himself to get us each a water, but not before reminding me that I was only babysitting and he was *not* giving me that pig.

While I waited for him to return, I let the music from the band flow over me and closed my eyes. I swayed to the slow, sensual beat as the singer crooned into the microphone.

"You look like a woman who could use a dance. Do me the honor?"

My eyes flew open to find Scott looming over me with one hand out and a softness in his eyes that did warm, melty things to my insides. I swallowed hard.

"Um . . ." I glanced down at the plush pig in front of me.

"Leave her. She'll be fine for one song." Scott reached down and grabbed my hand as I stood and untangled myself from the picnic bench. He moved with confident strides toward the makeshift dance floor. It was sanded plywood that creaked and flexed with our footsteps. I stood in front of Scott, and my heart thudded against my ribs—the same tender heart he'd broken when he left Redemption all those years ago.

"It's just a dance, Gemma."

I nodded and stepped into his space. My arms wound around his neck just as his hands found my hips. Bracing me, his hands flexed once before wrapping around my back and pulling me closer. Our hips pressed together.

It's just a dance.

The music played, and we moved together to the slow, sensual beat. It was a country classic about regret and love. Cowboys and second chances.

I'd always loved the singer's voice and the way she lamented over the man who'd chosen the rodeo over her, but came out stronger for it in the end. One of Scott's hands moved up my back, holding me close, and goose bumps erupted on my arms. A shiver raced through me.

"Are you cold?" Concern darkened his features as his eyebrows pitched forward.

Don't fall for it. You fell for his brand of cowboy charm once. Don't do it again. You won't survive it.

"No." Truth was, my skin was on fire. Every place our bodies touched burned through the denim and cotton. I let the heat relax the tense muscles in my shoulders. I leaned into him in immeasurable increments closer until I realized my head was flat against his shoulder. His forearms were locked behind my back as we moved together with the music.

A throaty tone vibrated from me as I hummed along to the lyrics. Scott's voice was hot against the shell of my ear as he leaned down. "You always had a beautiful voice."

My chest was tight, a hot ball swelling between my ribs. As much as I loved music, I never let anyone hear me sing. At least, not on purpose. Unless it was singing along with the car radio, music was something I kept for myself. The last scrap of my mother that I'd tucked away. One good memory to help offset the grime of all the bad.

"Don't. Don't stop."

When I realized I had stopped humming along, my breath caught. On an exhale, I picked up the melody where they'd left off, humming as I swayed in Scott's arms.

But this wasn't real life. We were lost in a bubble. Outsiders in a strange town. Sharing a moment.

Nothing more. We couldn't be.

My life was spiraling out of control, and I didn't need to get tangled up in a man who had made it painfully clear he could—and would—break my heart.

THE DRIVE back to the motel was a special kind of torture. Her juniper-and-wildflower scent billowed in the cab of the truck. It had felt good to hold her in my arms. Damn good. I had no right to want a woman as wild and free as Gemma. She was eleven years younger than me and the little sister of one of my best friends. Compounded by the fact she was under my protection. Her life was literally in my hands, and I couldn't stop thinking with my dick.

When we arrived back at the motel, Gemma was quiet. Too quiet. Dancing with her at the Wild Bronc Festival had been a mistake. Yet another lapse in judgment when it came to her.

Been a lot of those lately.

I opened the door to my room, carefully checking it first before using the connecting door to make a pass through Gemma's room. She stood in the threshold of the open door, her eyes hard as they raked over me.

"What is it?" I asked.

Her delicate arms folded in front of her. "I'm pissed at you."

I raised an eyebrow and held her gaze. "Thought you had a nice time."

The muscles in her jaw worked, and blood rushed between my legs as I imagined running my hands across her jaw and down her neck.

"I'm pissed," she continued, "because of what happened. How you left. You were gone *four years* in case you didn't notice. Then you come rolling in here with your demands and your rules." Gemma adopted a deep, mocking baritone as she puffed out her chest and barreled on. "We're leaving. Take the exit. Always enter a room behind me. Pizza in this town sucks, keep driving."

I had to focus on the flush of her cheeks to keep from smiling, but in the end that proved to be a mistake.

"—and then you have the *audacity* to be *nice* to me." She flicked her arm in my direction to emphasize her point.

I faced her and lifted my chin. "You want me to be a dick to you?"

She rolled her eyes and pushed past me into her own room before turning back. "No! I want you to be *normal*. And less . . . confusing."

I knew what she meant. I hadn't given her any kind of explanation about what had happened four years ago. She wouldn't understand that I'd gotten too close to her. Fucked it all up. I'd spent four years trying to make it right. But I could take her wrath. Hell, I'd done worse to myself every day since I drove away from the ranch without so much as telling her I was leaving.

But I never meant to toy with her emotions. Somehow with her I lost the ability to compartmentalize and maintain order. Seeing her hurt and falling apart was dangerous.

I took a small step forward. "Tell me what you want."

She started to speak but stopped herself. Her arms

dropped, and one hand toyed with the collar of her shirt. The air crackled between us. I took another step closer.

"I don't know." Her voice was tight, like she was losing the battle against a swell of tears.

I kept my voice low and calm. "How do you feel? Right now."

She was quiet until she found her voice. "Out of control. My whole life is full of people and situations where I have zero control over what happens to me."

My heart was pounding. My body roared to life. I wanted to fix it. Change everything to make it right for her. "Take control." I took a deep, steadying breath to show her what I meant. "Take it."

Her icy-blue eyes found mine, and the flash of desire that heated them was unmistakable. I gathered every ounce of my control to keep from taking one last step into her space and crushing her mouth to mine.

I stood, stone-still, energy buzzing through me.

Waiting.

"How?"

I swallowed thickly. "I'll do anything you ask. You want me to order that Chinese takeout? Fine. Tell me to go to hell. I'll turn around. Tell me—"

"Kiss me."

My mind went numb. I wasn't expecting those words to fly out of her mouth, but at that moment, I didn't give a shit.

Without hesitation, I slammed into her, crushing my mouth to hers. My hands gripped the back of her thighs as I hauled her legs around my waist. I turned, pinning her back against the wall, and kissed her as she'd demanded.

As I'd always dreamed of doing.

Frantic and passionate, my mouth moved over hers, swallowing the shocked gasp that erupted from her throat.

She opened for me, her tongue tangling with mine as her nails raked up the back of my skull. I couldn't press my body close enough to her. Her breasts pushed against me, and I could feel the hard pebble of her nipples through the fabric of her shirt. One hand left her ass to cup her breast. I dragged a thumb over the taut bud, and when she arched into me, climbing higher, I rubbed over it again.

I would have done anything Gemma told me to do. I prayed she didn't tell me to stop. Four long years. Four years I'd waited to kiss her, wondering what it would be like and cursing myself out for never having the balls to do it.

Gemma was everything.

That *kiss* was everything.

Breathless, I moved my mouth down the smooth column of her neck as I held her weight. At the base of her collarbone, I moved toward the other side when she froze. Her hands met my shoulders and pushed back. I looked at her as she dropped her legs to the floor. One hand tugged at the collar of her shirt.

Fuck.

I was centimeters away from Gemma's scars. While they had never bothered me—quite the opposite, in fact, they were a testament to what a badass she was—I knew she was guarded about them.

Gemma wiped her mouth and fixed her top as I adjusted the hard-on in my pants. I couldn't manage to get my breath, but I faked it anyway.

"Well." Gemma cleared her throat. "Agent Dunn. Good night."

I stared at her, desire flaring in my eyes as I took her in. Powerful and sexy as hell. She'd gotten what she wanted from me, and while I would have loved nothing more than to strip her bare and worship her for hours, it wasn't about what I wanted. She had admitted to feeling out of control.

This was something I could give her no one else could.

A grin spread across my face. With a nod, I walked to my room and shut the door. "Good night, Ms. Walker."

MY LIPS WERE SWOLLEN, and I could still feel the tingle of our kiss as I lay on my bed and let my fingertips smooth over my tender mouth.

Holy fuck. I kissed Scotty Dunn.

Not only had I kissed him, I'd demanded it, and he'd kissed me right back. The most controlled man I'd ever known had done exactly what I'd asked, the moment I asked it.

And then I'd kicked him out.

My mind was racing. I needed to talk this out with someone. I looked at the time—eleven p.m.—and toyed with the skin at the side of my thumb. I wasn't sure what the exact time zone difference was, but I knew it was later.

Screw it. I needed my best friend.

> You awake? I need advice.

<Incoming call: Kate Sullivan>

. . .

IMMEDIATELY MY PHONE LIT UP, and I smiled. I should have known Kate would answer no matter the time of night.

"Spill. What's happening?"

My eyes sliced to the door, and I lowered my voice. I didn't want him overhearing me freak out about the kiss, and I didn't trust the paper-thin walls of the motel.

"We kissed."

Kate's squeal was loud enough that I had to pull the phone from my ear. "Yes! I knew it! I knew there was something between you two and he wouldn't be able to keep his hands off you! Oh my god. I can't believe he kissed you!"

Her excitement only fueled the giddy feeling tingling inside me. "Shh," I demanded. "I am freaking out."

"So what happened? Where did it happen? Where is he now? Tell me *everything!*"

"He's back in his room." I looked at the wall again, wondering if Scott was as confused and turned on as I was.

"Oh." Disappointment dripped from her voice. "Well that sucks."

I laughed quietly. "Yeah, kinda."

"Did you kiss him or did he kiss you?"

"Well . . . we were kind of arguing, and I was unloading on him, and when he asked me what I wanted, I sort of . . . demanded it?"

"That is so fucking hot." Her serious tone had another bubble of laughter erupting from me, and I stifled it with a pillow.

"You have no idea." I groaned again, thinking of how he'd grabbed me by the back of the thighs and hauled me against the wall. I pressed my legs together just thinking about it, craving release from the incessant pressure.

"Did he freak out afterward or what? Why are you calling me and not getting railed by your hot bodyguard?"

"Kate. Seriously." I laughed with her again. "We kissed and were getting carried away when his mouth got really close to my scars. I kind of panicked and kicked him out."

Kate's voice grew quiet. "Oh, honey."

My jaw clenched. I didn't need or want her pity, but with her, at least I knew it came from a kind place. A place where she didn't ever want to see her best friend hurting. "It's fine. I just wasn't ready, that's all."

One thing Kate didn't know about me was that any previous sexual experiences were very well thought out. My scars were never fully visible. Instead, I opted for complete darkness or remaining mostly clothed throughout the encounter. It wasn't the sexiest way to handle my insecurities, but it kept me from seeing the pity and disappointment cross a man's face when he saw how truly damaged I was.

"You know what this means, right?" Kate was up to something. I could tell by the way she was barely containing another fit of the giggles. "Scotty Dunn likes a domme."

My face crinkled up. "A what? Like a dominatrix?"

No fucking way.

"I mean, maybe. You never know with those straitlaced types. Usually they like control in the bedroom, but sometimes they like to give it up for the right girl."

Holy shit. It was obvious I had a deeply rooted, primal urge to have sex with him, but I had chickened out. Too scared of being rejected, *again*, by him.

Would he have done it?

A warm glow bloomed low in my belly as I imagined what it would be like to be taken by Scott. Not just taken, but *fucked* simply because I'd demanded it. The image of him bending to my will was hot.

Too hot.

"How do you even know this?"

"I read *a lot* of smut."

We laughed together again, and I blew out a deep breath.

"Here's what you need to do," Kate continued. "Act totally normal tomorrow, but when he does something for you—opens your door, or hands you something you ask for, slip in a *good boy* and see what he does."

I rolled my eyes. "I am never doing that! You are no help at all."

"I'm telling you, Gem. You've got a hot sub on your hands."

"Good night." I shook my head as Kate continued laughing on the other end and hung up.

I spent the next thirty minutes in the cramped motel shower, scrubbing any trace of Agent Scott Dunn's cologne off my skin. I pulled a brush through my hair and tried to remember that Scott Dunn had broken my heart. I had no business fantasizing about our kiss and what could have happened if I had let him take it further.

MORNING CAME EARLY, and my dry, scratchy eyes proved I had tossed and turned all night. Another day on the road, stuck in my truck with Scott.

Good night, Ms. Walker.

I groaned and tipped my head to the ceiling. "Why does that have to be so hot?" I hurried and packed my clothes into my bag. Another town, another quiet motel was in my future. My eyes zipped to the red file folder that I'd placed on the nightstand. In it, the prosecuting attorney had pages upon pages of information so I could be prepared for my testimony.

Dread pooled in my stomach, and it lurched once. I flattened my palm against the dresser and leaned over. Flashes of how I'd been taken, what the men had done to me in that abandoned basement, rose to the surface.

I wanted to forget. I never wanted to be that frightened girl ever again. But faced with the realization that I would have to be in the same room as one of them again nauseated me. There was no way I could look any of them in the eye and not have the overwhelming need to cower. Flashes of a dark and dirty basement flooded my mind, and my heart raced.

I barely registered the soft knock on the door between Scott's room and mine. It was the low rumble of his voice that finally grabbed my attention.

"Time to wake up."

I straightened and sucked in a deep breath through my nose. My hair was smoothed, and although my eyes were rimmed with red, I could easily hide that behind my sunglasses. When I cranked the handle and pulled open the door, Scott was standing, hands in his pockets and a furrow set between his eyes.

"Ms. Walker."

A flutter of butterflies replaced the dread in my tummy. *Damn him.*

"Agent Dunn." I lifted my chin and turned my back on him to grab my small suitcase.

Before I could lift it, Scott was behind me, taking it from my hands. "I got it."

My mouth was parched, and I studied the side of his face as he stalked toward the front entrance of my room.

Say it. Just say the words. Good boy.

I pressed my molars together to hold my laughter in check. I would be mortified if I said that to Scott and he just stared at me—or, worse, *laughed*.

Instead, I quietly followed him out to the parking lot. Scott piled his luggage and mine in the back floorboards of the truck. We stood and stared at each other. I was thankful my mirrored sunglasses hid my tired eyes. I didn't need him analyzing the jumble of emotions I was sure was clear as day on my face.

After a beat, Scott sighed. "I'll take the first shift."

We bounced along another boring, lonely stretch of highway. The warm summer sun heated the cab of the truck, and I adjusted the vents to blow not-quite-cool-enough air across my skin. I shifted in the bench seat and tried to get comfortable.

Maybe taking my truck was a bad idea.

Not that I would ever admit that to Scott. Insisting we take the truck had been my one act of defiance—of taking control of this disaster of a road trip. But damn. It meant for really rough riding. My ass was numb and my back ached.

Scott's eyes never left the road. His hand rested on the bottom of the steering wheel, and the plains of Montana sailed past us. I took the opportunity to study the side of his face.

Long, dark lashes.

Cut jaw.

Full lips.

Those lips were so much more than I ever dreamed.

And those hands? Forget it.

My nipples twisted and sharpened beneath my top, and I angled myself away from him to prop an elbow on the window and gaze at the vast land around us. I crossed one leg over the other to lean as far away from Scott as I could manage in the small cab of the truck.

My movement caught his eye, and he glanced down at my ass. I covered a small smirk with my hand and turned my face toward the window. At least I wasn't the only one thinking about our kiss last night.

The lull of the road noise had my eyelids drooping, and I allowed myself to bask in the quiet. For the time being, I was safe. As much as I hated Scott for what he had done to my poor, naive heart, I knew in my soul he took his job seriously. He would never let something happen to me if he could prevent it.

After a few hours, the truck slowed, and I lifted my head. "Where are we?"

"North Dakota. Just a ways across the border. You fell asleep."

I looked out over the wide, rolling prairie. The rugged, unspoiled beauty of grasslands and sweeping vistas carried as far as I could see. Just over the hill, the beginnings of what appeared to be a small city came into view.

"We're staying here for the night."

My brows dipped down. I had assumed the entire day would be driving.

When I didn't speak, Scott clarified: "We made good time. This is far enough. The team will go ahead and secure the next stop."

I eyed him carefully. A prickle of awareness tingled the base of my neck. I couldn't tell if he was being weird about our kiss or if it was something else, but I couldn't help the feeling that he was still hiding something.

Scott didn't bother to use his GPS or a map when he pulled into a hotel chain I recognized. We also didn't take our bags before checking in at the front desk.

"Good afternoon." The woman behind the counter smiled brightly as we approached her. "Checking in?"

Scott gave the elderly woman an easy smile. "Yes, we have a reservation under Roberts."

Scott didn't look at me as I scanned his face, curious about the fake name. The woman clacked the keys on her computer as I glanced around the lobby. It was clean but plain. A couple with two boys, wrapped in towels as if they'd just gotten out of the hotel pool, walked by. The youngest peered up at me, and I smiled. His little green eyes dropped to my neck and went wide. I clutched the collar of my shirt and turned my attention back to the woman behind the counter.

"The reservation should be for two rooms. Top floor, preferably."

"Yes, sir. I have two king suites. Unfortunately, we do not have any available with an adjoining door, as requested, but these are just across the hall. Will that do, sir?"

I stifled the tiny part of me that was hoping she'd say they were all booked up and *Darn, you'll have to share a room,* but, alas, she did not.

Scott scooped up the key cards and the information she'd given up before heading to the bank of elevators across the lobby.

"I'd like to go check the rooms, and then I'll come back down and get our bags."

I hated how awkward things felt between us. All day we'd ridden in near silence, and now he could barely look at me. I was hurt and mad and turned on and frustrated and . . . hopeful, maybe? I liked it better when I could hate him from a distance.

Once he was satisfied our rooms were secure, he left me

alone to retrieve our luggage. My room was small, and the bed was harder than the one in the last motel, but it would do. I'd learned early in my life to be grateful for *any* bed, since there was a time my mother lost our apartment and we'd spent two months living out of her beat-up sedan. I flicked on the television and flipped through the channels, landing on HGTV and letting it serve as background noise.

My legs were restless. My body was in need of motion, and the small space of the hotel room was stifling. The need to run away was overwhelming. Thoughts of slipping into the night and starting a new life were tempting . . . until I thought of all the people who'd lined the entryway of Redemption Ranch as we'd driven away. Running felt easier than facing what happened in Chicago, but I didn't want to be that girl. I knew I'd miss my brothers and the family I'd found in Montana if I left it all behind.

When there was a light knock, I turned the television off and padded toward the door.

"It's me." Scott's deep voice made my heart flop in my chest.

I checked the peephole as I'd promised, and when I confirmed he was alone, I pulled open the door. Scott held my bag in his hand. Just the sight of his corded forearms flexing under the weight of my bag was enough to send desire coursing through me. I couldn't help but wonder if Kate was right about Scott, and until I could know for sure, the thought of him liking being bossed around would hound me.

I could test Kate's theory. Boss him around a little and see what he does. Worst-case scenario, we would go back to awkward silences and disdain for each other. Even that was easier than this jumble of uncertainness and arousal.

I tipped my head over my shoulder. "Put it at the edge of the bed."

No please, no asking.

"Yes, ma'am." A delicious thrill danced up my spine at his words.

Scott carefully placed my bag at my bed, and as he bent, the words slipped out: "Good boy." My voice was rough and thick, sensual in a way I didn't realize was possible.

He paused midway through standing straight. My heart hammered. His eyes sliced to me as a flush of crimson bloomed down his chest and neck.

Oh . . . OH.

Oh shit.

Kate could be right. There was no mistaking the desire swirling in his mossy eyes as they raked over me. I stepped closer to him. His rugged, masculine scent filled the air between us. A small smirk teased the corner of his mouth, and I wanted to taste it, *taste him,* as I gave into every fantasy I'd held on to since I'd first met him.

"Anything else I can do for you, Ms. Walker?" Scott stood straight, his thickly veined hands clasped in front of him. There was a whole hell of a lot I wanted Scotty Dunn to do for me, but I was still reeling over the information that he possibly *liked* when I bossed him around.

"No, thank you." I was secretly proud of my cool, smooth delivery.

He nodded once but didn't move. I turned my body, opening up the pathway to the door. Only then did his long legs carry him away from me. When he got to the door, he paused. "Since we have most of the evening to kill, there's a game tonight. If you're interested."

A game?

I looked around the plain motel room.

With a shrug, I said, "Beats reruns of *Fixer Upper*."

This time, Scott did smile. A devastatingly handsome grin that turned my guts into mush. "Pick you up at six."

EVAN

How's she holding up?

Fine.

EVAN

I need more than that. She's not giving you too much shit, is she?

Nothing I can't handle.

EVAN

Thanks, man. I know she's in good hands. Wouldn't trust her with anyone else.

GEMMA GRIPPED my elbow as we wound through the crowd. The contact sent bolts of heat up my arm and straight across my chest. Maybe I was having a heart attack. I shook off the possibility, knowing full well it was the fact that only twenty-four hours ago I had Gemma pressed upside a wall and had nearly lost control and ripped her clothing to shreds.

Bet her brother would have a few words to say about that.

Definitely not having a heart attack, though I'd nearly had one at the completely involuntary response my cock had to her calling me a *good boy* in her hotel room. It should have been funny.

It wasn't.

The way her voice had gotten thick and heady was the most potent drug in the world. I think it surprised her nearly as much as it had me. It took every ounce of composure I could muster to leave that room and not drop to my knees in front of her.

"I've never been to a baseball game."

I looked down at her wide eyes scanning the crowd, and I smiled. "I know."

A game in town was a nice surprise, and after her eyes lit up at the Wild Bronc Festival, I had mentally shifted my plans. If I could manage to pack in a few new experiences for her on this trip, I'd do it. When Ma suggested that a slower pace would help Gemma prepare for the trial, she'd inadvertently given me permission to make a few detours. With my team reporting zero movement from Billy Massaro's associates, I felt safer in the obscurity of Middle America.

Besides, if Gemma was going to have to face her worst fears in Chicago, I was going to be damn sure the trip there would be unforgettable.

My eyes scanned the crowd. A man in a plain black baseball cap caught my attention. His eyes were covered in the shadows of the brim. No kid with him. No friends or woman either. The hair pricked at the base of my skull, alarm bells pinging through my veins.

As quickly as I'd noticed him, he was lost in the crowd. I carefully cataloged the information—white male, black cap, buzzed hair, medium to large build.

I reminded myself that no one in Chicago seemed to be aware of Gemma or her plans to return to the city. Movement from Massaro's known associates had been minimal. Though it put me at ease, I still scanned the crowd again and committed as much as I could to memory—just to be sure Gemma was safe in the mass of people.

Old habits.

"Are you sure this is the right section?" Gemma asked as we moved down the stairs toward our seats. She scanned the ticket stub and looked up at the signs as we moved closer and closer to the field. "It seems really close."

Gemma's cool voice pulled me from my spiraling thoughts, and without waiting for my answer, she moved in the direction of our designated row. The stadium was filling up with families eager to enjoy a Friday-night minor league baseball game. Vendors walked up and down the stairs selling hot dogs, beer, cotton candy, and light-up trinkets for the children. The murmur of the crowd and the smell of fried food filled my lungs and brought a sense of hometown comfort. For the briefest moment, we didn't have to be a bodyguard and his charge. We could be two friends enjoying a baseball game together.

Only we weren't friends.

No, I had fucked that up royally when I left Montana. Gemma hated me, and she had every right. I'd let my control slip and led her on. I knew she was fragile, and I had taken advantage in a moment of weakness.

It couldn't happen again.

As we sat just behind the dugout, Gemma toyed with the collar of her flannel shirt. It was only mid-June, and we were months from the weather turning. She had to be roasting alive.

"Take it off if you're hot."

Gemma rolled the sleeves of the flannel and shook her head. "It just . . . it makes people uncomfortable."

I shrugged. "Not me."

Gemma looked around. No one seemed to be paying us any attention, and I could see her internal struggle play out on her gorgeous face. I hated that she'd been made to feel like she had to cover herself for other people. She was clearly uncomfortable in the stifling heat.

"Hey." I tipped my chin at her. "Fuck 'em."

A nearby mom looked sufficiently horrified at my vulgar language and covered her child's ears while shaking her head disapprovingly.

A slow grin spread across Gemma's face, and my chest tightened. Cautiously, she unbuttoned the front of her shirt, revealing a simple white tank top that hugged her curves. She looked around again before cautiously slipping the flannel shirt off her shoulders.

I had seen Gemma's scars. Four years ago they were much fresher—red and angry. Despite the fact they had faded to a paler pink, the long, jagged scars were visible from just above her collarbone, traveling in intersecting vines all the way down her arm to her delicate wrist.

I looked out onto the field, diverting my attention to the players warming up, while Gemma sat quietly next to me. After a few moments of silence, she slipped the shirt down the rest of the way and tied the sleeves around her trim waist.

A few players warmed up only feet away from us, tossing a ball back and forth and joking with each other. Gemma caught one player's eye, and he didn't hide the fact that he appreciated the warm smile that spread across her face. The cocky player razzed his friends, scooped up a ball, and continued to sneak obvious glances in our direction. I leaned back in my seat, lifting my chin and leveling him with a hard stare. He had the balls to grin at her and wink.

I ground my molars to dust.

What a fucking dick.

If Gemma noticed the attention, she didn't let on. I shifted in my seat, trying to get comfortable while actively avoiding any contact between us. It was still almost thirty minutes until the first pitch, but the stadium was filling up quickly.

Gemma's hands were folded in her lap as she looked around and took in the new experience. I used the opportunity to study the side of her face. Her profile was ingrained in my brain, but I still liked seeing her in a new light. Gemma had continued to grow into a stunning and elegant woman. While she still drove like a bat out of hell, she had a composure and grace that four years of stability in Montana had given her. It made me proud that Gemma seemed to have found herself in my home state.

I couldn't keep gawking at the slope of her nose or the length of her lashes, so I cleared my throat and attempted to act natural. "Would you like some nachos? Extra jalapeño? A poncho to eat them in, maybe?"

"Very funny." Her eyes scanned the crowd as people filtered down to take their seats.

The young player still couldn't take his eyes off Gemma. Not that I blamed him, but it annoyed the fuck out of me. "C'mon." I stood, blocking his view of Gemma's ass as she left her seat. "Let's get you something to eat."

∾

THE BADLANDS BIG Sticks won nine to three. The glow from the postgame fireworks bounced off Gemma's skin and danced in her eyes. With her head tipped toward the sky, she looked peaceful. Happy.

I did that.

Pride swelled in my chest that in that moment I could give something to Gemma no one else could. A new memory. A happy one. I hated to admit that there was little to nothing that I wouldn't give that woman if she'd only let me in.

If she'd only forgive me.

I'd spent the last four years trying to forgive myself, and all it had led to was another secret. If she knew the truth, I'd finally lose her forever.

Something in me shifted, and I realized, I couldn't let that happen.

The walk down the hotel hallway was silent. My fingers itched to lace with Gemma's, but I kept them fisted at my sides. We walked up to her door.

Gemma looked up at me and offered a small smile. "Thank you for tonight. It was a really fun time."

I nodded, then glanced down at her mouth as she sucked in a tiny breath. I wanted to lean in. To take her mouth and pour myself into her. It was wrong—she was too young, and I was responsible for her life. Gemma wasn't just some casual fuck.

She's everything.

I'd seen a spark of something earlier when she'd given me a command and I'd complied. We were in a standoff, staring at each other, neither knowing what to do about the crackling tension between us.

"I want to check your room." My voice was gravelly and thick. All I needed to do was make sure her room remained secure and walk out. Leave her be before desire took over and I made yet another mistake where Gemma was concerned.

Gemma silently opened the hotel room door and stepped aside to let me inside. She followed me in and leaned against the low dresser as I quickly made a pass through the small room.

I went to leave before I did something stupid like kiss her again, but Gemma's heady voice stopped me. "Wait."

I turned, my heart galloping, to see her with her hands braced behind her on the dresser. Her blue eyes danced with fire. "Why do you do what I tell you to do? Without me asking or being nice about it?"

"Because it's you." The truth came out heavy and swift, but I didn't regret it. Gemma deserved my truth, if nothing else.

"So you just do whatever I tell you to?" Gemma stood straighter, considering.

"Yes." My cock thickened at the endless possibilities, but I held tightly to my remaining tether of control.

"Like when I told you to kiss me."

"Correct. You can have anything you want from me." Considering how badly my body was aching for her, there was nothing I wouldn't do for Gemma. "You're in the lead here."

She needed to see, to feel for herself, that she was the one in complete control. No matter how I tried to fight it, I was helpless against her. I *craved* it. This was Gemma, my best friend's little sister and the woman I was bound by duty to protect.

Gemma stood, looking poised and in control. Confident. Handing over control to her was a turn-on I never expected, but I sure as hell didn't want it to stop.

She stepped closer as I took a wide stance and clasped my hands in front of me. "Tell me what you want me to do," I rasped, barely getting the words past the scratch in my throat.

Her eyes moved down from my face across my chest and lower. I shifted to hide my growing arousal, but it was painfully obvious behind my feeble attempt to conceal it. Gemma's hands moved over her own stomach and up to brush across her chest.

"Take off your clothes." Gemma was bold and assertive, and I was so fucking proud of her. Desire coursed through me as I did as I was told. I reached behind me to pull off my shirt and drop it to the floor.

"Pants too," she added.

"Yes, ma'am." I stifled a smile as I unbuttoned my jeans and lowered the zipper. Her eyes tracked every movement as I slid the denim down my legs and removed my black boxer briefs. I stood tall, no longer concerned about how my cock was rock-hard and jutted out for her. I wanted her to see what she did to me. I stood tall, waiting for her next request.

Gemma licked her lips. "Stroke your cock."

I gripped my dick and let loose the guttural groan at the back of my throat. My eyes never left hers. Gemma's pupils went wide as I moved my hand over myself.

"I want to watch you." Gemma began to unbutton her jeans and slide them down her muscular legs as she moved toward the bed. My eyes tracked her every movement as I tugged and stroked. I wanted to bury my cock inside her, but I couldn't. I wouldn't. Not until Gemma gave that to me. Instead, I watched as she lifted her white tank top over her head and removed her bra.

Standing before me, Gemma was a goddess. In only

panties and with desire flaring in her eyes, she was sexy and confident. The power she had over me was strange and complex but completely intoxicating.

She pointed behind me. "Sit in that chair."

I did as I was told and sat in the chair at the foot of the bed. Gemma moved to the corner of the mattress, where she spread her legs wide, propping her feet on the armrests beside me. The thin cotton between her legs had a spot of moisture, and I could only imagine how good, how wet, it would feel to slip my cock inside her.

"Anything I ask?"

"Anything." A sly grin spread across my face. "If you demand it." I wanted to hear the newfound confidence in her voice. I craved it.

"I want to watch you." Gemma's own hand moved down her side to brush over her pussy. She was in total control, and for the first time in my life, I could relax. Listen. My job was to do as she demanded, and I was surprisingly content to not be the one in the driver's seat. Not the federal agent or the protector or the man with a plan. My only job was to bring her pleasure, in whatever form she craved it.

I continued stroking my cock. With Gemma's eyes on me, I opened my palm, spit, and moved the wetness around my crown. She moaned and I reveled in the heady, sultry sound. I watched as her delicate fingers danced up her thighs and found her clit. She rubbed the outside of her underwear as she was spread in front of me. Gemma's head lolled back as her fingers moved past the edge of the cotton and into her heat.

My cock grew harder as a hot, needy ball of desire gathered at the base of my spine. I watched in jealous agony as her fingers pumped in and out of her. I wanted that delicious wet heat surrounding me as I stretched her open. My free hand gripped the arm of the chair, then moved up to hold her slim ankle as I struggled to maintain composure.

Gemma's mouth dropped open, and I wanted to go to her. Plant my mouth on hers and pour every emotion into her as I fucked her hard and dirty. My eyes moved over her curves as my desire spiraled higher.

"Look at me," she said.

My eyes sliced to hers in submission.

"Are you close?"

"Fuck yes, baby." A few more strokes and I'd be gone.

Frenzied energy sizzled between us. Gemma's hand gripped the side of the bed while she brought herself closer and closer to release. Her eyes ate up the lines of my stomach, and I flexed my abs just for her.

"I want you to come," she demanded, "come on my panties. Oh fuck. Fuck!"

As Gemma crashed over the edge, I did exactly as I was told. I stood, towering over her, and planted my hips between her spread legs. Gemma's body fell back as I pushed her knee to the bed with one hand and stroked myself with the other. On a groan, my release broke free. Over and over I emptied myself onto the thin cotton of her panties. As I finished, I dragged the head of my cock down her center, her breath sucking in as the head moved over her clit.

I struggled for air, breath sawing in and out of me as I processed what the hell had just happened.

Gemma fucking owned your ass, that's what happened.

I looked down at her before stepping out from between her legs. I took a step back, waiting for her to tell me our next move.

After a moment, Gemma blinked and pushed herself up

from the bed. Her hand found the errant hairs around her face, and she pushed them back and stood.

I waited, panting and altogether enraptured by her.

"I'm going to clean up." She moved toward the bathroom and shot a brief look over her shoulder. "Good night, Agent Dunn."

12

GEMMA

I CAUGHT the slow smirk that lifted the corner of Scotty's mouth as I'd dismissed him. The rising steam from the hot shower provided a welcome barrier from having to look at myself in the mirror.

I can't believe that just happened. I told Scott what to do—demanded it—and he did it. Eagerly, too, it seems.

I slipped my soaked, ruined panties down and kicked them away before standing under the hot spray of the shower. My mind raced as I cleaned myself and washed my hair. I let the soothing water soak into me as I replayed the most erotic experience of my life.

I needed to talk to Kate. Or Effie. Or Johnny. *Someone.*

After I turned off the water, I stood, listening. The room beyond the bathroom door was quiet. I quickly toweled off and listened again before opening the door and peeking into the room.

Silence.

Scott had left when I'd dismissed him, and relief washed over me. There was no way I could process what the hell had just happened without throwing myself at him. I moved toward the side table to grab my phone. Time zones be damned, I needed my best friend. When I reached for my phone, a small pad of paper and a discarded pen caught my eye. The small, blocky handwriting was so *male* that a tiny smile pinched my lips.

> MS. WALKER,
> WHATEVER YOU ASK OF ME,
> I WILL DO IT.
> —AGENT DUNN

Heat pooled low in my belly, and warmth spread across my chest. I thought him leaving after our encounter would make me feel cheap and dirty. That wasn't the case at all.

I was empowered.

My fingers raced over the recent contacts in my phone, and I pulled pajamas over my head as I waited for Kate to answer.

"Hey, Gem!" Music blared in the background as she answered. "One sec!"

I chewed the skin at the side of my thumb as I waited for Kate. When the music dulled, she was back. "Hi." Her breath was short. "What's up?"

"You were right about Scotty," I blurted.

"I KNEW IT!" Her shriek over the line made my ears ring. "Tell me everything!"

I gave her the quick rundown, sparing her only the most intimate details.

"You really said, 'Good night, Agent Dunn?' Holy shit. You're such a badass!"

I laughed. "I don't know what came over me. I just *felt*

like a badass in that moment. The fact that he seemed to get off on me being so bold is, like, a next-level turn-on."

"I can't get over this, Gem! You just hooked up with *Scott*. I can't even. That is so hot."

"Evan and Parker can't know." I thought of my older brothers and how epic their freak-out would be if they had any idea what Scotty and I had done on this trip. "What am I going to do now? We're back on the road tomorrow, and I'm going to be stuck in the truck with him, knowing how freaking good he looks naked."

She considered a moment. "Well, I think you have options. You either pretend like it never happened again. Tell him it was a mistake. Or . . ."

"Or what?"

"Or you embrace it. Take this time to explore this new side of each other and just have fun. There's no one there to stop you, Gem. No meddling older brothers. No rules at the ranch. Nothing."

The idea of another round with Scott, maybe even having actual sex with him, was enough to have flutters erupting in my belly again. All those years ago I'd wanted him to notice me so badly. Never in my wildest fantasies had I thought it would be as hot as it was.

"I hate him, Kate."

"Do you, though? Really?"

I could tell myself I hated how thick and low his voice got when he followed my orders. Or that it was a complete turn-on to see him bend to my will. That I hated how he enjoyed watching me as much as I enjoyed looking at him too. My best friend saw right through me.

"I hate what he did to me," I admitted. "That he wrecked my heart and . . . left me behind. We spent countless hours together on the ranch. When my fear and insomnia was at its worst, he was there—talking with me, playing cards, listening. It was more than just teaching me poker and gin rummy. I poured my heart and soul out to him."

"It was a crush."

A crush.

It sounded so simple. So innocent. Only Scott was eleven years older than me and one of Evan's best friends. We'd crossed a line, and I knew in my heart there was no going back. Kate was right. I could either pretend like it never happened or enjoy it while it lasted.

The music thumped in the background as Kate patiently waited for me to respond. I exhaled. "You're right. Thanks for listening."

"What are you going to do?"

My stomach clenched, but a shiver of anticipation raced down my spine. "I guess it's no use pretending like it didn't happen."

Kate chuckled. "That's my girl." She made a smacking kiss noise on the other end of the line. "Be safe. Have fun."

After ending the call, I curled into the plush comforter of the hotel bed and pulled the covers around my shoulders. I reached out to look at the note Scott left at my bedside, and Kate's words tumbled through my head.

Be safe. Have fun.

My entire life was tilted on its axis, and I was entertaining the idea of what sleeping with Scott would mean. He was older. Experienced. He had also proved that he was willing to put my needs ahead of his own. I smoothed my fingers over his handwriting.

Whatever you ask of me, I will do it.

His faith in me steadied me in a way I'd never imagined.

Scott Dunn had unknowingly unlocked a part of me that was confident. In control. It was the first time in my *life* I had ever been asked what I wanted. What I felt. How I wanted things to go. I was a woman making my own decisions.

And apparently one of those decisions was seeing where this new arrangement with Scott would take us.

SIENNA

Remember, when life gives you lemons . . .

VAL

Add tequila and salt?

EFFIE

Hell yes!

SIENNA

I was going to say, make lemonade but, yeah. That works too.

PARKER

Why are you drinking on this trip?

> 😊 I am not drinking tequila. And it's not a "trip." This wasn't a choice, remember?

EVAN

We remember, Gem. You good? Scotty taking care of you?

> It's going okay. Scott has been very accommodating.

PARKER

What the hell does that mean?

SIENNA

Relax, dear husband. I'm sure they're just finding their footing.

PARKER

That better be all he's finding.

Or he'll find my foot in his ass.

JOSH

Scott's a decent guy. He's making sure she's safe.

EVAN

We just want to know you're safe.

He's fine. I'm safe. GOODBYE.

Love you guys.

WHEN I INSISTED ON DRIVING, Scott only ground his molars together once before climbing up into the passenger seat. I used the radio to distract me from how good he looked sprawled out next to me. His large frame filled the cab, and his knees spread wide, encroaching on my space. Even in simple jeans and a white T-shirt, Scott looked sexy, and flashes of his naked body interrupted any rational thoughts. I'd opted to ignore the pangs of desire that coursed through me as we continued our long drive through the never-ending flat highways of North Dakota.

Finally, after hours barreling down Interstate 94 without so much as a glance in his direction, Scott turned the radio down and crossed his arms over his chest. "Are we gonna talk about last night?"

My eyes flicked in his direction, but I refocused on the

winding highway in front of me. During the silent drive, I had lost my nerve. My brothers' disapproving voices had wormed their way into my head. What if Scott lost his job because he fucked the person he was in charge of protecting? That was probably a thing, right?

My lips popped as I answered his question. "Nope."

I spared a glance in time to see his lips pressed together in a flat line. "Gemma, what happened last night was—"

"A mistake," I cut in, the lie bitter and burning with regret on my tongue.

A low grumble radiated from his chest. "I was going to say 'amazing,' but okay."

My head whipped in his direction. "Amazing?"

"I mean, yeah. I thought so." Scott smoothed his palms down his thighs.

A smile pulled at my mouth as I straightened in my seat. I gently cleared my throat. "I thought so too."

A self-satisfied chuckle rumbled next to me. Scott was cocky, self-assured, and it was sexy as hell.

I steadied my tone and tightened my grip on the steering wheel. "Evan can't know. He'll freak out." I sneaked another glance at Scott, and his eyes were trained on the road ahead of us. "Definitely not Parker. He may actually murder you."

For a moment, I thought he might argue and tell me that he didn't want to keep our newfound relationship—no, *situationship*—a secret.

Instead, he shifted his body to face me. "I told you before, you're in control here. If you want to keep whatever this is just between us, I'm fine with that. I'm not interested in losing my friend. Or my job."

I knew it.

I swallowed and lifted my chin in feigned confidence.

"Good." I shifted in my seat to help dull the low ache that was building between my thighs. "Now start navigating, because I think I'm lost."

Scott peered at the passing road signs and shook his head before smiling and pulling up the GPS on his phone. "Yes, Ms. Walker."

13

SCOTT

Status update.

AGENT WILCOX

Yes, sir. We're continuing to monitor any
calls to the jail. Informant interviews are
taking some time.

Fine. Make it happen. And Massaro?

AGENT WILCOX

Rotting in his cell as we speak.

Email the report of the property. We're en
route.

AGENT WILCOX

Done. Odd choice for a safe house,
correct?

Not your concern.

TO GEMMA'S CREDIT, her driving was slightly less terrifying on the deserted roads through North Dakota. I'd offered to take a turn, but she insisted on pushing through, and I let her. Gemma had always been at the will of those around her, so if she wanted to call the shots and drive all day, that was fine by me. Gemma was more than capable of taking care of herself, but that didn't mean I couldn't ease the burden a bit for her. There were other, subtler ways I could take care of her. Snacks at the gas station, choosing her favorite songs, finding ways to make her laugh.

My eyes fell to a small, tattered notebook tucked under her purse between us.

I gestured toward it. "Still writing songs?"

Her eyes flicked to the notebook, and a rosy blush crept onto her cheeks. "Sometimes."

That notebook was brand-new when I knew her four years ago, and once she'd admitted to writing down lines that inspired her, short quotes from poems she loved, and even words that popped into her head that she hoped might eventually turn into songs.

If I allowed myself, I could still hear the raspy, richly warm sound of her singing.

Gemma's posture stiffened, and I understood the topic was off-limits. I resettled into the uncomfortable cloth of the seat and crossed my arms. Thankfully the silence between us wasn't awkward, just . . . there. Knowing she was here, safe and under my care, was enough to settle my nerves for now.

But after several hours, Gemma's eyes were getting glassy, and whether or not I'd promised her control, it wasn't safe for her to drive any longer. We swapped at a gas station, and it took only twenty minutes for her eyes to flutter closed and her breath to become deep and even.

Gemma shifted in her seat. "You cold?" I asked.

She hummed but didn't open her eyes. I fiddled with the thermostat and shifted the vents away from her bare legs.

"I'm not sleeping. It's just a really long blink."

My low, satisfied laugh filled the truck as Gemma tucked one leg under herself. The small pink pig I'd won at the Wild Bronc Festival was peeking out at me from the nook of her elbow. Its happy, satisfied smile mirrored the swirl of emotions rolling through me.

"Yes, ma'am."

After my leg of the trip, I pulled the truck into the driveway of our temporary home. It was a small Airbnb on the outskirts of Saint Cloud, Minnesota. The agents ahead of us had ensured it was secure, and I gave them the green light to go on ahead to our next stop.

"Gem," I called softly. "We're here."

Gemma blinked and straightened in her seat, wiping the sleep from her eyes. She looked over the rustic river-view home.

"Where are we?" Gemma kneaded the tense muscles in her neck, and I wished I could reach out and soothe the ache that the cramped nap in the cab had caused her.

"Home." My dry, humorless laugh crackled between us. "For now, at least."

I turned off the truck and left her in the cab as I walked toward the rustic cabin. I heard Gemma following, so I punched in the code to access our temporary home. As I swung open the door, the heady mix of juniper and flowers wafted over my shoulder.

Goddamn, does she smell good.

She was determined not to talk about what happened between us last night, but once we were cooped up in a house by ourselves, she'd have no choice. Could I have arranged a nearby hotel for us to stay at? Of course. But the appeal of sharing a space with Gemma had been too great. I'd used its quiet setting and the distance between neighbors as a determining factor instead.

"A house?" Gemma asked over my shoulder.

"Welcome home." I turned to face her and held my arms out. "Hop up. I'll carry you across the threshold."

Gemma laughed and rolled her eyes at me as she pushed past me into the house. I stifled a grin and had no shame in watching how her ass moved in her tiny denim shorts. Gemma twirled in a circle, catching me staring, and shot me a quick, sly grin.

Heat raced down my spine. One look and that woman had me ready to drop to my knees and beg for the honor of worshipping her.

Gemma moved through the small home, her hand trailing up the banister toward the second floor.

"Wait." My voice came out harsher than I'd intended, and she flinched. "I need to go first. Just to be sure."

Realization dawned on her and her smile fell. I understood it too. On what felt like a road trip between two people finding their footing with each other, it was easy to forget that Gemma was still in very real danger.

She gave me a tiny nod, and I moved past her to ensure the home was safe. At the top of the stairs, a small landing with a sitting area and a bathroom separated two bedrooms. Downstairs, the entire home had been remodeled in an open concept. The kitchen had a large center island, and the space flowed into the general living area.

There was a plush sectional couch and big oak coffee table nestled by a fireplace. Above the mantel was a flat-screen TV. The entire home was decorated simply. It was elegant, with a masculine touch I appreciated. The large bay window looked out over the Mississippi River in the distance.

Gemma stood, staring out the large windows.

In another life, I could see her and me sharing a space like this. Styled but comfortable, with a piece of the land creating a gorgeous view. I'd want a porch swing or a set of Adirondack chairs for us to enjoy the sunset over a glass of wine or laughing over something funny our kids had done that day.

Jesus fucking Christ.

I scrubbed a hand over my face. I needed to get my head in the game and stop mooning over my best friend's little sister. My responsibility.

My Gemma.

Christ, I was totally fucked.

Gemma turned toward me. "Here till morning?"

"Here till morning," I confirmed with a nod.

"I'm going to go get my bags. Is that fine with you, or am I going to get ambushed if I set foot outside by myself?"

I'm sure she would have been fine. Not only had my team secured the area, but I'd done a sweep myself. Once Gemma had planted that thought in my brain, though, I couldn't let it go.

I strode toward the door. "I'll get them."

Her mocking laughter bounced off my back as I left her in the house to gather our bags and clear my head. Deciding to stay in a quiet house with Gemma had definitely been a mistake. I wouldn't last five minutes before I was begging her to let me touch her. Taste her. I couldn't spend the next several hours alone in that house with her.

Once back inside, I dropped my bags to the ground. "Get ready. We're going out."

∽

> Does Gemma still sing?

EVAN

Great voice, like our mom. But no. Why?

> Just trying to get a read on her.

EVAN

Good luck, brother.

∽

THE OFFICE WAS a decent-size local bar in Saint Cloud. The signs outside promised cold drinks and daily specials. Plus, it was a Thursday—karaoke night. Once I'd seen that, I veered left and pushed my way into the establishment. A sign above the bar read, "Tell your wife you had to stay late at the Office," and T-shirts with the same slogan hung for sale next to the register. I couldn't help a light snort.

The low chatter around us was a surprising comfort. Gemma and I could talk without being bothered, but if the conversation between us grew awkward, there would be plenty of people watching and bad karaoke to keep us distracted.

I thought back to the weathered notebook Gemma had in the truck. I was curious what was written on the worn, tattered pages. From one of our late-night conversations, I also knew that while music and lyrics filled her soul, she'd never really sung in front of anyone but me.

Sitting across from me at a table, I took in her beautiful face and wondered why that was still true.

A deep ache formed in my chest with thoughts of all the things I no longer knew about Gemma.

It was getting late, and the dinner crowd was slowly being replaced by groups of people gathered close to the makeshift stage, drinking pitchers of beer or random cocktails. We ordered, and our food came surprisingly quickly. I tried for small talk, but Gemma's eyes kept drifting to the singers fumbling through renditions of familiar songs. A trio of girls shout-sang their way through "Baby Got Back," and Gemma's hearty laughter floated above the crowd.

It was the most beautiful and heartbreaking sound in the world.

"You should go next."

Gemma's blue eyes were icy as they sliced toward me. "Very funny."

I lifted my brows. "I wasn't joking. Don't forget—I've heard you sing, Gem. You can run circles around these people."

She shifted and played with the edge of her short-sleeved tee. I was proud she seemed to be getting a little more comfortable with her scars in public. I wondered if they were a part of the reason she never performed for anyone or if it truly was stage fright.

I leaned my elbow on the edge of the table and inched closer to her. "Remember that time you sang 'Fast Car'?"

"*You* remember that?" Her face tipped down to try to hide the bloom of color on her cheeks.

I smiled at her. "Still my favorite song."

She looked up, and something passed over Gemma's face—confusion or shock, I couldn't tell—but she tamped it down just as quickly as it came.

"Why? The lyrics are *so* depressing."

I huffed a quiet breath out of my nose and shook my head. She had no clue. When Gemma had sung it, it felt as though my chest had cracked open. The soulful sadness in her voice was heartbreaking and addicting.

"It's a great song."

When she stayed silent but looked longingly back at the stage, I pressed harder. "It's not like you're ever going to see these people again. Come on. One song."

She toyed with her lip, and I knew I had her. With a determined nod, Gemma pushed off the tall stool and strode toward the DJ at the side of the stage. She leaned in close, stating something in his ear, and he nodded and gestured to his right.

She straightened and stayed next to the stage as the singer fumbled his way through a country ballad. Whoops and hollers from the crowd had him leaning into the bit, and he winked and pointed out into the crowd. They cheered and called out, not minding in the least he was absolutely butchering a beloved country classic.

It was the perfect crowd for Gemma to get over her fear of singing in public.

When the man finally finished and took an excessive amount of time bowing and blowing kisses to the crowd, the DJ lowered his headphones and pointed Gemma in the direction of the mic.

She took a visible gulp. Her arms crossed over her trim stomach. A loud catcall whistle pierced through the crowd noise, and I tensed in my seat, looking around. Once Gemma made it to the microphone, she glanced at the DJ and gave a soft nod.

The opening chords of Journey's "Don't Stop Believin'" rang out, and she was greeted with more claps and apprecia- tive hollers from the crowd. I grinned at her, though she still looked nervous as fuck. Her eyes moved around the crowd, and her fingers toyed with the hem of her shirt. I followed her gaze to see a table of women whispering and pointing in her direction. Gemma saw it too, and her hand moved over her exposed scars above her elbow.

My heartbeat ticked faster.

I whispered a prayer. "Come on. Come on. You got this."

As the intro to the song continued, Gemma missed the start. My stomach plummeted. She looked at the DJ, who only nodded in encouragement and looped the song back on itself, starting over.

"Come on, honey!" a man yelled over the music.

I was on my feet and heading toward the stage, my heart pounding.

What the hell are you doing?

I moved in front of the DJ's table, swiping the second mic off the black fabric. Gemma began to move away from the microphone in retreat. She was giving up. As the song began, my voice cracked over the first few lyrics. Gemma froze, her gorgeous blue eyes growing wide as I fumbled my way through the opening lines.

"Yes!" A man at a table in front of me started cheering.

"Woo!" The table of women clapped along to the beat.

Shouts of encouragement from the crowd infused me with confidence as I read the lyrics on the monitor and tried to focus my attention on Gemma, who was still frozen in shock. Finally, I let it all go and did an awkward spin to emphasize a lyric, and the crowd roared to life.

Cheering and singing along as I did my best to make an ass of myself and tug a smile from Gemma.

Finally, she covered her gaping mouth and laughed. Gemma stepped up to the microphone. On the beat drop, her velvet voice rang out. As she sang into the mic, the crowd went absolutely wild. Gemma's voice was raspy and warm and miles better than anyone who'd performed tonight. The entire bar was on their feet, singing and clapping along as we gave the performance of our lives.

Gemma's insecurities seemed temporarily forgotten as she got into the song and belted her heart out along with the crowd.

I was so fucking proud of her.

Somewhere in the song I'd stopped singing to just stare at the goddess in front of me. The crowd adored her as she moved in front of them. When the song reached its peak, my heart was hammering. Gemma hit the high notes with power, and the crowd lost it and was whooping and hollering just for her.

When the song ended, Gemma was breathless and her eyes were wild. Seeing her adored and appreciated was a high I'd never expected. Our eyes locked, and it was the happiest I'd felt in years.

Four to be exact.

With a little hop and a twirl, Gemma replaced the microphone on the stand and flounced toward me. Before I could second-guess it, I scooped her up in a hug and spun her around. Gemma shot one fist in the air, and we received another round of applause.

I set Gemma on her feet, but my hands didn't leave her hips. Her breath was sawing in and out, her breasts plastered to my chest.

"I can't believe I just did that!" She was panting, and I could feel her heart beating in a wild rhythm against mine.

I smiled down at her, willing my heart to dislodge from my throat. I was high on her, on this moment, and without thinking, I planted both hands on her face and dragged her into a kiss.

14

GEMMA

THE SHORT DRIVE home crackled with sexual tension. I was still coming down from the unexpected kiss and the thrill of my one and only performance in front of a crowd.

I had actually done it.

Sure, I had completely frozen and made an ass of myself in the beginning, but Scott had rescued me. He'd made a fool of himself so that I could gather the fraying ends of my confidence and pull it together. Once I'd let go and just sang, the support and encouragement from the crowd had been invigorating. They didn't see the poor, timid girl with the scars. They saw someone who loved good, fun music and wanted to share it with them.

They saw *me*.

Scott clutched my hand in the center of the truck's bench seat as he drove wildly to our temporary home at the edge of town. With my other hand, my finger pressed against my bottom lip. I could still feel the warmth of his kiss.

I wanted it again.

And soon.

We both hurried out of the truck, and Scott's long strides ate up the distance to the front door.

I didn't want time to second-guess myself. I flew into his arms before the front door was even open. He caught me, pressing his large frame against my body as he swiveled us inside. My insides were humming with electricity, and I wanted to climb him.

Feel him.

I braced my arms at his shoulders and pushed him back so I could see the lust bloom in his eyes. A zip of exhilaration raced through me. "I want to see you naked."

"Do I get to see you naked?" A cocky gleam shone in his eyes.

I lifted an eyebrow. "Take my clothes off. Now."

His jaw flexed to hide the smirk, but I caught it. "Yes, ma'am."

God I love when he uses that strong, deep tone with me.

Scott's hands moved under my T-shirt and splayed over my ribs for the briefest second before he lifted the shirt over my head. His eyes roamed over the curve of my breasts, and his fingertips trailed down my sides toward the button of my jean shorts.

I toed off my canvas shoes as he unbuttoned and unzipped my shorts, letting them drop to the floor. I stepped out of them, then out of my socks, and kicked them away as he stared at me. Satisfaction pulled a smile from me as he clearly appreciated the gauzy black-lace bra-and-panty set I had worn.

"On your knees."

Scott immediately lowered himself in front of me, his hands moving over my ass.

Fuck. He didn't even hesitate.

I looked down at him and raised an eyebrow. "Do you like that? When I tell you what to do?"

His Adam's apple bobbed. "I do."

"Good. Because I want you to fuck me. Hard."

It was filthy. Naughty. I had never demanded anything in my life, let alone to be fucked by the hot older man who had starred in every one of my salacious fantasies. I took one step closer, pressing my stomach to his face, and he placed a hot, wet, open-mouthed kiss just below my navel. It was languid and delicious, and I squeezed my thighs together to relieve the mounting pressure.

I ached to be filled by him. Stretched and used up until I could finally stop thinking about him.

"Stand up." He towered over me but I held the power. "I said *fucked*."

"Yes, ma'am." On a dime, Scott turned me and grabbed my hip bones, dragging my ass against his front. He was hard as steel, and I loved knowing I'd done that to him. That he reacted to me in such a primal way.

He moved us toward the couch, where he bent me over the armrest, my ass tipped high into the air. One hand snaked up my back and fisted in my hair. I looked over my shoulder as he released me to reach behind his neck and whip off his shirt. He made quick work of removing his pants and boxer briefs before returning his hands to me.

As I'd demanded, Scott wasn't delicate. He didn't treat me like something precious and breakable. His palms were rough, and they pulled the sides of my underwear down over my behind and let them stay just above my knees. His long fingers found the seam of my ass and ran between my cheeks to my pussy.

"Do you have a condom?"

He nodded and swiped his pants from the floor and dug

out the wrapper. As he worked to open the packet, I reached back to feel how hard and ready he was for me.

Scott gripped my hip with one hand. A deep moan rattled my throat as I pressed my hips back. He held his cock in his hand and used the bare tip to tease my entrance. I was already wet. Ready.

"Bury that cock inside me." My breath became frantic with anticipation. I swallowed hard. "Now."

I watched over my shoulder as he rolled a condom down his thick shaft. A deep, aching pulse squeezed between my legs. I planted my feet wide as Scott positioned himself at my entrance. Without warning, he used his size to bend me at the waist, my ass level with his cock. In one thrust, he pushed inside of me. His force and size had tears burning at the corners of my eyes.

More.

I wanted so much more. His hand found my hair again as the other gripped my hip. He pumped in and out, fucking me as I had demanded.

"Fuck, baby." He moaned.

"Yes. Tell me. Talk to me."

"You're so tight and wet. I can feel you stretch over my cock. Am I hurting you?"

"Shut up." A hot coil tightened inside me. "More. Tell me more."

"You have no idea how long I've imagined this. You bent over and taking my cock." His thrusts were punishing. His size teased the edge of painful. I ground my hips back to take even more. I reached forward, arching my back and tipping my ass higher in the air.

We moaned in unison at the new, delicious angle.

Thoughts dissolved as Scott continued to pound into

me. His words became a jumbled stream of dirty and delicious syllables.

"Next time I'm going to taste that pussy. Lick up every drop of your cum as it runs down your thighs."

"Oh my god." My voice was hoarse and felt like someone else's. This filthy, gorgeous man was fucking me senseless, all because I'd taken control. The legs of the couch scraped against the wooden floor as we lost ourselves.

Scott thrust up into me, and one thick finger teased my clit. "Yes," I panted. "I'm almost there. Don't stop."

"I won't stop, baby. I won't stop until you've taken it all." Scott slipped his fingers down, feeling the way my pussy stretched around his cock and moved back up toward my clit.

"Do you like that?" I was so close. I needed to hear the deep rumble of his voice as I hurtled over the edge.

"Do I like feeling how my thick cock stretches you open?"

I nodded, unable to speak.

"God, yes. You take it so well."

At his words—his praise—I came undone. Wave after wave coursed through me as I came around him.

"Tell me," he panted. "Tell me I can come for you."

Lost in my bliss, I squeezed my inner muscles tighter. "Yes. Come for me. Now."

On a growl, he covered me with his weight. His cock flexed and spasmed inside of me as he finished.

We were slick with sweat. Panting breaths filled the living room as we both came down from an incredible high.

"Holy hell." Scott's voice was thick and rusty.

A bubble of laughter tickled my chest, and I couldn't hold it in. As Scott slipped from me, I turned to sit on the arm of the couch. He stood, looking down at me with his hands planted on his hips. The deep scowl between his eyes as he stood naked in front of me renewed my laughter.

"What's funny?" He crossed his arms, not at all concerned with his still-hard dick jutting out between us.

"You. This. Us." I stood and cupped his neck, pulling him into a brief kiss. "Let's clean up and maybe we'll have another go."

Emboldened, I sauntered off in the direction of the shower, knowing full well he was only steps behind me.

15

SCOTT

HOLY HELL.

In the span of moments, Gemma had absolutely owned me. It was the hottest thing I'd ever experienced. Sad to admit, but it had been way too long since I'd been with a woman, and even then it had never even come close to being the whole-body experience it was with Gemma.

Her appreciative mewls and moans were enough to have me spiraling and craving more orders from her pretty mouth.

When we'd finally caught our breaths, I followed Gemma into the cabin's bathroom. She stepped into the shower, and I joined her. Warm water ran over the slope of her shoulders and down her back.

Tiny pale freckles dotted the top of her right shoulder, and I ran my fingertips across it. I wondered if her freckles would darken and multiply when she allowed her skin to absorb the summer sun. My eyes moved to her left shoulder, where the scarred skin held no melanin. No freckles or visible pores.

With her back to me, Gemma squirted a dollop of

shampoo in her palm and began working it into her blonde hair.

My fingers moved to her scalp. "Let me."

As I massaged the suds and ran my fingertips lower, a rumble vibrated through her neck. I softly moved down, letting my fingers trail over the base of her neck and the slope of her shoulders.

When my hand met her scars, she stiffened. I lowered my mouth to the delicate skin below her ear and kissed. "Let me take care of you," I whispered.

Gemma's breath was still shallow as I used the soap from her hair to run my palms down her shoulders, across her elbows to her wrists. I tangled my fingers with hers.

Gemma's scars had never bothered me in the way she'd assumed. Yes, it pained me to think of her injured and in pain, but more so they were a testament to her tenacity.

She was a warrior.

My hands moved back up and across her chest as her head lolled to the side. Her weight sagged into me, and I wound my arms around her. For a moment, I simply held her under the hot spray.

Steam and water crashed over us, and I shifted, turning and positioning her so I could rinse the soap from her hair. Gemma's wary eyes never left mine as I focused on the task of rinsing the silken strands of her pale, blonde hair.

My large palm brushed over her chest and landed at her heart. Dangerous words threatened to spill, and I ground my molars to keep from ruining the moment by flaying myself open for her. Instead, my hands moved to knead the small muscles at the base of her skull, and I tilted her head until our mouths fused.

We broke away from the kiss, breathless and wanting.

Everything about that moment was wrong. Gemma was

Evan's little sister. He trusted me. Ma trusted me to do my job and do it well. Neither of those included risking everything to worship the woman in front of me, but I couldn't bring myself to care.

It may be wrong, but it was perfect.

We finished the shower and dressed. Gemma chose a loose, matching pajama set, and I simply pulled on a pair of gray sweats, but I didn't bother with a shirt.

While it was late, we were both too charged to go to sleep just yet. I motioned toward the small table and two wingback chairs that made a small sitting area in the upstairs landing. "One round of gin rummy. What do you say?"

Gemma smiled and pulled her towel-dried hair into a loose knot on the top of her head.

I nodded. "Give me a minute."

Gemma looked at me curiously, but I disappeared into my bedroom. I dug out a small pocket-size notebook, a worn deck of cards, and a pen from my duffel bag. She was settled into a chair, one leg tucked underneath and the other propped up. Her chin rested on her knee. I tossed the little notebook on the table and watched it spin toward her.

Her eyes grew wide as she lifted it, and her fingers fumbled through the pages. "Are you fucking kidding me right now?"

I fought the smile that pulled at the corner of my mouth. "What?"

"You know what. I can't believe you have it . . . after all this time."

I shrugged like the tiny notebook wasn't my singular prize possession.

On the long, lonely nights when Gemma had first come to the ranch, I'd used her bouts of insomnia to spend time with her under the guise of being a decent human, when really even then I'd craved her presence. I'd taught her Texas Hold'em at first. Then gin rummy. That quickly became our nightly game.

Gemma's fingers moved down the column of tally marks, counting as she went. When she reached the last group of tallies, her index finger tapped. "Ha. I'm up by nine."

"Yep." Pressure built in my chest. My guts were reorganizing themselves to make room for the swell and discomfort around my heart.

Gemma flipped through the first few pages again, shaking her head.

I shuffled the deck quickly and dealt without another word. After a few rounds in relaxed silence, Gemma flipped her losing hand onto the table.

"You still cheat, I see." Gemma folded her arms across her chest.

I chuckled. "Cheat? Not a chance. You're just a sore loser." I tallied my win in the notebook.

Truth was, I never cheated. I simply knew her tells so well I could anticipate how the game would play out. If she had a high-value face card, she'd die before she gave it up. Gemma was the type of player who'd rack up points as soon as she could, while I'd lie in wait, ensuring I positioned myself with the highest score I could manage.

"Sandbagger," Gemma grumbled.

I reshuffled the deck and dealt another hand. Gemma carefully arranged her cards, back to the front, groups to the left. I hadn't quite figured out the exact system she used, but face cards were always pulled from her right. On her first move, she discarded a two, which I happily scooped up.

She scowled.

I laughed and said, "You know in this game a two has absolutely the same value as a nine, right?"

Gemma was adamantly against low-number cards, and I secretly loved that hadn't changed.

"Fuck them twos."

We both laughed. The ridiculous phrase was something I'd heard countless times when I'd played a set of twos that nudged my score ahead of hers.

Gemma's eyes lowered to my bare chest. Her gaze flicked over the set of wings and script, but landed on the small tattoo over my heart. Her gaze burned like a brand. I had hoped she hadn't noticed, and a rock lodged in my throat.

My fingertips brushed over the tiny number two perched above the red heart before shuffling again and trying not to fumble the cards.

She softly cleared her throat. "Deal up. I need to stay ahead."

LATER, in the quiet hours of the night, with Gemma's limbs wrapped around me, I stared up into the darkness.

After a few more rounds of gin rummy, we'd called it a night, and instead of going to our respective bedrooms, Gemma went with me to my bed. For hours we explored and tasted and brought each other higher.

I'd gone years trying to forget the competitive glint in her eye or the way her blonde hair fell over her face and made my mouth go dry. I'd fought my attraction to her while we both lived and worked at Redemption. Despite the friendship I valued with her brother, despite knowing I was risking a job I loved, I couldn't help the feelings that had developed over late-night card games.

She didn't know, mainly because I'd been a prick and never told her, that after shit went down at the ranch and she was nearly taken from me, something inside me snapped. She came to me that night after the incident, afraid but hopeful, and she'd poured her heart out. She'd claimed to love me. She was nineteen, and I was a thirty-year-old man with no right to stifle her life by claiming her.

I was pissed. At her for saying it out loud. At myself for loving her back and being too much of a coward to admit it.

Instead, I channeled that rage. The overwhelming need to punish anyone who'd wronged her took over my life. For four years I hunted. Now we were so close to making them pay.

Whatever you ask of me, I will do it.

I wrote the words because they were still too painful to admit aloud. But I meant them.

With Gemma it had always been that way.

I gathered her closer, hoping to not disrupt her sleep as I dropped a soft kiss on the top of her head.

Gemma's soft, sleepy voice cut through my spinning thoughts. "You didn't even say goodbye."

Emotion burned in my throat. I knew when I left it would hurt her. God, how I had fucked things up with Gemma. Handled it all wrong, and here I was still making it worse instead of better.

"I know."

16

GEMMA

I am so totally fucked.

KATE

Scott or Chicago?

Both?

SOPH

Okay. Okay. One thing at a time . . . Scott?!
(Please say yes!)

Yup.

SOPH

I don't know if I am supposed to be this
excited, but I LOVE a road trip romance!
swoon

And if this blows up in my face and he
breaks me again?

KATE

Then together we pick up the pieces. No
matter what happens.

～

"HEY, what if we don't make the trip through Wisconsin today?" Scott's voice cut through my racing thoughts as I reorganized my suitcase.

He stood in the doorway of what was supposed to be my bedroom. The bed was still made since we'd spent the night tangled in his sheets instead.

"What do you mean?" I asked.

Scott rubbed his palm over the stubble on his chin. He hadn't bothered to shave in the past few days, and I'd recently learned that I loved the rasp of his stubble against the tender skin of my thighs. My breath hitched and I squeezed them together, ignoring the glorious soreness that resided there.

He shrugged. "Just thinking. Your meeting isn't until Wednesday. It's just over seven hours to Chicago. Even if we broke that up over two days, as planned, we'd still be getting there early."

The mere mention of Chicago had my heart galloping and a sick roll rippling through my stomach.

"The more I think about it," he continued, "the more I think it might be safer in the long run to not be in the city too early. Rather than holing up in a safe house surrounded by agents, maybe we spend a day or two just taking our time."

I blinked at him. A day or two hiding in a safe house with federal agents I didn't know or spending an extra few days in a fantasy bubble with Scott? Yeah. No question.

"What will Ma say?" Scott had a lot of power to make decisions, but ultimately my care as a witness fell on the shoulders of Ma Brown.

Scott winked at me, and a flurry of bees rioted in my belly. "Let me take care of Ma."

I smiled down at my suitcase. My unease over testifying had been mounting. I nearly vomited any time I thought of actually having to face one or more of the men who had thrown me in a basement for the sole purpose of frightening me and punishing my brother.

It was a relief to not face it. Not yet, at least.

A few more days with Scott.

I didn't even know where we stood, but for the time being, it seemed that we were both enjoying our newfound arrangement. I still clutched my youthful heart and tried to protect it, but last night I could practically hear the thoughts jumbling in Scott's head.

I had tried to be brave and voice my sadness over him leaving me behind at the ranch. It was hard to articulate how it had taken me *years* to understand why he had left so abruptly. I still wasn't sure I understood or knew the real reasons.

In exchange he offered no excuses, no explanation, just *I know.*

I was smart to guard my heart. Giving it up to him again would be so easy. After I testified, Scott would no longer be charged with protecting me. Would he leave again? Request to be assigned back at Redemption? Did I want that?

I took a breath and lifted my face to the ceiling.

One day at a time.

I zipped the bag closed and walked toward the doorway of the room we had shared. Scott was bent over the bed, trying to rearrange the sheets and comforter while a voice came over the speaker of his phone.

"And Ma approved that?" *Evan.*

"Course. Just keeping you in the loop, like you asked."

I should have walked downstairs, but instead, I planted myself out of view and listened to Scott talk with Evan.

"Is Gem holding up? She says she's fine, but everyone around here is worried about her. I appreciate you taking care of her."

I smiled at the concern laced in my brother's deep voice and the knowledge of what had developed between Scott and me.

"Yeah." Scott cleared his throat. "Yeah, she's fine. It's good."

"This has been a long time coming for you with this case. Just keep an eye out. Don't let her run. It's not like she's known for her stick-to-itiveness."

Scott laughed in assent. "She'll do it. I'll make sure of it."

Shame rippled through me. Two very important men in my life were talking about me like I was a child. Sure, I hadn't always been the most responsible woman in the room, but I'd worked hard to leave the scared little girl I was in Chicago behind.

I was Gemma Walker now.

I'd started over—gotten through school, gotten a decent job, made friends. Hell, I had a hot-as-hell thirty-four-year-old man on his knees, begging for me as recently as last night. I was doing pretty fucking okay.

I couldn't listen any more. It felt wrong to listen in on Scott's conversation with my brother and only fueled my desire to put my past to rest. I also wasn't ready to let go of the decadent, soul-shattering sex Scott and I had been having.

Why did he have to ruin it by talking to my brother?

I was opening and slamming cabinet doors, desperately

searching for a coffee mug, when Scott appeared downstairs.

"That cabinet piss you off or what?" Humor danced in his voice, and I scowled in his direction. Something was off with him. Was he hiding something? Now that he was downstairs, I couldn't read anything in his expression besides contentment. Maybe even affection.

"I need coffee," I grumbled and continued looking for a mug.

Scott's large frame came up behind me, his warmth seeping into my back. I closed my eyes and leaned into him despite my unease.

"I've got a better idea. Instead of beating up the cabinets, I want to take you somewhere today. We'll grab coffee on the way out of town." His hands smoothed up my arms, and I relaxed into him.

A few more days. I can pretend for at least that long.

I would deal with whatever this was between Scott and me later. Right now, I wanted nothing more than to get lost in the magic of pretending he was mine.

WE ROLLED along a lonesome highway with the windows down and the radio up. Wind whipped through the cab to tangle my hair, but I still kept one arm stretched out the passenger window.

I let the earlier tension of the morning dissolve and focused on enjoying the ride as Scotty drove us north up a quiet stretch of road.

"You really won't tell me where we're going?"

He grinned. "Nope."

I rolled my eyes. "Fine." A wicked thought danced through my mind. "And if I demand to know?"

Scott shot me a sideways glance and dragged a hand down the denim on his thighs. "Are you?"

I let the thought roll around in my head. In the bedroom, it was exhilarating to be in control. Scott did anything I asked with enthusiasm. It turned him on as much as it did me to exude that power over him. But here, in the confines of my beat-up old pickup, I liked that he wanted to surprise me. He may not think of it as a date, but I was already considering it the first date I'd been on in a very, very long time.

I twisted my lips, considering whether or not to demand to know our destination, then shot him a wink. "Not yet."

Scott smiled and turned the dial on the radio to find a station. As the music played, I sang. The melodies and harmonies flowed from me, and I was unafraid for Scott to hear me. I'd even jotted down a few random lyrics that popped in my head on the short drive to our destination. Most of them centered on the broad-shouldered man behind the wheel.

"You're a very talented singer. I'm not just saying that." Scott shifted his focus from the road to me.

A hot flush tingled my cheeks and ears.

"When all this is over, have you ever thought about singing? As your profession?"

I smiled at him but shook my head. "No."

"My sister Maggie lives in Chikalu Falls. One of her husband's friends has a popular band. He used to be some big name in the music business. I could make a call . . ."

I looked up from my notebook. His hopeful eyes speared me. "Scott. No. The other night was a fluke. I can't really sing in front of people. I'm too . . ." I glanced at the scars on my arm, bare without the protection of a long-sleeved shirt. "Broken."

I could feel the tension radiating off him. I knew he wanted to push, but he didn't understand. My eyes refused to leave my notebook as I flipped a page and pretended to continue writing. My eyes burned with tears.

Singing was in my soul, but I could barely get through singing a cover, let alone sing an original song. I knew in my heart the vulnerable lyrics I'd spent years scribbling in a notebook would always be safely tucked away in my bag.

Had I ever gotten over my stage fright long enough to actually have a chance as a singer, I would have done it in a heartbeat. Trouble was, it wasn't just my scars that prevented me from having the confidence to get up on stage.

It was fear.

What if someone from my past recognized me? What if the life I'd spent the last four years creating was destroyed because bad men wanted to punish me? What if Evan was right and I lacked the grit to stick with something?

Thankfully, Scott let the conversation die, and I lost myself in the radio and watching the rural landscape as we drove. When the truck finally slowed, I read the passing signs.

Darwin, Minnesota—home of the world's largest ball of twine.

I looked at Scott, my eyebrows pinched. He shrugged. "Saw it on the map and figured why the hell not."

Scott pulled into a small parking lot and put the truck in park. He stretched his long legs as he got out and rounded the hood to help me down. I slid my arms into a chambray shirt and made quick work of fastening the buttons.

Just ahead of us, a glass-walled gazebo had visitors peering inside. As we walked up, the massive ball came into view. People from all over the country were posing in front of the gazebo and snapping selfies. Several held signs that said things like *Twine Ball or Bust* and *Drove from California, and all we saw was some twine.*

Scott held out his arms. "Now you can say you've officially seen the world's largest ball of twine."

My smile spread. "A sentence I never thought I would say."

Scott wound his arm around my shoulders, and we took our time walking through the small museum and back outside to look at the absolutely gigantic ball of twine.

I paused to read from the sign in front of the twine ball. "Look at this." I drew Scott's attention to the sign outside of the gazebo. "He worked on this from 1950 until 1979. It says he had to stop because he developed emphysema." My heart twinged for the elderly man. I knew from residents at the nursing home that it was a painful and aggressive disease. "His family says he never smoked, and they believe his illness was from twine ball dust. He died in 1989."

"The thing he loved most is what killed him." Scott dragged a hand through his short hair. "Holy shit, that's depressing."

I tucked myself into his side and looked at the massive brown ball again. "This is the worst date ever."

A bubble of laughter exploded out of me as Scott shot me a bland look. His annoyance only fueled the fit of giggles, and he took one step toward me.

My feet mirrored his, taking one step in retreat. My hand shot up. "Don't. Don't you dare do it." I laughed again.

When I saw challenge in his eyes and he took another step, I winked over my shoulder. I took off in a sprint through the grassy field next to the gazebo. A sick, primal thrill raced through me. I wanted to run. I wanted him to chase me. To catch me. My feet were swift, but I could hear his heavy footfalls closing in on me, and my heartbeat ratcheted higher. Unrestrained, wild laughter raced through me.

It took fewer than twenty steps for Scott to catch up to me, scooping me in his arms and turning me around. The rumble of his laughter echoed through my back as his powerful arms held me.

Together we tumbled in the grass, leaves and dried grass sticking to my hair. We were both panting and laughing as the afternoon sun filtered through the puffy summer clouds above us. On our backs, we looked up at the clear sky.

When my heartbeat finally calmed, I tilted my head toward Scott. "It wasn't a terrible date."

"No?"

I shook my head. "It's quirky and fun. Totally random." My hand found his. "I love it."

He squeezed once, and I fought the sting of tears and the troublesome fact that my foolish heart was once again falling for Scott Dunn.

MA

You missed your status update report. I've called twice.

Apologies. It won't happen again. I will be updating the entire team shortly.

MA

Everything all right with our girl? Will she be ready?

All going according to plan.

IT BLEW my mind that something as simple as a ball of twine could make Gemma happy. Then again, I should have known better. She was everything strong and sweet and good in the world. It was no wonder she would be completely charmed by an old farmer who set out to save something everyone else would have discarded.

The fact it killed him in the end was a bit of a downer

though. To make up for it, I planned a proper date. Not that I was calling it that.

Dinner.

Just dinner.

Maybe a walk down the riverfront tacked onto it.

Definitely not a date.

Evan's words from earlier stuck with me. When he'd mentioned her tendency to cut and run when things got tough, I immediately wanted to jump to her defense. That wasn't the tenacious, determined woman I'd grown to know. Despite his offhand assessment of his sister and my urge to defend her, I knew Gemma was growing more anxious the closer we got to Chicago. But she had to do this. The last four years of my life hinged on her testimony.

Gemma needed more time to be prepared to be hammered with questions from the defense attorney during cross-examination. This trip had nothing to do with seeing the surprised delight glow on her face and the warm tingle that ran through me from a single look.

I could feel my grip on the situation loosening with every second I spent with Gemma.

I rapped twice on the doorframe to her room, and when she turned from her position on the floor, my breath seized in my chest.

Breathe, man. She's just a woman.

Gemma was sitting cross-legged with the packet of information the attorneys had provided. A frown deepened the line between her eyebrows. Her shoulders slumped.

An uncomfortable tug between my ribs had me moving toward her. When it came to Gemma, I couldn't help the riot of emotions she stirred. Namely, a protectiveness that was unrelenting.

I moved silently, unfurling my body behind hers,

moving my legs around her and resting my arms on top of my knees. My head rested on her shoulder as I looked onto the paperwork. Her floral juniper perfume surrounded me.

"Hanging in there?" I asked.

She lifted a slim shoulder. Gemma shuffled the papers, organizing the chaos and tamping them into a neat pile.

"Two of them." Her voice was soft but strong as I waited for her to continue. "It says here that my testimony could potentially put two men in federal prison for a lifetime." She shuffled through the papers until she found what she was looking for. "This guy," Gemma pointed at the all-too-familiar name. Billy Massaro's mug shot was a grainy black-and-white photo. He had the fucking audacity to smirk at the camera. "He wasn't there that night."

I hummed in agreement. I knew the case file well. Billy Massaro was too high up to actually get his hands dirty. He was the twisted man behind it.

"But this guy was." Her index finger covered the face of one of the lackeys that Billy had ordered to take Gemma. The only one who got the drop on Evan and managed to slink away in the rainy darkness.

"I hate thinking about it. Mostly I try to forget it ever happened. They want me to give a detailed account of that night. What happened in that abandoned house. How Evan found me and killed those men. How this happened." Gemma lifted her arm and glanced at the scars.

"They already know what happened. They just need to hear it from you again. On record."

"But what if something I say gets Evan in more trouble? I mean, he *killed* people for me."

I wrapped my arms around her middle and pulled her closer to me. "Evan's plea was already settled. This is about punishing the men who took you and wanted to hurt you.

Only you have the power to do that. They're bad men, and you can relay the information you know from the inner circle. It's why you're here and your brothers are not."

Mostly.

Gemma nodded and swallowed thickly. After a beat, she covered the papers with the manilla envelope and pushed to her feet. I rose with her and watched as she stuffed the stack of papers on the top of her suitcase without bothering to place them back in the file folder.

"I don't want to think about it right now."

I dipped my chin. "Not a problem." I wanted to replace the sad look on her face immediately. "Be ready in twenty minutes."

I left Gemma to get ready for our not-a-date dinner. When she walked down the stairs in a tight black shirt tucked into a short, fluttery skirt with flowers on it, my mouth went dry. Her long, tanned legs were endless, and my eyes roamed over her from hip all the way down to the white sneakers on her feet. Gemma made casual look cute and irresistible all at the same time.

I dragged a hand across my chest and hoped the ache that resided there would ease up.

After the short drive, we made our way through town. My eyes kept moving over the hem of that damn skirt. Friday night at the Office looked even busier than Thursday's karaoke, so we'd opted for a small restaurant a few doors down. The sign out front promised the best tacos in the Midwest, so we figured what the hell.

The place was busy, but after a short wait we were led to a small, high-backed booth in the rear of the restaurant. Gemma chose one side and scooted across the bench seat to the wall. Instead of sitting opposite her, I took over the remaining space at her side. She only lifted an eyebrow at my choice and then smiled down at the plastic menu in front of her.

After we ordered, Gemma shifted in the seat to face me, leaning her back against the wall. Our knees brushed, and my cock thickened at the contact. I shifted my weight, using my shoulders to block the outside world from the intimacy of our booth. With Gemma it was easy to pretend like there was nothing and no one more important.

Because there isn't.

I tamped down the reckless thought and focused on our conversation, ignoring the way my body hummed at her closeness.

My T-shirt was casual and snug at the biceps. Gemma teased a fingertip under the hem of one sleeve. Her fingertips brushed against my inked skin. "I don't remember you having all these."

My left hand found her thigh and ran along the hem of her skirt. "A lot are new."

A small smile lifted the corner of her mouth. "They suit you. Straitlaced on the outside but underneath is a different story."

Gemma's delicate fingers danced over the thin skin on my inner arm. My fingers brushed slightly higher on her bare thigh.

Her hand moved over my shoulder to land on my chest just above my heart where the two-of-hearts tattoo was inked. "Are you going to tell me about this one?"

I looked deep into her cerulean eyes. "You already know."

The din of the restaurant fell away as she shifted toward me. She was the sun, and I was lost in her orbit. Her sweet, minty breath washed over me as I leaned closer.

"Scott."

"Yes, Ms. Walker."

A wicked grin spread across her face. "I have a surprise for you."

Heat prickled the back of my neck. I glanced around the restaurant. We were protected in the bubble of a busy Friday night. Gemma leaned close, her lips brushing the shell of my ear as I stared ahead.

"I forgot to wear underwear tonight."

My cock instantly throbbed, and my fingers fisted the hem of her flimsy skirt. My hand ached to move upward and confirm her secret.

Instead, Gemma shifted away, crossing one leg over the other and letting a low, throaty laugh hang between us. I couldn't stop staring at her thin skirt, knowing her sweet cunt was bare and that gauzy fabric was the only thing separating us.

I groaned. "You're trying to kill me, woman."

Gemma laughed again and lifted a toned shoulder. "Maybe."

When the server came back with our food, Gemma beamed at him. She shot me an innocent but knowing smile as she thanked the man. I scowled at my plate and shifted against the raging hard-on beneath the table.

I managed to get through dinner while actively battling thoughts of driving my hands up her skirt and over the swell of her bare hips. I wanted to drag her onto my lap and grind her against my cock until we were both screaming. Instead, Gemma ate with a smug smile, and every time she licked her lips, I grew more desperate.

When the server delivered the check, I practically threw bills at him and dragged Gemma out of the crowded restaurant. As I stomped outside, Gemma let loose another throaty laugh. I tugged her under my arm and pulled her close.

"You're pure evil, woman."

Gemma laughed again, and I didn't bother to fight the playful energy that bounced through me. As we walked down the sidewalk, Gemma twirled in front of me, her skirt fluttering softly and dangerously high in the late-summer evening.

A limestone walking path veered off the main sidewalk toward the riverfront. A small park and open fields separated the busy downtown with the neatly manicured trails that hugged the shoreline. It wasn't late, so the summer sun still hung above the tree line, but the yellow glow of the old-timey streetlamps lining the path added a romantic glow to the walkway.

I walked us down the crushed-stone path toward the water. Up ahead, the limestone shifted to red bricks and a small sign indicated fourteen acres of winding botanical gardens.

"Can we?" Gemma clasped her hands beneath her chin and widened her eyes at me.

I gave her a small smile and swept a hand in front of me. "After you."

A little delighted squeal pealed out of her and she ran a hand along the tall flowering bushes lining the path. As we moved deeper down the redbrick pathway, the flower beds got denser, more artistic and intricate.

"This is unreal." Gemma's voice was full of wonder. "I've never seen anything like it."

As far as the eye could see were winding, redbrick paths lined with an explosion of flowers and plants. The gardens were meticulously maintained, and each section was prettier than the last. As Gemma walked slightly ahead of me, time slowed. She was happy. Peaceful. I wished more than anything I could freeze time and always remember her with a smile on her lips and early evening sun in her hair.

I had missed out on four years of her.

What a dipshit.

Though I knew in my gut I had done the right thing. Doing what I had to do to truly set her free. I hoped that in a few more days it all would finally be done. Laid to rest.

"What's with the grumpy face?" Gemma's soft voice broke me from my thoughts of Chicago.

I cleared my throat and shook my head. "All good."

She smirked at me. "Good." She lifted a finger and made the cutest little scowl. "No grumps allowed on this date."

I was still convincing myself this wasn't a date, but I didn't have the heart to correct her. Gemma looked around, and a streak of mischief crossed her gorgeous face. Her eyes darted around, confirming that we were in a secluded section of the gardens and we hadn't passed any other visitors in several minutes.

Her fingertips teased the hem of her skirt.

"Don't," I growled, knowing full well she didn't listen for shit.

Gemma shot me a flirty look over her shoulder, her lips tucked under her teeth.

Then she did it.

In a swift sweep of her hands, Gemma flashed me her smooth, bare ass.

Little shit.

I caught her around the waist before she could run off, and I pulled her into my chest. Her laughter exploded around me, and a happy, unfamiliar swell filled my chest.

I tucked my lips next to her ear and wound one hand

around her hip, inching up the hem of her skirt. Her skin was smooth beneath my weathered hands. My fingertips brushed the apex of her thigh and felt only smooth, tender skin.

"Such a tease." My voice was rough and desperate.

Gemma's laugh was throaty, and my cock throbbed in response, pressing into her ass as I held her.

I brushed my fingertips over the smooth lips of her bare pussy.

Fuuuuck.

Gemma swiveled in my arms, standing in front of me and planting her hands on my shoulders. I looked down on her, ready to take her in the middle of a park if she'd let me.

"I can show you a tease," she threatened as one hand snaked down my chest and over the rock-hard cock behind my zipper.

Gemma looked around and spotted a small greenhouse at the edge of the path. It was shrouded by shadows in the darkening evening.

"Get over there." The deepening of her tone had my stomach swooping to my knees.

I swallowed past the gravel in my throat. "Yes, ma'am."

My immediate compliance had her smile widening. My pulse skipped as I looked around again to confirm no one could see us. If I was about to rail Gemma against a greenhouse, then I'd be damned if anyone dared interrupt that.

Once we slipped behind the far side of the greenhouse, the lack of sunlight cooled my skin. Earth and flowers mixed with Gemma's perfume. She guided my shoulders and walked me backward until I was pressed against the greenhouse. She molded her body to mine, and my hands found her hips, hiking her flimsy skirt higher. Her skin was puckered with goose bumps, so I ran my hands up and over her hips in an attempt to warm her.

"Uh-uh." Gemma's eyes flashed. I paused. She walked two dainty fingers up my chest and slid her hand across my cheek. "Listen to me. You will not come."

I shot her a quizzical look, my eyes bouncing between hers to try to understand. Gemma's hands found my belt and began to unfasten.

"Do you understand?" she asked, loosening the leather and pausing at the zipper.

Oh, hell.

I swallowed past the dry knot in my throat. "Yes."

She tipped an eyebrow.

Goddamn, I love how this woman bosses me around.

"Yes, Ms. Walker," I corrected.

She bit back a smile as she lowered my zipper, dropping to her knees at the same time. A brief worry of her scraping her tender knees against the earth dissolved as she took my cock in her mouth.

I groaned, clenching my fists at my sides. Gemma pulled me in long and deep, and there was no way I was going to be able to hold back if she kept sucking like that. One hand worked the base of my cock, and she took me to the back of her throat.

Over and over she sucked my cock and hummed while her hands stroked. I wanted to come. Fuck, I wanted to. To feel my release hit the back of her pretty throat.

But I wouldn't.

For her.

She needed to be in control as much as I needed the relief from giving it up.

One hand brushed the hair from her face.

"Yes," she panted and looked up at me. "I like that."

Wanting to make it good for her, I gently wound my hand into her hair as she continued to work my cock. Watching her mouth stretch over me was so fucking hot that I had to look up at the evening sun sagging over the trees in the distance.

Soft mewls worked in tandem with her mouth, and I looked down to see her free hand sliding up her skirt and dipping into her pussy.

Jesus Christ.

"Gemma, you've got to stop doing that, or I am definitely going to come."

She paused to give me a wicked grin. She held my stare as she wound her tongue around the crown of my cock. "No. You are not."

I closed my eyes and leaned my head against the greenhouse, thinking of anything I could to not let my release build. To not tangle my hand in her hair and fuck her mouth like my body was screaming at me to do.

Gemma sucked my cock as she played with herself. The evening sounds of water lapping on the riverbank and birds and insects blanketed us from the outside world. Tucked away from the walking path, no one would find us unless they came looking. I could have hauled her up and fucked her rough and dirty against the building or pounded into her as she lay across the soft earth.

But it wasn't about me.

Gemma needed the spark in her eyes when she forgot about the limits and expectations continually placed upon her. When she let go of the stress she carried with her.

She could just *exist*. With me. I could be the answer to her pleasure, and she was free to use me however she needed. In those moments, I was as free as she was. No rules. No complications.

Complete freedom.

My teeth ground together as I fought back the wave of pleasure that she so easily dragged from me. Gemma's fingers pumped into herself, and on a cry she plunged them deeper and took me to the back of her throat. My heart nearly stopped, and my balls rioted against me, but I did as I was told and held back.

Gemma released me as we both panted in the growing darkness. My fingernails bit into my palms. Once I regained some semblance of composure, I tucked my stiff cock back into my jeans.

When she stood, I grabbed her wrist, her fingers still wet from her pussy. I pulled her hand to my mouth, sucking on her delicate fingers. Her sweet flavor exploded on my tongue as I ran it between her fingers. Her eyes rolled back and closed as I tasted her.

"Let's go home." I gripped her face in my hands and looked deeply into her crystal-blue eyes. "Let me worship you."

HOURS LATER GEMMA was dozing on my shoulder. Her toned thigh was draped over me, and I trailed my fingertips absently up her spine.

I didn't fully submit to Gemma. It may start with her in control, but we both took turns taking the lead. Back and forth we surrendered to each other in an intricately woven blanket of comfort, trust, and power.

I never wanted the moment to end. I wanted the fantasy life where Gemma and I could set out on our own adventure. Attorneys and federal agents and best friends and brothers be damned—just Gemma and me making a go of it.

I leaned down to inhale the sweet scent of her hair and savor it. As much as I wanted that life—could see it in painful, blissful clarity—it was not our reality. It was late, and once the sun came up, we'd be making our way toward Chicago and, very likely, the end of us.

18

GEMMA

FIRM HANDS ON MY SHOULDERS.

An abrupt shake.

"Goddamn it. Hey!"

On panicked instinct, the heel of my hand stuck upward and connected, but I was then met with a firm grip around my wrist. My body rioted against being held down.

"Gem! Gemma, stop!" Familiarity broke through my confusion.

My heart was hammering, and a clammy sheen of sweat was sticky between my breasts.

My head whipped to the side, and recognition and relief washed over me. "Oh my god. Scott. Did I . . . did I hit you?" I scrambled to my knees.

Scotty shifted from his hip to sitting upright as my fingers moved over his face and paused at a small red mark blooming at the corner of his right eye.

"Did I do that? Shit. I am so sorry!" Worry was quickly replaced by embarrassment as I realized I'd just hit Scott square in the face.

He gently pushed aside my worried fingers. "It's fine.

You grazed me. But damn. Have you been working out?" He gingerly touched a finger to the red spot, then checked for blood.

Heat flamed at my cheeks. "Val and I still spar at the gym a few times a week."

His full lips pressed into a flat line that I was learning meant he was either annoyed or worried or trying to work something out in his head. I still couldn't tell which. "Good. That's good."

"I am really sorry," I said again, despite Scott shaking his head and dismissing the apology as unnecessary.

"You were having a nightmare." His voice rumbled in the pale morning light.

I glanced at the clock. *Four a.m.* I brushed the sweaty strands of hair off my face and sucked in a steadying breath. "I, um . . . I don't remember."

Worry. That line was definitely worry etching his face.

"Does it happen a lot?"

Not really, because I never sleep through the night long enough to dream. "No."

"Hmm." He clearly knew I was holding something back.

The steady drum of my heartbeat was deafening. I sat, awkwardly tangled in the bedsheets and looking at Scott, trying to decide how much of my issues to enlighten him on. Exposing myself and being vulnerable was not something that came naturally to me, and at one time Scott was the only person I'd ever opened up to outside of Evan.

And he left you behind anyway.

The errant thought didn't have a chance to take root, because Scott moved, shifting his body so he was lying on his back and staring at the ceiling. His outstretched arm was a welcoming cocoon for me to snuggle into.

He tipped his head toward his arm. "Get in here."

A shy smile bloomed on my face as I wiggled down to fit into the cozy nook of his arm. My body had cooled so the warmth of his skin was a welcomed blanket of comfort.

"I'm sorry I beat you up," I whispered.

A low chuckle reverberated through his chest, and Scott shifted our bodies to spoon. He tucked himself around me and hiked his knees up to cuddle. A gentle kiss at the base of my ear had me wrapping an arm around his and bringing his hand to rest under my chin.

"You've got a good palm strike, I'll give you that much."

His large hands swallowed my small ones, and I pressed one hand into his to compare the size.

"It started with self-defense. With Val. I think you were still here then."

"I remember. She's a good sparring partner. I got my ass handed to me by Val a time or two."

A soft laugh filled the air between us. I would always credit Val for helping me feel less weak. Less vulnerable. Empowered. We'd started with some basic self-defense moves, and when Val had returned to Montana after her time away, we'd continued with my training. Self-defense, tae kwon do, a little jujitsu mixed in.

I had picked up some more advanced techniques, and it was interesting to note my instincts were ready, if I ever needed them. Though I did feel terrible I had accidentally hit Scott in the face.

But I could never be defenseless again. That was the price for surviving.

The air between Scott and me had shifted. With him I was safe. Warm. Cuddled in a bed where I was just . . . *me.*

My voice was quiet but did not shake. "It was the middle of the day. When they took me."

Scott listened in silence when I told him exactly what had happened to me. Every frightening, stomach-churning detail. He didn't say a word, somehow knowing one syllable from him would rattle me. Instead, he held me, protected me from my own thoughts and worries and anything in the outside world that could come for me. The cottage was our refuge, and I was safe and warm in his embrace. It was there, as he patiently listened to my story in the predawn darkness of a stranger's bedroom, it happened. For the second time in my life, I let my stupid heart tumble recklessly in love with Scotty Dunn.

BEFORE WE POINTED my beat-up pickup east and set out on the road, I had convinced Scott to make time for one last walk through the quaint Minnesota town. I found a ridiculously fabulous pair of oversize sunglasses and a hot latte.

"Hot coffee? Really? It's summer."

I stuck out my tongue and pushed my movie-star sunglasses up my nose with one finger and circled the hood toward the driver's-side door. Scott crossed his arms over his chest and glared down at me.

I held out my hand. "It's my turn."

"Fat chance. If anyone's driving this death wagon, it's me."

My mouth dropped open. "Death wagon? This truck is a classic."

He smirked and huffed a breath out his nose. "A classic piece of shit." Scott shook his head. "Only *you* would be able to convince Ma to let you drive this disaster across the country." He flipped his chin toward the other side of the vehicle. "Get in."

I dipped my chin to raise an eyebrow over the top of my sunglasses. "Okay, bossy."

As I walked away, he smacked my ass, and my playful yelp floated over the morning air.

I like this dynamic.

No more drama. No more painful, messy feelings.

Just the painful, messy disaster of you being eyeballs deep in love with him.

I pulled myself into the passenger's seat and ignored the skittering of panic that my scattered thoughts tried to drum up.

Scott cranked over the engine, and it roared to life. He buckled his seat belt while I looked at the map app on my phone.

I turned the screen to face him. "Seven and a half hours?"

He looked out onto the road and nodded at a mother and her son crossing the street. "Give or take."

"Straight shot?" I asked.

He seemed to consider my question for the briefest moment. Maybe Scott was also feeling the high of our road trip and didn't want it to end quite so soon either.

He pulled out onto the roadway. "Yes."

Then again, maybe not.

The beginning of our trip was quiet. Scott fiddled with the radio, and when he landed on a station of classic rock, he paused and drummed his thumb on the steering wheel. A time or two I caught a glance in my direction, probably wondering if I would spontaneously burst into song again.

As much as music was a part of me—bone deep and fused with my soul—it was also intensely personal. Singing filled my cup but also made me feel exposed. Raw. After the intensity of the last few days, I needed to be more careful with my tender heart.

Scott's expression was hard to read, and his quiet demeanor was unsettling.

What the hell was that guy thinking?

I chewed my lip and quietly pulled up my texts.

> So things have . . . changed.

KATE
> Like escalated to full-on bondage changed? 😈

I rolled my eyes and stifled a giggle.

> No. Like, catching feelings changed.

I watched as the text bubble popped up and disappeared several times.

KATE
> Fuck.

> Yeah. It's bad. What the hell am I going to do?

I sliced a glance in his direction, but Scott was singularly focused on the long drive toward Chicago. The rough planes of his unshaven jawline sent a dirty thought of its rasp against my inner thigh and a tingle down my back. His palm rested on his thigh, and my hand itched to reach out and slip my hand beneath his.

KATE

The obvious answer is to tell him.

Not. Happening.

KATE

I figured. How much longer till you get there?

We should be in Chicago late tonight.

KATE

Then enjoy it while it lasts. Then focus on putting those assholes behind bars so they can rot in hell like they deserve.

I smiled at her ferocity. Kate was a keeper.

Thanks. Love you.

KATE

Love you more.

Now go tie that man up. He'll like it, I promise.

A tiny laugh broke free as I tucked my phone into my bag.

Scott turned his head toward me. Heat bloomed across my cheeks as I thought of him bound and willing as I straddled him. Hot as that image was, I wasn't quite sure I was ready for that level of dominance. Nothing excited me more than commanding Scott as foreplay, but when we got down to it, there was no denying he was just as feral in the bedroom as I was. It was downright hot to see that switch flip.

I scissored my legs together and cracked a window.

"Are you hot?" he asked and began to adjust the air vents.

I gave him a small smile. "All good. Thanks."

My heart squeezed at his innocent and immediate reaction to take care of me. Younger, stupider me would have taken that errant thought and ran with it—coming up with all variations of Scott and me living a life together with kids and a dog and a happily ever after.

I watched the road signs zip past me as we barreled east. With every passing mile, I was closer and closer to facing what happened to me all those years ago. I didn't want to do it. I had let that part of me die along with the men Evan killed that night. Sure, the men higher up in the organization were still out there, but in my secluded section of Montana, I felt safe.

Somehow the people responsible for my kidnapping had been tracked and brought in, dragging me back to the life I had worked so hard to forget. Though I knew the US attorney was just doing her job, I still resented everyone involved.

Why couldn't they just let it go? Leave me alone?

Tears pricked my eyes, and I shifted to face the window.

A warm hand brushed across my thigh and squeezed. "You okay?"

I swallowed thickly and nodded. I couldn't even look at him. "Just tired."

Hours passed as I sat, miserable and alone only inches from the man I wanted to comfort me. When I was lost in him, I found myself. I didn't have to think about the frightened, disfigured woman staring back at me from the mirror. I could be the Gemma that *I* chose to be—strong, in control, desired.

The closer we got to Chicago, the harder it was to remember that woman ever existed. Maybe I had left her in a remote cabin in Minnesota and hadn't realized it.

"Can we stop?" I finally asked, stifling hot, over-whelmed, and on the brink of panic.

His eyes scanned my face, but if he noticed my mounting despair, he didn't show it. With only a nod, he scanned the next several road signs. When we came up on a town, he pulled off the interstate and into the parking lot of a large gas station and truck stop.

Without looking at him, I fumbled with my seat belt and swiftly pushed open the creaking metal door of the truck. "Just going to the bathroom. I'll be back."

I moved as quickly as my feet would allow and ignored the clerk who greeted me at the door. I made a beeline for the ladies' restroom and was pleasantly surprised to see it was large and bright and clean.

The smell of lemon cleaner and disinfectant greeted me, and I pushed open the large stall at the end of the row. Overwhelmed, I sank to the ground. A sob from deep within my chest broke out, and I covered my mouth with both hands.

I can't.

I can't do this.

Over and over, horrible, heartbreaking thoughts—how panicked and scared I was the night I was taken, the sacrifices Evan had made for me, the patchwork family I had left behind in Montana, knowing Scott would up and leave again once his assignment was over—tumbled over each other as I cried.

The stall door opened, and I didn't move from where I huddled in the corner. Warm arms wrapped around me, and Scott's familiar scent of fresh laundry and spicy after-shave surrounded me. A fresh round of sobs echoed in the bathroom as I shifted to bury my face into the comfort of his broad chest.

As he soothed and held me, the tension in my shoulders melted. He murmured words of comfort that I didn't register—just the warm, soothing rumble of his voice. Finally, when I was wrung out, my sobs quieted.

Scott continued to hold me as I steadied my breathing. Shame and embarrassment crept in at the edges as I realized we were huddled on the bathroom floor of a gas station as I had a total meltdown.

I harshly brushed away the tears beneath my eyes and tried to gather an ounce of dignity.

"I'm sorry, I—" I gulped in the air and tried to calm myself. "I just needed a minute."

Scott's arms never left mine. "Take all the time you need."

My legs tingled and my back ached by the time I was steady enough to stand. Scott pulled me up and into an embrace, not caring he was in the women's restroom and I had completely fallen apart.

I wanted to crawl into a hole and die of embarrassment. Scott led me out of the building and back toward the truck. The line of worry had permanently etched itself onto his forehead, and I used the reflection of the window to assess the damage to my face.

My eyes were puffy, cheeks red, nose a total disaster.

"Ma, we got an issue." My attention was drawn to Scott and his stern tone as he spoke into his phone.

Fuck. He's ratting me out to Ma.

A fresh ache made residence in my chest.

Everyone will know I'm not strong enough to do this after all.

"Not an emergency, but we have a flat." He avoided my eyes when I looked at him again.

I glanced down at the truck. All four tires seemed perfectly fine.

"Yes," he continued. "I will update our location. We're not too rural, so I can arrange for it to be fixed, and we should be on the road by the morning." He waited. "Of course . . . understood."

When he dropped his phone in his back pocket, I pinched my brows together. Scott moved his large frame toward me. Instead of the embrace I was expecting, he bent low and removed a knife from his boot and plunged it into the rear tire.

19

SCOTT

AGENT WILCOX

We've received the update from Agent Brown. The team can circle back to provide additional support. I'll send the ETA.

No need. Just a flat tire. We'll be on the road again by morning.

AGENT WILCOX

That's against protocol, sir. I will have to document this.

Understood.

WAS LYING to my boss a bad move? Probably.

Was I risking everything I'd worked for the last four years? You bet.

But slashing my own tire in order to have one more night with Gemma? Totally fucking worth it.

I frowned down at the flat and then shifted my focus to Gemma. "We're not going to get too far with that."

Her eyes widened. I casually stretched my back and looked at the mechanic shop attached to the truck stop. I was four steps away when I turned to find her gaping at my back. "You coming or what?"

Gemma scampered to my side, still a bit shell-shocked.

The kid at the counter was helpful, though he took his time taking down our information. My toe was tapping a rhythm on the oil-stained concrete floors by the time he called his boss. The mechanic, who seemed to own the place, walked in from the back of the shop. He assured me that fixing the tire shouldn't be a problem. I slipped him the keys and made a quick call for a ride to a local motel.

When I closed the door to our room for the night, Gemma still hadn't spoken a word.

I dropped our bags on one of the beds. We wouldn't be needing the second one. I'd be damned if Gemma was spending this stolen night anywhere other than wrapped around me until sunrise.

"Looks like we have some time to kill." I glanced around the cramped motel room. I should have planned this better, but . . . fuck it.

"Do you want to relax? Take a nap?" I asked. "It's your call."

With a shake of her head, Gemma surged forward and threw her arms over my neck. My arms banded around her middle, and I held her body close to mine.

"Thank you." Her breath whispered against the skin on my neck, and I squeezed harder.

I released her and brushed my thumbs across her cheekbones. The swelling in her eyes had started to recede, and that helped the band around my heart loosen. I stared down at her.

Gemma's hand moved across my cheek and over the tender, blackening bruise developing beside my eye, where she'd struck me after her nightmare. "This looks terrible."

"Does it make me look cool?"

Her immediate burst of laughter brought levity, and I could finally—*finally*—exhale a tiny breath of relief.

She looked around the small space. "Do we have time to get out for a little while?"

"You heard the mechanic. The truck won't be ready until the morning. We've got all the time in the world."

While Gemma freshened up, I secured our room and did a general sweep of the property. It was an outdoor entrance–style motel. Not ideal, but it was in a populated part of the small town. The friendly waves and assessing glances I received from the townspeople also indicated that they were acutely aware of any strange faces. That was good considering a town like that, with a healthy neighborhood watch, would likely alert the local authorities if they suspected someone was up to no good. At a time like this, nosy neighbors were an asset.

Once I was satisfied that there was no immediate threat to Gemma's safety, we decided to take a short cab ride to the town's center and pick a restaurant once we got there.

One last hurrah.

The town was simple, as far as Wisconsin small towns go. Gemma and I walked side by side down the sidewalk. She paused and bent to retie her shoelace. I had the perfect view of her heart-shaped ass, and my palm twitched. I wanted to squeeze her curves and mold her to me. Let every man within eyesight know she was mine. When she popped up and started walking again, I averted my eyes and tried to play it cool.

As we walked, I maneuvered around her, placing myself between her and the street. Gemma didn't call attention to it, but a slight blush stained her cheeks as she tucked a strand of light-blonde hair behind her ear.

She knew.

The warm summer air was shifting. Whispers of cooler temperatures floated on the breeze, and as the sun sagged low on the horizon, Gemma hugged her middle.

"Cold?"

Gemma only shook her head, but I wrapped an arm around her anyway. My lips immediately found her hair and dropped a kiss on the crown of her head. A slim arm banded around my waist, and my heart galloped.

So much had changed in four years, yet so much had remained exactly as I remembered it.

I had spent countless nights fighting temptation and pretending to not be affected whenever Gemma stepped into a room. Honor was ingrained in me—my earliest memories of my father included talks about responsibility, respect, and taking care of others. Nowhere in his talks of duty and responsibility had he covered what to do with the mounting feelings toward the nineteen-year-old little sister of your best friend.

So I'd done the only thing I knew how to do. I buried those feelings so deeply even I couldn't find them and slathered them with a layer of cool indifference. Because there was no other option when it came to Gemma.

The fallout was everyone else that came after her. Women who tried to find the man buried beneath the rubble. Who gave up when it became painfully clear that there was nothing left but an empty cavern where my heart had once resided.

Because I'd given it to her a long time ago.

Now that space in my chest was aching and swollen, pushing painfully against my ribs as Gemma took over every corner of my soul. Even the simple act of breathing was nearly impossible with juniper and flowers dancing in the air around her.

Gemma's shoulder bumped into my side as we walked, breaking me free from my spiraling thoughts. We'd stopped in front of a small storefront that promised *Wisconsin's Best Cheese Curds from the Renowned Mars Cheese Castle.*

"I vote beer and cheese." Excitement danced in her eyes, and there was zero chance I was telling her no.

I nodded. "I mean, I guess. It is from the *Cheese Castle,* after all."

Gemma's soft laugh and gentle eye roll was a punch to the gut.

Christ, I fucking loved that eye roll.

We loaded a small handcart with more dairy products than were medically sound and a six pack of New Glarus. When Gemma reached into her purse to pay, I simply scowled in her direction and gently hip checked her out of the way.

No woman of mine is paying when I'm around.

The swell of protectiveness—*no, ownership*—was staggering. If I could help it, Gemma would want for nothing for as long as she drew breath.

She was mine and I was hers.

The realization hit me like a freight train. There truly was no going back.

Maybe we could find a way to deal with our age difference, our history, and her mistrust. Evan, Parker, even Ma would just have to deal with it.

That is, if she'll still have me once the truth comes out.

There was no way I could live the rest of my life without Gemma as a central part of it. I'd just as soon empty my own chest with an ice cream scoop than live the rest of my days knowing I had a shot and was too much of a pussy to take it.

After such an emotional day, Gemma remained quiet but content on the ride back to the motel. The shadows behind her eyes had lifted, and the lightness in her laughter had returned.

Holding one of the several bags we'd left with, Gemma turned a small circle in the little motel room. "Should I pull that little table over?"

"Mmm." I shook my head, then tipped my chin toward the spare bed. "Picnic."

A slow grin widened on her face, and my heart flopped again. Pleasing Gemma was the easiest thing in the world if you paid attention, and my attention on her was unwavering.

Gemma grabbed a small hand towel from the bathroom and spread it out over the comforter. Then, one by one, she inspected and arranged our makeshift picnic. A small wheel of baby swiss, bite-size chunks of fresh cheese curds, something called hoop cheese. She had also added a small box of crackers and a tube of summer sausage to our purchase. Rustic, and not a vegetable in sight.

It was perfect.

I sat cross-legged in front of her and didn't even try to hide the fact that I appreciated the long line of her legs as she sat across from me. We tasted and sampled and completely ignored the fact that, come morning, there could be no more excuses.

Chicago was waiting.

Gemma plucked a cheese curd from the package. "Want to see my special talent?"

I grinned at her. "You've only got the one?"

She leveled me with a playful look. "It's one of many."

When I waited, she tossed the bite high in the air, tipped her head back, and caught it with her mouth.

"Nice. Got some height on that one." I chewed a cracker and grinned at her.

"You try." Gemma pushed the bag toward me.

"Pssh," I teased. "Child's play." I tossed the curd high in the air, intentionally higher than hers, and had to move right to track it. "Oh shit."

The curd came down, bouncing off my nose and tumbling across the carpet. Gemma squealed in delight.

"See?" she said, pointing at me between fits of laughter. "You got too cocky."

She plucked a fresh, golden nugget of cheese from the package and felt its weight in her hand. "It's all about patience and skill." She tossed it high and caught it easily, shooting a wide grin at me as she chewed.

"Show-off."

My annoyance pulled another laugh from her, and I couldn't help but join her. Gemma's playfulness was infectious.

"Here," she said. "Open up."

Gemma aimed a cheese curd at me, and I clamped my mouth into a tight line.

"Come on. Don't be a drag. I bet I can make it."

After a second, I reluctantly opened my mouth and tried to track the bite of food as it went sailing through the air. With only a slight tilt of my head, I caught it.

"Yes!" Gemma shot both arms up and cheered. "I am amazing!"

Laughing, I swallowed, then surged forward and wrapped my arms around her middle. Shifting my weight, I lifted her from the mattress and turned so we tumbled onto the opposite bed.

"Who's cocky now?" I looked down at her perfect features. The same face that had haunted my dreams for years. "You are such a show-off."

"Admit it." She grinned and playfulness radiated from her. "I am perfect in every way."

My voice dipped low as hot air simmered between us. "Gemma. You are perfect in every way."

A deep-red blush crept its way up her neck and into her cheeks.

"Gemma," I repeated. "You have always been perfect."

She tried to look away. A heavy breath whooshed between us. "Don't say that."

"Why? It's the truth."

"Because my stupid heart wants to believe you." Her breathless admission broke the last shreds of resolve I'd been carrying. Any restraint I'd been clinging to was gone.

My mouth moved over hers, soft but demanding. I poured into her as her hips molded to mine. I wanted Gemma to feel every touch I'd ever denied myself. Every time I had looked at her across a game of gin rummy and wanted to kiss her. Every conversation I'd tucked away in my memory because I knew she could never be mine.

But she was mine. Gemma had *always* been mine.

I looked down at her. Gemma's lips were puffy and wet and *mine*. "Believe me. I have wanted you longer than you can imagine. Longer than I like to admit to myself because I know that makes me a shitty friend and a terrible person. But it's you. It's always been you."

The truth hurt too much to look at her, so I captured her

mouth again, sliding my tongue over hers as she granted me entrance. Her arms wound around my shoulders and pulled me closer.

Her hot breath swept over my neck and ear. "Take me. Show me."

I lifted my weight just long enough to meet her gaze. "Is that an order?"

Her eyes nearly rolled to the back of her skull as she ground her hips against me. "Fuck yes, it is. I want you to own me, Scotty."

Her heady, breathless admission was all the permission I needed. "Yes, ma'am."

Gripping behind her thighs, I hauled her higher up on the mattress. One hand swept the bed clear so I had room to worship every inch of her. My hands gripped just above her knees and spread her legs open, granting me access to press against her heat. I left a trail of wet, sucking kisses as I moved down her neck and kneaded her muscles in my palms.

Her perfect tits pressed into my chest, and through her shirt I could feel the hard pebbles of her pert nipples. My hands moved up the sides of her rib cage. I groaned at how perfect and tight she felt beneath me. I dragged my fingertips over her body—from the tender, thumping base of her throat down the center of her chest, stopping at the top button of her shirt.

"Do you like this shirt?" I asked.

She swallowed hard and tried to answer. "Um. I don't know."

Fuck it.

I gripped the shirt in my hands and ripped it open, exposing a plain white tank top beneath. "I'll buy you a new one."

My hands were rough as I yanked the neckline of her tank down, beneath her breasts. Her rosy nipples taunted me through delicate, sheer lace. I wanted—needed—my mouth on her.

When my teeth scraped against a tight, tender bud, Gemma cried out and tangled her hands in my hair.

My cock ached from behind the zipper of my jeans. I wanted to bury myself balls deep in Gemma and let the world melt away around us.

I shoved the tank top—along with her bra—high on her chest, capturing her breast in my mouth without the tease of lace. My tongue rolled around her nipple, lavishing it with sucks and less-than-gentle pulls of my teeth.

My nails raked down her stomach and snagged on the waist of her shorts. In one pull, I dragged her shorts and underwear down her thighs and tossed them aside. Gemma shimmied out of her tank and bra and lay back, watching me from the bed.

I took my time, drawing down the zipper of my jeans and shoving the denim low enough so that the base of my cock was visible where the material came together in a V. Lust swirled in Gemma's eyes as she licked her lips, and my cock pulsed in response.

I reached behind me and pulled off my shirt, tossing it away with the rest of our clothing. Her blue eyes were locked between my legs, where my aching cock was still hidden.

"See something you like?"

Fire sparkled in her eyes as they flew to mine. "I see something that's mine."

I inched off the bed, planting my feet, and pushed my pants and underwear to the floor in one aggressive move.

My cock jutted out to show Gemma what she did to me—how rock-hard she made me.

"I want you to tell me." Her fingertips moved over her sweet cunt as she spoke. "Are you going to take my mouth or this pussy?"

A growl rumbled from the depraved depths of my chest. "Trust me, I would love nothing more than to fuck the back of your throat, simply because you told me to, but right now, I need to fill this pussy."

I reached forward, yanking her legs and positioning her at the end of the bed and tucking her thighs at my sides. I gripped the base of my cock and squeezed. I was so fucking close to blowing my load all over her perfect, pristine body.

Instead, I ran the tip over her clit and down her seam. "So fucking wet."

Soft, mewling sounds floated up from beneath me. She was wet and hot and ready for me to show her just how singular my obsession with her had become. Gripping my cock, I slapped it hard against her pussy before sliding up and down, teasing her entrance.

My body screamed at me to plow into her, pin her to the mattress, and claim what was mine, but I dragged out the pleasure for the both of us. Her tiny muscles quivered as I barely entered her tight, wet hole.

"Yes, Scott, yes." Gemma gripped my hips and tried to pull me deeper.

I placed one hand on her chest at the base of her throat. Her pulse hammered beneath my fingertips. "Easy, girl. I've got you."

Gemma's hips bucked as I fed her another slow, aching inch. I eased back and slid my way forward, back and forth, deeper and deeper until I had stretched her open and filled her completely.

Grinding my hips against her, I began a slow, steady rhythm.

With too much on the line, I couldn't form the words to tell her just what had shifted. That things had changed between us and they wouldn't ever be the same.

But I could show her.

THE WATER in the cheap motel was barely above freezing. After running his soapy hands over my body and washing my hair, Scott wrapped himself around me and held me in our bed. The muted sounds of the highway filled the background, and I lay there, listening to his even breathing.

Scott had owned me, as I'd requested, and there was no doubt—my heart and soul were lost to him. My heart would never recover from this reckless road trip across the country with Scotty Dunn.

I didn't want it to.

Even if that meant I was picking up its shattered pieces when he left.

"I can hear you thinking." Fatigue made his voice rumbly and thick.

I shifted in his arms, turning nose to nose with Scott.

"It was different. Earlier," I whispered to him.

A slight flash of concern deepened the furrow in his brow.

My soft laugh filled the space between us. "Different good," I corrected.

He let out a deep sigh and smiled. "You could have led with that."

I smiled back and ran a hand over his forehead, then raked my nails through his short crop of hair.

"Mmm. That feels good."

I studied his face as his eyes closed and he enjoyed my hands on him.

In the morning, this is all over.

Tears burned the corner of my eyes and tingled in my nose. I held a quiet breath and tried to keep the tears at bay.

"Scotty, I'm scared."

His eyes opened and looked deeply into mine. "I know."

My vision got blurry behind the fresh wave of emotion.

"You can do this, Gem. You have to."

"Do I?" I tried to laugh through the tears. "What if we just run away? Be nomads or convert a school bus into a traveling tiny home. A skoolie sounds perfect. I just saw it on the DIY network."

"I'm not that handy, babe," he joked.

I frowned at him, and Scott shifted his legs to tangle with mine. "I can't even imagine you with another job."

He looked at me and paused. His eyes drifted down to my mouth and back over my face. "It's not just a job. It's who I am."

"I know," I responded into the darkness. Being an agent was what he lived and breathed. It was what he wanted out of his life.

"I want a life. Unafraid. But what if that never happens?"

"Do this and it will. I promise you, it will."

Do this thing that someone else wants you to do. They always say it'll be good for you.

I huffed a humorless laugh. "My whole life has been painted by decisions made by other people—my mother, my brothers, Ma at the ranch. Decisions that are 'what's best for me,' but you know what? It doesn't always feel that way."

Scott stayed quiet as he studied my face. I was unloading some heavy shit on him, and instead of offering to fix it or giving suggestions, he just . . . listened.

"I watched my mother give up her dreams of becoming a singer for drugs and men. Faceless boyfriends I can't even remember now kept her compliant and needy and in a box. Do you know how hard it is to see her face every single time I look in the mirror? She stares back at me and just looks . . . empty."

"You're not empty, Gem."

I looked away. It was too painful to be so honest with him after years of pretending to be someone else. He deserved to know the truth—how messy and fucked up I still was on the inside.

Scott deserved to know my feelings for him ran deep, but I was so afraid of opening myself up to him again, only to have him disappear on me. Instead, I shared the only grain of truth I could. "This thing. With you? It works for me."

Scott's strong arms pulled me so there was only a sliver of shared air between us. "This works for me too."

"And tomorrow?" I let the question hang in the air. It was more than tomorrow. It was all of my tomorrows—every single one—wrapped up in a tiny package and placed at his feet.

"Tomorrow you show up in Chicago and show them who you really are."

~

WE WOKE EARLY the next day, neither of us seeming to have gotten any rest with the looming heaviness of the upcoming days.

Scott had avoided my question about our future as a couple, and it seemed that was the end of it. As the miles ticked down, the tension in his shoulders got tighter and tighter. His eyes darted to every car that passed and then flicked to the rearview mirror. Several phone calls updated his team of our location and estimated time of arrival.

When we got closer, my truck was flanked by unmarked cars. Scott looked down into the car at his side and nodded. "We've got company."

My eyes widened, and he squeezed my hand. "The good kind. An escort to where we're going."

Our time pretending this was just a road trip was officially over.

As we drove down the interstate toward Illinois, I wasn't greeted with a longing or nostalgia. The roads seemed too crowded. The cars too fast.

I missed Tipp.

My brothers had each called to check on me and give me a pep talk. Evan was encouraging and positive, as always. Parker simply grumbled and said he could still "call a guy" if I changed my mind.

My heart ached for home.

Before long, Chicago's skyline bloomed over the horizon. Scott's thumb circled on the back of my hand, and I offered him only a tight smile.

This is it.

The city traffic buzzed around us. Crawling, zooming,

horns honking—it made my skin crawl and the cab of my beat-up old truck entirely too small.

"So what's the plan?"

"They're expecting us at a secure location. A safe house, of sorts. There you will be protected around the clock."

"By you?" I toyed with the soft skin on the inside of my lip.

A barely perceptible shake of his head was his only response.

"What about you? Where will you be?" I tried to keep the panic from creeping into my voice but only managed to make it sound tight and frantic.

"I'll debrief the team. Check in with Ma at the ranch. But I will be a part of the team responsible for your safety." Scott looked at me long enough to gather strength from his hard glare. "I will not let anything bad happen to you."

He squeezed my hand, and instead of feeling comfort, my heart thunked, heavy and hard, against my breastbone.

"And this?" I gestured with my hand between him and me.

A muscle in Scott's jaw ticced, but he didn't answer my question.

He knows exactly what I'm asking.

"Will your job be at risk if anyone knows?" I could guess the answer but needed to hear him confirm it anyway.

Scott turned the car down a city street and continued on our path toward the safe house. His eyes stayed locked on the road. "When people find out about our relationship, I will be removed from the case."

"If, you mean. *If* people find out."

Scott finally glanced in my direction and slowed the truck. "When, Gemma. I have no interest in hiding you away like some dirty little secret. I will need to report to my supervisors and inform them that the situation between us has changed."

I thought of Scott getting into trouble because of me. Because I'd thrown myself at him and we both got off on our unique power dynamic. I couldn't stand the idea of him being reprimanded, or worse, because of me. "No," I ground out.

Scott ignored my harsh tone. "An agent needs to remain impartial in order to make the many difficult decisions that can arise in cases like these. If there were to be an emergency, I can't be trusted to make decisions without my emotions getting in the way."

I straightened in my seat. This wouldn't do. I cleared my throat. "I said no. I feel safest with you. I trust, without a doubt, that you'd make any decision with my best interest at heart. Whatever is happening between you and me is no one's business. We'll deal with it once we're back in Montana." I lifted a brow. "Is that clear, Agent Dunn?"

A slow smile crept up the corner of his mouth. "Yes, ma'am."

21

SCOTT

I CIRCLED the neighborhood of the safe house four times, taking long, winding side roads and crisscrossing over the streets until I was satisfied no one was following us. When I nodded at the driver escorting us, he drove ahead and disappeared down the street.

After turning in the driveway, I punched the code to the garage and pulled Gemma's truck into the empty space next to the unmarked vehicle already parked.

The heavy door closed behind us, blanketing us in darkness. Gemma's breathing filled the cab of the truck, and beside my own heartbeat, it was the only sound. I squeezed her hand again and brought her knuckles to my lips.

Our eyes locked. She looked scared but ready. I nodded at her. "This is it."

I gathered our bags and punched in the access code on the door that led to the interior of the home. Two federal agents stood from the small kitchen island and walked to shake my hand. The men wore casual clothing, but their weapons at their backs and ankles were visible to my trained eyes.

"Agent Dunn, Ms. Walker. I am Agent Kelly McMichaels, and this is my partner, Agent Donovan Proctor. I trust the trip here was uneventful?"

Her eyes sliced in my direction, but I continued to stare forward. She gently cleared her throat. "It was."

"Excellent. Agent Dunn," he reached out his hand to shake mine. "Agent Proctor will show you to your room, Ms. Walker."

"Thank you." Gemma stepped forward as the federal agent walked her down a cramped hallway at the back of the house.

Once she was out of earshot, Agent McMichaels dropped his professional demeanor and bumped me in the arm. "How the fuck are ya, Scotty?"

He clamped a hand on my shoulder and gave me a friendly handshake. Kelly and I had crossed paths on various cases. He was a good old boy from the Boston area and was known for taking on cases that required extensive undercover work. His nondescript Irish American looks were unique, but easily forgettable. Perfect for when you wanted to be a nobody.

"What brought you to Chicago, Kel?"

"You kidding me? The chance to see Billy Massaro locked up? Plus, I'm hoping he squeals under pressure and I can get a little intel for a case I'm working."

I scoffed and dragged a hand across the back of my neck. "Always have an angle."

Kelly grinned at me. "Damn right I do."

I stared down the dark hallway again, wondering how Gemma was settling into her room.

"Hot little piece of ass, huh?"

My head whipped in his direction, and rage bubbled in

my chest. I did my best to tamp it down, to hide it, but it was too late.

When he saw the flare in my eyes, he chuckled and raised his palms. "Easy, boss. I'm just fucking with you."

"It's nothing." I bent down to pick up my duffel bag and set it on the island. I aimlessly rifled through it, needing a distraction from Agent McMichaels. Apparently hiding my true feelings for Gemma was going to be tougher than I'd anticipated.

"Don't tell me you fucked her. You're not that stupid, right?"

I continued rummaging through my bag. "I'm not a fucking idiot. I know."

Kelly chuckled. "Good. Because if the deputy director found out you were banging a star witness in a federal case this size, shit would hit the fan, and you know it. And the US attorney?" Kelly shook his head. "She's a fucking nightmare, but a hell of a prosecutor. Lorene would wear your balls around on a necklace just for risking the case against Massaro."

I swiveled in his direction and took an aggressive step. "I know what's at stake. So shut the fuck up about it."

Donovan returned to the kitchen after getting Gemma settled. I wanted to go to her. Check her room myself and comfort her rather than dump her into a dingy room and leave her all alone. But Kelly was right—outing my relationship with Gemma would cause all hell to break loose, and we were so close to this finally being over.

Four years of my life and it all comes down to this.

All Gemma had to do was go through with it.

When my phone buzzed and Ma's number flashed across the screen, I frowned down at it. I had texted her just before we'd arrived and couldn't think of a good reason she'd be calling so soon.

"Agent Dunn."

"Scott. I've just gotten off the phone with the special agent in charge of Gemma's protection unit. There's an issue. What is your status?"

I turned my body away from the two agents in the kitchen and took two steps toward the hallway. Toward Gemma.

"We just arrived and Gemma is getting settled. What's happening?"

"A development. We have reason to believe that Massaro is now very aware of Gemma's involvement and impending testimony. His attorney was notified during discovery and must have shared that information with his client."

Acid burned the back of my throat. "Tell me exactly what you know."

"Nothing has been corroborated yet, but the communications team did detect something odd over a phone call of his. Massaro received a call from a known associate when he asked if the precious stone he'd wanted had been located."

Precious stone? Precious stone. A gem. Gemma.

"Fuck."

"Yeah, I said the same thing. The team in Chicago was alerted as soon as they received the information and informed me as well."

I scanned the joke of a safe house. Gemma was a sitting duck, and there was fuck all I could do about it.

"She can't stay here. She isn't safe."

"Agent Dunn, Gemma is exactly where she needs to be to fulfill her obligation. I assured the team in Chicago that you could, and would, remain impartial. Is that correct?"

My fist clenched at my side. "Absolutely."

I ended the call as my thoughts spiraled further out of control. I wanted to stomp to the back bedroom, kick open the door, and carry Gemma away to safety like a caveman. Back to Montana.

Home.

Instead, I boxed up my emotions and left her in the care of Agents McMichaels and Proctor.

22

GEMMA

THE FOUR WALLS in my new room were painted creamy beige. It was the same shade my mother's living room had turned after years of smoking inside. When she'd died and I was left to clear the house, Evan and I had taken everything off the walls. It was then we'd noticed that they weren't golden yellow, but actually white, and had been stained with years of smoke and filth. I had looked up at the perfect circle of grime the clock had revealed and dropped it at my feet. It was then I told Evan I wanted nothing from that house and walked out the front door.

There was nothing left for me there. There hadn't been for a very long time.

My stomach turned to be in the center of a room painted that exact shade.

Against the left wall was a queen-size bed with a simple green plaid comforter and two flat pillows. A small dresser was on the right-hand side, and next to it was a mini fridge. It had a variety of beverages and a few sad-looking pieces of fruit.

I moved toward the small window in front of me.

Frosted glass.

I cupped my hands to see out of the window, but the world outside was obscured. I fiddled with the lock and tried to pull the window open, but it was no use. Locked—or nailed shut, I couldn't be sure.

Through the thin walls I could hear voices in the other room but couldn't make out what they were discussing.

My breathing came in sharp pants. Like a caged animal I wanted nothing more than to run. Get away from this pathetic room and my pathetic life.

I dropped my bag on the bed and walked back toward the voices in the kitchen. When I stepped into the room, both agents stood at attention. I glanced around the small house.

My heart sank at the realization that Scott was not with them.

One of the agents—McMichaels, I think—cleared his throat. "Agent Dunn is reporting to the field office."

I pressed my lips in a flat line and nodded once. I tried to control my obvious disappointment as my heart twisted.

Gone, without a goodbye.

Again.

It shouldn't have stung. We'd agreed to keep it professional and quiet until we could sort everything out when I was back in Montana, but his abrupt departure was jarring.

"Is everything settled in your room? You're comfortable, miss?" Agent Proctor's kind, dark-brown eyes helped ease my rattling nerves.

A small, pathetic smile was all I could muster. "Sure. Thank you."

The other agent stepped forward. "We are on rotating shifts." He gestured with his head toward his partner.

"We'll be here until the morning, then swap out with a new team. In the meantime, we stay put."

I glanced over my shoulder at the darkened hallway toward my room. The house itself was cramped, and it felt as though the walls were already closing in. "Just stay here indefinitely?"

He dipped his chin. "Yes, ma'am. If you're to be moved or receive a visitor—like the attorneys, we'll be notified. Other than that, we wait."

"I'll make the dinner run. How does an Italian beef sound? Probably been a minute since you've had a good Chicago beef."

My stomach roiled at the thought of food. "Great," I offered.

Agent Proctor jingled his keys in his pocket and gave me a kind smile.

"And hey," Agent McMichaels said. "I want mine dry. None of that soggy dipped shit you like. And hot peppers."

Agent Proctor lifted two fingers in salute over his shoulder as he exited the safe house and bolted the door.

I SMOOTHED my palms over the sleek oak conference table. The view of the city through the floor-to-ceiling windows of the high-rise was a welcome sight after four days without leaving the safe house. I had hoped things would move quickly and I could get this over with, but that wasn't the case.

Three days and not a single word from Scott. Two agents whose names I'd yet to memorize stood in the room with me, drinking stale coffee and chatting while we waited.

After what felt like hours, Lorene Shipman pushed

open the conference room door and sailed into the airy space. "Ms. Marino, it's a pleasure to meet you."

I stood and awkwardly straightened my shirt. "It's Walker now."

Her eyes pinched, and she offered a tight smile. "Of course. Ms. Walker." She stuck out a hand. "Thank you for meeting with us today."

I shook her hand, and she gestured for me to sit. Several other attorneys flanked her. One leaned down and whispered something in her ear, to which she only shook her head, prompting him to scamper off.

Her eyes raked over me. Assessing and obviously finding me lacking in some fundamental way by how her lips tipped down at the corners. "Gemma. Can I call you Gemma? I'd like to think of us as friends."

There was no way in fuck I'd be friends with this woman. "Sure."

"Lovely. Today is just a way to prepare you for the upcoming trial. The judge is primed, and we are ready to move forward swiftly. As you can imagine, you will be our primary witness. The nail in Massaro's coffin, if you will. Your testimony and victim impact statement must be perfect."

She didn't bother waiting for a response. Without pause, she went through the trial proceedings, what had already occurred, and what I could expect on the days I would be asked to testify. She explained cross-examination and how the defense attorney would no doubt try to undermine my testimony by attacking my character, my family.

My head spun.

I wanted to dive under the covers of some plush king-size hotel bed and bury myself until I woke to find Scotty and I were still tangled in each other.

Nothing about it felt right. Chicago may have been my old life—no parents and no rules and skirting the law to run numbers or packages for the men my brothers worked for—but it was like putting on your favorite cozy sweatshirt and finding it no longer fit. It was too tight, the worn fabric too thin to warm you.

I wanted the broken-in, dusty jeans like the ones I'd found myself in Montana.

"Can I just stop you right there?" I lifted a hand, interrupting the presidentially appointed US attorney midsentence.

Her eyes widened at my audacity, and she bit back her annoyance with a smooth, practiced smile. "Of course."

"Do I have to do this?"

She gave a thin smile. "I'm not sure what you mean."

My fingers itched to fidget, but I clasped them in my lap. "I have been doing my research these past few days. I found a few cases where witnesses were able to provide their testimony through video or a written statement. Something along the lines of protecting the witness from undue psychological harm by forcing her to be in the same room as the accused."

A light scoff was hidden by a cough behind the US attorney, and her shoulders rolled. She folded her hands in front of her, mirroring mine.

"In some cases, yes. That may be true. However, I must stress the importance of the jury being able to identify with you. To truly see what these men are capable of."

She paused, hesitating on something as her eyes moved over me, but ultimately she decided to say it anyway. "We'll also want you to wear something modest, but with bare shoulders. The jury needs to see exactly what you went through because of that monster. Is that going to be a problem?"

And there it was.

I would be exposed.

Exploited.

"You want me on display." I bit back the angry words that wanted to tumble from me.

She only lifted a brow. "That's correct."

I didn't have time to be shocked at her honest response. To be truthful, I respected the fact that she was finally being straight with me. I knew all along my scars and the fact I had a pretty face would help make the jury sympathetic and angry at the men responsible.

When I hesitated, she continued, "Isn't it worth it to put the man who did this to you behind bars?"

I shook my head. "The men didn't actually cut me or do this directly. When Officer Rivera arrived, I was confused. Frightened. I ran and didn't see the sliding glass door. It shattered and"—I lifted my arm—"this happened."

She shot me a hard, icy stare. "I am aware of what happened to you that night. However"—she tapped her pen aggressively against the yellow legal pad—"the jury needs to understand that none of that would have happened had you not been kidnapped. Thrown in a basement for days and frightened into silence because Billy Massaro ordered it. The narrative we weave for the jury will be the very thing that will put away these men for the rest of their lives."

Nausea bubbled up, and I pressed my hand to my stomach to quell the way it pitched and rolled.

A younger man in a suit leaned down to whisper something into Lorene's ear. She shot me a look, and I straightened in my seat.

Her jaw flexed, and a nervous sweat trickled down my spine as she pressed. "You should also consider what this would mean for Agent Dunn."

My thoughts jumbled. *Scott? What this would mean for him?*

I swallowed past the thickness coating my throat. "I'm not sure I understand."

"I'm surprised you didn't know." A sculpted eyebrow raised, and one corner of her mouth lifted. "Well, it is thanks to Agent Dunn you're in Chicago at all." She clasped her manicured hands in her lap.

I cleared my throat. "Yes, I understand. He made sure I was safe on the trip here." My vision became unfocused as I nodded to soothe my rattled nerves.

She hummed, and I thought there was something thinly veiled in her response, but she only added, "Among other things, but yes. We are all relieved the trip here went according to plan. It would be a shame for that to be in vain."

Her words scooped on another helping of guilt as I thought of nothing but running away. Burying my head in the sand until this was all over.

Where I was safe.

Where I wasn't Gemma Marino, star witness, but just Gemma—the woman who got funny looks when she wore long sleeves in the broiling summer heat. The woman who laughed in the face of anyone who said she was an atrocious driver. The woman who wasn't a shitty daughter and a bad friend, but who smiled through uncomfortable moments and showed up early to decorate for family birthday parties.

My head throbbed.

Everyone was counting on me to be strong. Make the

right choice —whatever that meant. Evan, Parker, Ma, even Scott. My entire family unit was watching me toe the ledge of a cliff, waiting to see if I flew or sank like a stone.

And at that moment, all I wanted to do was turn and run toward home.

MA

Unfortunately, there is nothing more I
can do.

> You knew the deal. I get her here and
> ensure her safety.

MA

She's in good hands.

> Not good enough.

MA

I can make a call, but don't forget who
you're talking to.

I TOSSED my phone on the table and watched in
frustration as it spun away from me. If I didn't see Gemma,
and soon, I was going to lose my fucking mind.

It had been four days since I'd left Gemma behind at
the safe house, and every minute had been consumed with

thoughts of her. After briefing the field office and updating Ma at the ranch, I spent the rest of my time finding an angle that would allow me to see her again.

All I knew was she was meeting with the attorneys and making plans for her upcoming testimony. She had to be freaking out. She was thrown back into a city that brought her worst nightmares screaming back to life, all while everyone told her she was in imminent danger.

Don't let her run.

Evan's words about his sister came racing back to me. What if she did run? Four years of my life would be for nothing. If she didn't testify, Billy Massaro would weasel his way out of those charges and be back on the street in a matter of days. There would be no stopping him from coming after her.

I raked a hand through my hair.

Fuck.

After Gemma and Val were attacked in Tipp, I was gutted. I couldn't stand the thought of her not being protected.

So I made the deal.

Four years ago, I marched into Ma's office and let her know that I'd gotten clearance from the district director to follow up on leads that would directly impact Gemma and Evan's case. If I could haul those motherfuckers in, no one would continue looking for the Marino siblings. She could live the new life she deserved. A life free as Gemma Walker.

So I left.

I'd never allowed myself to regret that decision. Until today.

Now that I was faced with the fallout of my choices, I wasn't as confident I'd made the right one. In four years, there hadn't been another incident with Gemma or Val or Evan at the ranch. Instead, I'd devoted my time to hunting the men responsible. Found them. Then dragged Gemma back into the viper pit.

Gemma was strong as fuck, but it gnawed at me that she was in Chicago at all.

A target.

Because of me.

I stood, pocketed my phone, and swiped my keys.

Fuck this. I'm getting my girl.

A PRICKLE DANCED across the back of my neck before I'd even turned down the street where the safe house was located. It was midday, but there were no kids playing in the yards. Very few cars came in and out of the neighborhood, and there was an eerie calm on the side street when I'd pulled my rental car into the drive.

Gemma would have no use for her truck once we'd arrived in Chicago, but I still needed to get around, and I would have stuck out like a sore thumb in her piece-of-shit rig. Instead, the nondescript sedan I'd rented was perfect for blending in and being forgotten.

As I pulled the car up to the safe house, I willed my breaths to be even. I punched in the code to the garage door.

Error.

"Motherfucker." I steadied my shaking hands as nerves vibrated through me.

I finally got the code right on the third attempt and shook my head—at myself and partly to try to pull it together. Beside the gut feeling that something was off, I had no reason to suspect Gemma wasn't safe in the house and likely bored out of her mind.

I entered the security code to enter the house. First try. When the door came open, my heart sank.

Silence.

Eerie quiet.

My hand rested against the gun at my hip as I glanced around. No television. No agents milling around eating or talking on the phone.

I quickly moved through the kitchen and into the adjoining living room—both empty.

"Gemma!" I shouted down the back hallway, praying she would pop her blonde head out of the doorway.

I was met with deafening silence.

I yanked the refrigerator door open and found exactly what I suspected. Totally empty.

That told me three things—Gemma wasn't moved in haste, she definitely wasn't here, and I'd been edged out of the inner circle of knowledge regarding her whereabouts.

After a sweep of the remaining rooms in the house—all empty—I unlocked my phone and dialed.

"Deputy Director Neil Walsh's office. How may I help you?"

"I need to speak with Walsh. Immediately." My eyes scanned the empty house again as my anger stacked and grew.

"And who may I ask is calling?"

"Agent Scott Dunn. Tell him I'm one of Agent Dorthea Brown's men working the Massaro case."

"Hold, please."

After what felt like a lifetime of listening to a shitty Muzak rendition of Bruno Mars, the line finally connected.

"Agent Dunn. This is Deputy Director Walsh. How can I help you?"

"I need to know the current location of Gemma Walker immediately."

A soft laugh drifted over the line, and I clenched my fist to keep from ramming it through the drywall.

"Ms. Walker is preparing for her testimony. I can assure you she is in a safe location."

"I'm currently standing in her *safe location*, and there's no one here."

Walsh paused. "You knew Ms. Walker when she was first assigned to that remote little shithole Dorthea loves so much, did you not? In fact, you specifically requested to work this case, if I'm not mistaken."

I bit back the venomous words I wanted to spew when he'd insulted Redemption Ranch. Pissing off my boss's boss wasn't going to get me what I needed. "I did."

"Frankly, I'm shocked you weren't immediately removed from duty considering the sexual nature of your relationship with the young Miss Walker."

My brain stuttered and blanked at his words. Surely, he was talking about when Gemma first arrived in Montana, but as far as I knew, no one knew about what had happened between us, and I wouldn't call one drunken kiss a *sexual relationship*.

When I made no indication of responding, he added, "I have information that four years ago, while Gemma was under your protection, you engaged in an inappropriate relationship with her."

"Your information is wrong."

"So you have never had an inappropriate relationship with Ms. Walker?"

Unsure where to go with this conversation, I gave as

much truth as I could. "Ms. Walker's care and protection have always been of utmost importance to me."

"I see."

"I have direct orders from Agent Brown to escort Ms. Walker to Chicago and provide protection for the duration of her stay."

"Son, I have a long history with Dorthea. I know more than you might think."

I ground my teeth together at his condescending *son* and waited for him to continue. He sighed. "Frankly, I'm getting tired of you cowboys thinking you can skirt the rules and not be held to the same standards as the other field agents. Thank you for your service, Agent Dunn. You may return to Montana before receiving your next assignment."

And with that, the line went dead.

24

GEMMA

ON A SCALE *of 1 to 10, how bad would it be to steal a federal agent's phone?*

Looks like I was about to find out.

"Hey, Donovan?" I injected sweetness into my voice and swallowed back the wave of nausea.

The young agent looked up from his slice of pizza and wiped his mouth before setting the napkin on the table. "Yes, ma'am."

A soft little snort escaped through my nose. Those words didn't have quite the same ring as when Scotty voiced them. My heart twisted. A jumble of nerves and worry vibrated under my skin.

"When do you think I might be able to get my phone back?"

His dark eyes sliced toward the two other agents holed up with us, both eating pizza with various degrees of boredom written on their faces, but they didn't seem to notice. "Oh, I . . . I'd have to check on that."

The fake smile pinched my cheeks, and I lifted my shoulders. "It just feels, you know, a little like I'm the criminal here, since you took my phone and I'm not allowed to leave."

Donovan straightened and ran a hand down his light-blue Oxford shirt. "Oh no, Ms. Walker, I assure you that we're just making sure that you're safe. You're in good hands."

"Still, it feels a little . . . kidnappy."

He smiled at that and nodded once. "I get that."

I leaned back in the wooden dining chair. "I'm just *really* bored." I glanced down at the black mirrored screen of the phone to his right. "Any chance you have any games on that thing?"

He followed my gaze to his phone and picked it up. The kind agent smiled at me, and I returned the smile and prayed my guilt wasn't obvious. "Actually, yeah, I do." He unblocked the phone, and my heartbeat ticked faster. "I'm stuck on a level in Candy Crush. Maybe you can try."

"Mmm," I hummed. "Worth a shot." I eagerly grabbed his phone as Donovan returned to his pizza, and I moved to the corner of the couch, where I could have my back to a wall.

Swiping up, I lowered the volume but left Candy Crush open in the background. My nervous fingers fumbled, but I opened the messaging app and typed a cryptic text to Kate. I prayed she knew what to do with it.

UNKNOWN NUMBER

It's me. Safe but need help ASAP. Pls tell Johnny "ordering an Angel shot. Brian's court has nothing on the Rasa." Don't text back 🖤

As quickly as I'd typed it, I deleted the message and

swiped to close the messaging app. When I looked up, Donovan was shooting me a curious look.

A laugh that I hoped sounded less panicky than I felt slipped past my lips. "You were right. This level is brutal."

He nodded and joined me on the opposite end of the couch. I let the timer on the game run out and handed it back to him. "No luck."

When I stood, Donovan was swiping through his apps, clearly checking that I was on only the game. When he slipped the phone back into his pocket, I exhaled and stood.

"I'm going to call it a night. Another long day tomorrow with the attorneys. Will I see you?"

"Day off. But I'm back on shift in a few days. Take care of yourself." His kind eyes slathered on the layers of guilt.

If this worked and Scott found me, Donovan would be in a heap of shit for letting me use his phone—even if I did it behind his back. I walked a few feet toward the small bedroom. This safe house was similarly sized to the last one and just as bare-bones and shitty. My skin crawled thinking about the unknown number of nights I was going to be stuck here.

As I lay on the lumpy twin-size mattress, I focused on the ceiling's popcorn texture and whispered a prayer to the universe. "Come on, Tipp. Do your thing."

THE KNOCK at the door startled me, and I pressed a hand to my chest. "Yes?"

"Ride's here, Ms. Walker."

I swallowed and checked myself one last time in the splotchy mirror hanging on the back of the bedroom door.

It had been days since I'd haphazardly texted Kate,

pleading for help and trying to be as guarded as possible on the off chance someone would find it on Agent Proctor's phone. I'd lost any hope that my pathetic attempt to contact Scotty had worked.

My eyes burned from lack of sleep. I was facing yet another draining day of going over testimony, being peppered with questions, and telling the same story over and over that my memories began to feel fuzzy, even to myself.

Is gaslighting yourself a thing? Because I feel fucking scattered.

The faces of the agents who changed shifts and watched over the safe house began to run together and blur. I hadn't seen Agents McMichaels or Proctor in days and lacked any interest in getting to know the new ones.

With a *thank you* nod to the agent who escorted me to the unmarked car, I slipped in the back seat. The air was stale, and I tipped my head back, closing my eyes and letting the outside world fade away as the locks clicked.

Tell me again this isn't a prison.

"Ms. Walker."

The deep, rumbling voice sent a bolt of electricity through me. My spine stiffened and my head whipped up. In the rearview, I could feel the intensity of his stare behind the dark sunglasses.

"Don't move," Scott commanded. "We need to get out of the garage without drawing attention."

I swallowed past the knot that had formed in my throat and nodded.

Scott reversed the car out of the driveway and only lifted two fingers in salute to my escort. When we pulled out of the drive and he drove slowly down the neighborhood road, I released the sigh in my chest.

"You found me." I still whispered despite us being alone in the car.

Scott had barely looked over his shoulder when I saw the smirk lift his lips. "Course I did."

I rolled my eyes at his cockiness, and excitement replaced the leaden lump of dread that had taken residence in my stomach.

Dressed in a suit and tie, Scott had left his broken-in denim and dusty boots behind. Just as I had suspected, he looked damn good in a well-tailored suit. His wide palms gripped the steering wheel as he drove us through the neighborhood toward the city.

I wanted to launch forward, wrap my arms around him, and squeeze. I pressed my palms together to keep from mauling him from the back seat and peppering him with kisses.

"You need to keep your appointment with the attorneys. They're expecting you. Just had to see you again and know for myself you were okay."

I hated that he was implying this encounter was short lived. That our time together was finite and rapidly ending as we drove toward the attorneys' downtown office. I pushed those feelings aside to get answers to the thousands of questions rolling through me.

I settled on the two most demanding ones. "How did you find me? How are you here right now?"

Scott smiled at me through the rearview mirror again. "Your little Nancy Drew stunt actually worked."

I looked at him and smiled when I realized what he meant.

"Kate texted Johnny your message, exactly as you'd asked," he continued. "He immediately went to the Rasa to show Al. Al understood." Scott continued to drive in the direction of the city, but he slowed as we talked. "So what the hell is an angel shot?"

I smiled at the memory of Al, our beloved, cantankerous bartender. "It's Al's way of taking care of us. About a year ago, we had seen this trend on TikTok. If a woman ever feels uncomfortable or creeped out by someone at the bar, she can order an angel shot, and that signals the bartender that something's not right. He loved the idea, and now behind the bathroom door in each of the stalls at the Rasa, there's a little note that tells girls about it and how to use it."

Scott shook his head. "I'll be damned. Well, your text rallied the troops, because Al understood you were serious, so he went straight to Evan. Evan has a number to a burner phone of mine, and I was able to figure out the rest. But why tell Kate to go to Johnny and not straight to Evan or even Ma?"

"Do you even know Johnny Porter? I couldn't risk someone not taking it seriously, and he is *always* at a level ten. I think it's because he and Effie listen to too many murder podcasts. I knew if he thought something was really wrong, he'd be screaming it in the middle of Main Street by sundown."

I huffed another breath. *I can't believe that shit actually worked.*

Scott turned serious. "I'm sorry it took me so long to get here. The text must have autocorrected to 'Brian's court,' but it was enough of a start for me to connect the dots to the safe house location on *Briarcourt*."

I smiled at him, my chest aching to be closer. "You found me. You came back."

"I will always come back for you, Ms. Walker."

Tightness stole my breath, and I fought a wave of tears. Through the city, Scott drove past small buildings that gave way to high-rises. As we approached the building that housed the many attorneys working on the case, instead of pulling to the front, Scott turned the car and drove through the dim parking garage. In a darkened corner, he pulled into a secluded space and put the car in park.

Without thought, I unbuckled and launched myself across the space between the front seats. Scott twisted his body to meet me, and our lips crashed together. His hands raked across my temples and tangled in my hair.

Our moans filled the interior of the car as his tongue slid past my lips. I opened for him and pressed forward. Scott's grip was fevered and demanding as he pulled me from the back seat across his lap. I adjusted so I could straddle him.

In the front seat of a federal vehicle, I emptied myself into that kiss. Days of tension and worry poured from me, and Scott drank every last drop.

His erection pressed against the seam of my jeans, and I ached for more. For all of him. I ached for that look in his eyes when I told him exactly what I wanted, and he was more than happy to give it to me. His hands ran up my shoulder blades and pressed my chest to his.

Hours.

Days.

A lifetime passed before we came up for air.

Our breath mingled as I rested my forehead against his. "Let's leave. Drive out of here and never come back."

"I can't do that." Regret deepened the intensity of his voice.

I ground my hips into his lap and smiled. "That's an order, Agent Dunn."

The appreciative rumble of his laugh was fleeting as he rubbed his hands up my arms. "Trust me, baby, nothing sounds better than running away with you. But if we do that, you're leaving behind everything. Montana. Your family. Running isn't the answer this time. This is better."

I sat back, still straddling his hips and resting my hands on his broad shoulders. I was so tired of everyone telling me what was in my best interest. "Better for who? For you? The attorneys? It certainly doesn't feel better for me."

"We can't. You'll lose everything. So instead you'll go. Tell everyone what happened to you and make sure it can't happen to anyone else again."

I huffed a humorless laugh and shook my head. Deep down I knew it was the right thing to do. What *needed* to happen, even if it meant I relived a part of my past I had hoped to leave buried in Chicago.

Scott moved slowly, melting his mouth over my neck with open-mouthed kisses.

"You're awfully convincing. What's in it for you?" I asked, only half joking.

He stayed silent but looked at me, and a flicker of something crossed his face. It was gone before I could figure out exactly what it was.

Was there something more to Scott bringing me to Chicago?

His hands framed my face. "The woman you found on this trip? The fierce badass who lives here"—he gently ran a finger across my scars, my heart thunking beneath his touch —"the one who takes no shit? Find her. That's who needs to show up in court."

"Come with me," I pleaded.

"I'm working on it, but it's time to go." He leaned forward and kissed me gently.

"Will you be in trouble for kidnapping me?" I stared into his hazel eyes.

"You got here safely. I knew Kelly was your driver

today, so I convinced him to take the scenic route around the city. I highly doubt anyone will notice you had a different driver. But only if you're on time to the appointment."

I sighed and straightened my shirt. Scott ran a thumb over my swollen lips. "You should also probably try not to look like you just got fucked in the front seat of the car."

I laughed and shifted to the passenger seat before wrinkling my nose at him. "Ha. I wish."

Scott grabbed my hand and kissed my knuckles. There was so much I wanted to say to him, but fear held me back. There'd be time once we returned to Montana to figure everything out. For now, I just had to keep moving forward. Get this over with.

"An agent will be waiting to escort you up to the office. I'll drop you off in front." Straitlaced Agent Dunn was back, and I smiled to myself.

As I righted my clothing and dragged my hands through my hair, Scott pulled out of the secluded parking space. Midmorning sun blinded me as we exited the dark garage. He drove around the block and stopped in front of the familiar building. Scott nodded to an agent who stepped up to the passenger door and opened it for me.

"You're late," the agent barked.

Scott scoffed. "Five minutes. I got turned around with all the damn one-way streets here."

"Everything okay, miss? You look a little . . . frazzled."

I couldn't help the laugh that bubbled from me as I ran a hand down the back of my hair again. "Yep. Great." I straightened and exited the car and sailed toward the high-rise building without looking back. My chin was high. My steps were confident. And my heart was left somewhere in the front seat of Scotty's car.

25

SCOTT

EVAN

Did she look okay? She's safe?

Great.

VAL

Looks like we owe Al and Johnny . . . again.

SIENNA

Reason 856 why Tipp is the BEST.

EFFIE

Agreed.

JOSH

Bring our girl home. It's not the same around here without you two.

Working on it.

SIENNA

swoon

PARKER

What the hell are you swooning over, wife?

~

"DO I look like a fucking idiot to you?"

I stared at Deputy Director Neil Walsh's reddening face and considered my answer carefully. He did, in fact, look like a pompous douchebag, but an idiot? Definitely not.

"No, sir."

"I thought I made myself clear when you called my office and started making demands that you were *not* in charge here. In fact, your very involvement with this case puts one of the most high-profile organized crime cases we've seen in years at risk."

It had been two days since I'd dropped Gemma off at this very high-rise, and now I found myself standing in a drab conference room in an attorney's office getting my ass handed to me.

My back was stiff, and my hands remained clasped behind me. I stared at a spot on the wall just over his left shoulder. "Yes, sir."

"And don't get me started on your little cross-country adventure. You're lucky you didn't get that girl killed. Jesus Christ, what a headache." Deputy Director Walsh squeezed his forehead, and chances were good he was about to pop a blood vessel.

My gut rolled at the thought of Gemma's safety at risk. In truth, there were times we had acted recklessly. Selfishly. Times where my focus was not one hundred percent on getting her to Chicago safely. Times when I was thinking with my dick instead of doing what I knew was in the case's best interest.

But I didn't regret a second of it, and fuck this guy and anyone else who tried to make me feel bad for having stolen a week with Gemma and fallen head over heels for her.

Again.

A soft knock had us both turning toward the door. Walsh's long strides tore through the space between the table and the entrance of the conference room. When Ma Brown walked in, my jaw popped open, but I quickly slammed it closed and repositioned myself at attention.

"Dorthea," Walsh said with a shake of her hand.

"Deputy Director. Congratulations on the promotion." Ma had replaced her typical jeans and leather gloves with a starched navy pantsuit. She was put together. Strong, in command, and scary as fuck.

"Position could have been yours had you finally left that godforsaken cattle ranch. You could still come to work for me though."

"Come on, Neil, you know better than that." Ma provided a polite smile, but just as she often did at Redemption, the conversation was shut down when she deemed it over.

"Well, this one's a piece of work." He threw a thumb over his shoulder in my direction. "Where the hell do you find them? Someone needs to get those cowboys in line. They're reckless."

"Happy to take him off your hands, Deputy Director."

A slight tingle of relief washed over me. As surprised as I was to see Ma in Chicago, dealing with her was significantly better than Walsh. In fact, the prick didn't even bother to say goodbye; rather, he sailed out of the conference room without so much as a backward glance.

My eyes flicked to Ma's face. She looked me over with what I could only imagine was disappointment thinly veiled as anger.

So much disappointment.

My chest pinched. I had enjoyed my time working

under the direction of Dorthea Brown. Redemption had been a stone's throw away from my own hometown, and the comforts of Montana made it easy to transition to life as a US marshal.

As a young agent, I'd had the opportunity to travel and feel as though I made a difference through law enforcement. Redemption allowed me to cling to my roots and get my hands dirty when the ranch needed it.

When work took me across the country, it was Redemption, and Montana, that called me home. Ma Brown was a large part of that, and her disappointment was a tough pill.

She lowered her voice. "How you answer the next series of questions is vitally important. Do you understand me?"

I searched her face for answers, but she gave away nothing.

"Yes, ma'am."

"Four years ago when Gemma Marino came to Redemption Ranch, did you engage in a sexual relationship with her?"

My pulse spiked. "No, ma'am."

Ma only lifted an eyebrow.

"Ms. Walker," I clarified, "as I knew her, came to the ranch, and I was one of many agents charged with caring for her safety. During that time we did develop a friendship."

Ma crossed her arms. "Did that friendship ever develop into an inappropriate relationship?"

"Again, no. However, at one time, Gemma was intoxicated on the ranch." It was strange to be talking with Ma so formally, but I pressed on and gave her the information she needed. "She claimed to have snuck alcohol after a traumatic incident with Ms. Val Rivera. As I attempted to escort Ms. Walker to her cottage, she did attempt to kiss me."

The almost-kiss that I would always remember and had

fueled years of Gemma's hatred of me. The kiss that nearly killed me to stop. The pain of rejection in Gemma's eyes was something that haunted me every day for four long years.

I caught a slight twitch in the corner of Ma's eyes. She was not happy to be learning this information. A kiss with Gemma when she had been a newly placed witness in protection, topped with the fact she'd been nineteen and I was eleven years older than her and charged with her safety, was not a good look.

At all.

I cleared my throat and continued: "I put an end to it and escorted Ms. Walker safely home. The next morning, I requested a transfer."

"Did you have any contact with Ms. Walker during the four years you were not in Montana?"

"No." *And it nearly killed me to walk away.*

"Very well." Ma placed both palms on the table in front of her and bowed her head. She exhaled a deep sigh. "Special Agent Scott Dunn, you are hereby relieved of your duties for the United States Marshals Service, effective immediately."

I took a small step forward. "What? Ma, please—" I pleaded.

She cut me off with a raised hand and ice in her eyes. "You will be placed on *temporary* administrative leave until a review of your conduct and performance is completed." Her eyes softened, and she placed an open palm in front of me. "I need your service weapon and your badge, Scotty."

My jaw clenched, and words begged to be spoken, but my duty and loyalty to her kept me silent. I removed my gun from the holster, ensured it was safe to handle, and placed my badge next to it on the table.

Ma looked down at the table and sighed. It took only a moment to compose herself, and she looked up. "Ah, well, now that that's taken care of."

I looked at her in confusion as she smiled and rounded the table. She placed her hands on my shoulders. "You fucked up, son."

I fought a smile. "Yeah, I know."

Ma dipped her head to meet my eye. "Switching places with the drop driver? Really?"

I raked a hand through my hair. "Had to see her."

Ma's eyes rolled toward the ceiling. "You cowboys and your misplaced sense of romanticism." She poked a slim finger into my chest. "You boys are going to kill me."

"Can I see her?"

"That I can't do," Ma said. "This is messy. Dangerous. Whatever business you and her have needs to wait until she's untangled from all of this. You need to go home to Montana and wait for it to be over."

I shook my head and had started to argue when she silenced me with a glare. "You've done enough, Scott. The pressure on Gemma right now is incredible. When I drove here to discuss things with the attorney team, I saw her. Gemma was in tears. Inconsolable."

My stomach pitched and rolled at the thought of Gemma being so upset. I wanted to ram my fist through the wall. Pick up a chair and toss it through the high glass windows.

I was fucking helpless.

"I also need to tell you this too." Ma's words had me lifting my head and looking at her carefully. "She backed out yesterday."

No.

I shook my head. "She wouldn't." My thoughts scattered in a thousand directions. "She can't. Four years." I paced like a caged animal in the small conference room. "But I found them. I tracked them down and—she can't just *not* testify. Massaro will walk."

Ma flattened her lips in a sad smile. "Yes. Most likely without her testimony in front of a jury and a signed statement, Massaro will weasel his way out of this."

Blood drained from my face. My hands tingled.

Four years of my life, gone. For absolutely nothing.

"Gemma wouldn't do that. She can't."

Ma gripped my shoulder and squeezed. "She already did."

EVAN

Don't pull a stunt like that again. You nearly gave me a heart attack.

Noted.

I STARED down at the neat stack of typed papers in front of me.

"All you have to do is sign." Lorene leaned her hip against the desk in her office and held a pen in my direction. "We've transcribed your testimony into a written statement that can be read aloud to the court in your absence."

I thumbed through the several-page document. The words *kidnap* and *plate-glass window* and *basement* jumped out at me, but the rest blurred together. "It'll be enough, right? You said it would be enough to show the judge how dangerous those men are?"

She lifted a slim shoulder as if she didn't give a flying

fuck whether or not Billy Massaro was stopped. "Hopeful-
ly." She looked down at her manicured nails and then back
to me. "I don't go to court to lose, but if I'm being honest,
without the impact of your direct testimony, it's a long shot."

My fingers buzzed with energy. After six hours of being
prepped by an endless stream of attorneys and testimonial
experts, I'd had a complete breakdown. Exhaustion and
haunting memories consumed me. Tears flowed, and the
agonizing thought of being faced with the men responsible
for my kidnapping danced through my mind.

I couldn't do it.

It was just too much.

I sobbed in an office chair until I was wrung out. One of
the lawyers had taken pity on me and gotten me a napkin
and lukewarm glass of water. My only other option to
standing in front of the court was to provide a written
statement.

A much easier way out.

"Sign the statement and we'll proceed without you.
Your obligation for providing testimony as a witness under
protection will be fulfilled, unless the court requires it
again."

"Again?"

"In the case of a mistrial, retrial, appeals . . . things like
that."

I shook my head. "I don't want to do this again."

She shrugged. "It's the position we're in. No one wants
to go through this again, but it happens."

She abruptly flipped the pen toward me and pressed a
button on the telephone sitting on the table. Moments later
another lawyer with a stack of files entered the conference
room. He set the files beside Lorene and stood with his back
to me.

"She's signing now," she said.

"Dibs on not being the one to tell the marshal he wasted four years of his life on this," the young lawyer muttered to her.

I glanced up, the pen dangling from my fingertips. "Four years? What . . . what are you talking about?"

The attorney turned her attention to me and hummed with a nod. "Yes. There was a US marshal who spent the better part of four years undercover, tracking down the individuals responsible for your . . . unfortunate detainment. No one had even come close, but he worked every lead until we got enough information for an arrest and charges. I'm guessing he'll be pretty disheartened to hear all that work was truly for nothing."

A buzzing whooshed in my ears as my heart pounded. The floor fell away as my head spun.

Four years. Four years. No . . . it couldn't . . .

"The agent," I choked out. "Who was it?"

Lorene flicked open a file folder and raised an eyebrow as though she was surprised I was even asking. The world fell away at her words. "Agent Scott Dunn, of course."

Four Years, One Month, and Nine Days Ago

The pad of my fingers started at my neck, circling the red, angry scars that crept past my collarbone.

What if the glass had hit an artery?

My fingers trailed south across my chest and lower on my arm. The inside of my biceps no longer had soft, tender flesh. Instead, chaotic intersections of red slashes and bumps littered my arm and burned a path past my elbow to my wrist. My wounds had been repaired, but they would never be gone. My finger paused on the marks near my wrist. One extended a centimeter or two onto my palm.

What if it had been deeper?

I shook the frightening, intrusive thoughts from my fuzzy mind and lifted the bottle of dark liquid to my lips. I shuddered as I swallowed it down.

Fucking bourbon.

I'd lifted it from Evan's secret stash and, at the time, didn't give a shit if he found out I'd stolen it. He could continue to be the responsible one. Tonight I was getting shitfaced.

I didn't want to go back to my cottage, so instead, I dangled my feet off the dock of the small pond just west of the main lodge. It was peaceful. Secluded. I could get hammered and feel sorry for myself without anyone clicking their tongue and shaking their heads in disappointment.

I took another sip.

Maybe I am just like my mother after all.

Only hours ago my life had been tipped sideways—again.

How long had I spent resenting my oldest brother, Parker? Thinking he was the man who had made the order to kidnap me? His voice still ran an icy chill up my spine.

Now he was here and everyone, including Evan, was telling me that Parker wasn't the man responsible.

Well, fuck that. No matter who is responsible, I'm the one who looks like a cut-up rag doll. If it were a man, women would fawn over him and say his scars were sexy. But me? I was just a broken, discarded little thing.

"Pity party for one?" The deep timbre of Scotty's voice had butterflies erupting low in my belly.

I closed my eyes against the darkness and soaked it in.

My head swam with bourbon. My filter dissolved in the bottom of my glass.

"Fuck yeah, I'm having a pity party. Wanna join me?"

I kicked my dangling legs and leaned back on the dock, the bottle settled between my thighs. Scott's dusty boots came to pause right next to me.

"Looking for me to kick your ass in gin rummy?" I teased.

"Let's go to bed, Gem."

I only hummed.

How I wished those delicious words meant something else entirely. I had had sex only once, and it was pretty uneventful, but any red-blooded woman could assume that Scotty Dunn definitely knew his way around a bedroom and a woman's body.

The slimy ooze of jealousy ran through me. Surely, women had been in his bed. Women who were older and sophisticated. Beautiful and unscarred. My eyes landed on my bare, disfigured arm again, and I slipped it into the sleeve of the flannel shirt at my side. My eyes burned.

Women who weren't broken.

When I continued to sulk and stare out onto the black mirror of the pond water, Scotty sighed and sat next to me. His masculine aftershave wafted over me and, mixed with the bourbon, did dangerous things to my insides.

Shoulder to shoulder, I let myself lean into his warmth. Over the months that our friendship had developed, I'd learned to soak in the rare and fleeting moments of contact.

"What's going on with you? Are you drunk?" He was more concerned than annoyed. Just another tick mark in the column of things I loved about him.

"Trying to be." I smiled and lifted the bottle to my lips

again when Scotty's hand reached up and stopped me short of another long pull.

My eyes flashed to him. He held my gaze—far longer than he ever had before. His eyes were more brown than green in the moonlight as his gaze moved over my face and landed on my lips. He gently pulled the bottle from my hand.

He paused with the bottle midair, and I fully expected a verbal reprimand from the always straitlaced Scotty. Instead, he lifted the bottle to his lips and took a long pull. I watched the column of his throat work as he swallowed. My eyes flew to the slick sheen of bourbon still resting on his lower lip. I wanted to be brave enough to lean forward and swipe it with my tongue. To finally—finally—do with him what I'd been imagining all those months.

Scotty's eyes held mine. He took another quick drink without breaking our eye contact. Heavy heat pooled in my belly. Scott shook his head as if he couldn't believe he was sitting here, with me, slowly getting drunk in the darkness.

Scott set the bottle behind us. My tongue darted out and pulled my lower lip into my mouth, sucking off the drop of bourbon that clung there as he continued to stare.

I knew that look in his eyes.

Hunger.

My chest pinched. I wanted to be brave. To lean in and kiss him like I'd dreamed about for months and months.

"I don't like to see you sad," he said.

His deep voice was like a blanket, and I let it smother me. Soothe me. I closed my eyes to imagine a world where Scotty Dunn scooped me into his arms and made everything better. But in that fantasy, I wasn't some broken, sad little girl. I was a fierce woman with power and control. A woman I could never be.

Against my will, my body hiccuped, and I tried to hide the fact that my brain was feeling fuzzier by the second.

I pouted toward the water, letting my thoughts tumble out of me. "What if no one thinks I'm pretty?"

A low harrumph rumbled next to me. "That's impossible."

I yanked up the unbuttoned sleeve of my shirt, revealing the worst of the scars on my forearm. "Look at me. I'm hideous. Disfigured."

Scott shifted his body, but I kept my eyes focused on the knotty boards of the dock. "Gemma, I am looking at you. I've been looking at you for a long time."

He scrubbed a hand along the back of his neck and let go of a deep, resounding sigh. I finally mustered the courage to look at him again as he continued: "And you're the most beautiful woman in the world."

My heart soared. Rainbows and unicorns and twinkly stars burst through my imagination.

Scotty Dunn thinks I am beautiful.

That was it—everything I had imagined between us was coming true, and things would totally work out. I was finally getting to be a winner in my loser of a life.

I hiccuped again and giggled, covering my mouth with my hand.

"All right, drunkard, time to go." Scott pulled a leg beneath him and shifted to stand.

I scrunched my nose at him. "Drunkard? You are such an old man."

He stifled a groan as he got up. "Yeah. Don't I know it."

Scott held his hand out to me as I stared up at him. "Come on, let's go."

When I moved to stand, the earth shifted below me. I

ended up on all fours as the wood swirled beneath me. "Whoa. Okay. Nope. I'm good."

Scotty laughed, and his strong hands gripped my rib cage as he pulled me up. His closeness made it hard to breathe.

I righted myself, but the world still pitched and rocked like waves slamming against a boat. "Thanks," I breathed. When I wobbled again, I gripped his shoulders. "Whoa."

Scott rolled his eyes and bent to scoop me in his arms.

Every point of contact lit up—from my arm looped around his neck to the length of my thigh pressed against his torso. I nestled into him like a cat.

It was a bit of a walk to my cottage, but Scott didn't put me down. He didn't strain as he carried my weight across the gravel path toward home. I stared up at the sharp line of his jaw set against the star-filled night sky. My heart leaped.

This is it. This is finally it!

When we reached the cottage, Scott was careful to set me down. His fingertip moved a strand of hair away from my face as he assessed me. I reached up and smoothed the faint line that formed between his eyebrows with my thumb. We'd never been so close, sharing air and wrapped in the silent darkness of a Montana night.

"What are you thinking? Right now?" I asked.

"Your brother would kill me if he knew what I was thinking."

I let my hand trail down the muscular slope of his shoulder, gathering every bit of courage I could. "My brother isn't here. And he's not my keeper."

Scott's eyes dropped to my lips, and the hunger returned to his gaze.

"Do you really think I'm beautiful?" I asked. My insecurities raged as I stood on my front porch with an older, experienced man, and hope hummed through me.

"More than I have a right to," he admitted.

Pinching my eyes closed, I stepped up on my tiptoes and pulled his mouth to mine.

Scott stilled. His hand clutched the back of my shirt. A soft moan bubbled up my throat at the softness of his lips, but instead of taking me, pulling me closer, his hands gripped my hips and gently pushed me away from him.

Confusion clouded my mind and was quickly replaced with embarrassment and shame.

"Gemma. I—we can't."

I swiped the kiss from my lips and looked away. My cheeks burned. Scott couldn't even look me in the eye.

"Pfft. Whatever." I blew a raspberry with my lips and tried to hide my mounting shame. Suddenly freezing, I clutched the collar of my shirt and pulled it closer, hiding any trace of my scars.

I drunkenly fumbled with my keys, then moved away from Scotty and into the cottage. I slammed the door behind me and sank to the floor with my back pressed against the wood.

"Gem. Come on. Open up, Gemma. We can talk about this." His voice was soft and only made the cracks in my heart break wide open. Scotty was a good man. A good friend. No matter how long I'd let my juvenile fantasies run away from me, he would never see me as more than that. His friend's little sister.

I stifled a sob behind my hand and refused to open the door. When I heard two footsteps recede, I braved a peek out the window at my side. Pulling back the curtain just enough, I saw his silhouette, crouched on the top step of my little front porch.

Scotty rested his elbows on his bent knees and held his

head in his hands. He raked his fingers through his hair and stared out into the darkness.

I stared at him. So long I stared, as he stood guard outside my cottage door, until fatigue and alcohol pulled me under.

But in the early hours of morning, when I awoke on the floor of my cottage, with a pounding head and aching back, he was gone.

SCOTT

THE BURNER PHONE in my pocket buzzed, and I put it to my ear. "Dunn."

"Scotty, we need to talk." Ma Brown's smooth voice came over the line.

"How did you get this number?" Her silence had me shaking my head.

Of course she could somehow get this number.

I could imagine her unamused face perfectly as she waited. "What do you need?"

"Gemma would like to see you before her meeting with the attorneys." My heartbeat ticked higher as I swallowed past the fist-size lump in my throat. "However," she paused, "it will be brief and supervised. Be at the attorney's office in one hour. There's a Starbucks on the first floor. Gemma will meet you there."

Ma hung up before I could react, but it was for the best. My windpipe was so tight there was no way I'd be able to speak. I was across the city, packing my shit and trying to find any way I could fix the mess I'd made.

When I arrived downtown, I was early. The sun was

shining, and the air was already warming in the summer morning. I sat in the plaza at the base of a small fountain. Men and women in suits hustled past me; a bike courier was already making deliveries. A few people sat nearby on the fountain ledge or on the benches and drank coffee or ate a hurried breakfast. The fast pace of the city buzzed around me, and I missed the long stretches of silence found in quiet Montana mornings.

I let myself imagine slow mornings with coffee on a wide front porch, Gemma tucked under a blanket with a book in her lap. I'd kiss the top of her head and nestle in behind her even though there was another chair. She'd laugh and shake her head but then sigh and cuddle in closer.

The striking clarity of my imagination was a cruel bitch. My chest ached thinking of the maybes and what-ifs.

Goddamn, I need to fix things.

I checked my watch and made my way into the high-rise a few minutes before our arranged time. The coffee shop was, as Ma had indicated, on the first floor. It was busy, so I got in line and ordered Gemma's favorite and a black coffee for myself.

Not long after the order was up, a man in a suit with assessing eyes made a lazy loop in the coffee shop. An agent, no doubt. We were shockingly easy to spot, if you knew what to look for. I took a casual stance near a table in the back and waited.

Moments later, Gemma walked through the door. My heart stopped. Her platinum hair hung in smooth, beachy waves, and her oversize band T-shirt had been cropped high on her stomach. Her jeans were high waisted, and she had a flannel tied around her waist. She looked chic. Effortlessly stylish, and more than one chump in a suit turned their heads to drink her in.

Possessiveness burned in my veins.

That woman is mine. And I am hers.

I stood straighter and moved forward when I caught her eye. The ice in her glare nearly paused my steps, but I trudged ahead. Only a few paces behind her was Agent Kelly McMichaels. He kept a respectable distance as I faced Gemma.

I kept my voice low, hoping to soothe her glare with my voice. "Hey, babe."

Her nostrils flared and I tensed.

Yep, she's pissed.

"Don't. Even," she warned.

I lifted the paper cup in my hand. "Grande skinny vanilla latte. Extra shot, extra hot."

Her eyes flicked down to her favorite drink, and I swear I saw her soften for the tiniest fraction of a second. My heart held on to that hope.

She swiped at the cup aggressively but offered a curt, "Thank you."

I sipped my black coffee and tried not to smile.

God, I love her fire, even when it's aimed at me.

I motioned toward an empty table nearby, but she stood her ground.

"I found out some very interesting information yesterday."

"Okay . . ." The anger in her voice made my tongue go thick. The distinct feeling of knowing you'd fucked up but not quite knowing what you did crept up the back of my neck. Honestly, it could be any number of things, from manipulating our road trip to convincing Kelly to let me be the one to be her drop-off driver to a thousand microdecisions in between.

"Tell me why you left Montana."

My jaw clenched and I widened my stance. *Here we go.* "I had a job to do."

"That is such bullshit!" When heads turned, Gemma lowered her voice and stepped forward, poking a hard finger into my pec. "It's bullshit and you know it."

This time, frustration rattled through my veins. She didn't get it. She didn't see how everything I had done had been with singular, unwavering focus—*her.*

"It isn't," I ground out. "I spent four years of my life tracking them down. *For you.*"

When I emphasized the last two words, fire danced in her eyes. "I didn't need you to do that," she hissed. "Jesus! Why can't you see that? I was getting past it. I was finally moving on. Happy."

Tears burned in her eyes, and my heart filled with lead.

For so long, I'd convinced myself that everything I was doing—following every lead, making allies with the scum of the earth, sacrificing a life with Gemma at my side, had been because she needed me to.

The revelation that maybe she didn't really need me to do those things roiled in my gut.

I fucked it up. Right from the very beginning.

"It is so infuriating having everyone around me make decisions without ever asking *me* what I want. I hope you know you left for *nothing.*" When a tear tumbled over her lower lashes, my heart twisted. Gemma brushed it away and turned. I reached for her, and time slowed.

Out of the corner of my eye, Kelly made a movement. A barely perceptible dip of his chin. The hairs on the back of my neck stood. My eyes sliced to the back corner of the coffee shop, where a man stepped through the crowd.

Familiarity bloomed in the back of my mind.

A man in a black baseball cap. The same man from the baseball game in North Dakota. Build. Haircut. Brooding energy.

I was sure of it.

As time and sound warped, the man surged forward, and I instinctively reached for my service weapon.

A gun I didn't have.

Pivoting, my feet carried me forward, lurching toward Gemma. Her back was to me, but my hand reached out, and one arm pushed her behind me as I blocked her body with my own.

I called out a warning as the man tangled his body with mine. A sharp pain shot across my flank as we wrestled to the ground.

The crowd gasped and a woman screamed. As we tussled on the floor, an agent tackled the man and pulled him off me. I rolled in time to see Kelly grip Gemma by the shoulders and drag her to safety.

"No!" I called. Kelly was in on it; that much I knew for certain. The pain in my side bloomed upward, and I gripped it. When I pulled my hand away bloody, I realized I'd been stabbed.

Mostly a flesh wound, but it had been intended for Gemma.

My Gemma.

Pain and hatred radiated off my body as I righted myself to my knees and attempted to stand. I was seething. All hell broke loose, and I was surrounded by helpful Samaritans and then more agents as security and medical help arrived.

Gemma had been scurried away, and I couldn't get

through the crowd to find her before she was, undoubtedly, moved to a secure location.

I shrugged off the offer to go to the hospital, instead opting for a primitive wrapping of gauze and tape.

"This probably needs stitches." The pointed look of the EMT told me she was probably right.

"It's fine." I looked past her to find where they'd taken Gemma. I wouldn't stop looking until I knew she was safe.

"Your call." The EMT sighed and shook her head as she finished the wrapping.

The area was cleared by police and agents as I stood by to provide my statement. Without my federal identification, the police were hesitant to release me, and I was getting pissyer by the second.

When Ma Brown came stomping down the hallway, looking like she was breathing hellfire, I sighed in relief. She was always someone I could trust. She'd believe me when I told her about Kelly, and she could ensure Gemma was truly safe.

The crowd parted for her, sensing the authority in her steps. She flashed her ID at the officers who were standing guard by me. "He's with me." She dismissed them with a jerk of her head.

When Ma stepped up to me, she lifted both hands. "What the hell?"

"I'm totally fine, thanks for asking."

She sighed and softened, fractionally. "Are you?"

I stood and stifled a pained groan. "Perfect. But we need to talk."

Ma looked around and pulled me into a quiet corner, away from curious glances and eager ears.

"It was meant for Gemma."

"Clearly." Ma was not known for her patience, and it showed.

"Kelly McMichaels is in on it."

Her eyes widened. "That is a serious accusation."

"I'm sure of it. He gave a signal. I've been working it out." I gestured to the side of my head. "When we were in North Dakota, I saw the same man who attacked today. He was tracking us. No one outside the agency knew our locations. Someone on the inside was providing information, but it was delayed. Had to have been someone carefully probing to not raise any red flags."

Her lips flattened. While it was a serious accusation, I was convinced of its truth. "What's his angle? Why risk it?"

I exhaled, and my side rioted against the muscle contraction. I grunted against the pain. "My guess is it's his case. He told me he was hoping Gemma's presence would drum up some information for a case he's been working on for years. Best I figure is nothing was coming up, and he was getting desperate. When she decided to walk, he knew his chances were slipping away."

Ma's gaze looked out onto the people standing around and staring at the scene. "It's possible. I'll look into it."

"Let me back on. She needs someone to protect her."

Ma's eyes flew to mine. "No."

With the conversation over, Ma whirled in her suit and walked away from me, leaving me desperate, without answers, and with an angry aching heart that rivaled the wound at my side.

PULLING onto the interstate and driving away from Chicago was one of the hardest things I'd done in my entire fucking life. Second only to leaving Montana after Gemma kissed me. Back then I had spent the night on the top step of her front porch, willing myself not to bang on her door and demand she kiss me again.

All so I could kiss her back proper. To show her the way a woman like her deserved to be kissed.

Both times I knew in my gut that leaving was the right decision, but the tether Gemma had lassoed around my heart made it nearly impossible to go.

Ma insisted I give Gemma the space she needed and to not fuck this case any more than I already had—her actual words.

While on administrative leave, I didn't have a leg to stand on to continually insert myself in the case, so Ma encouraged me—aka pointed her finger at me and insisted, "Go. Home"—to leave Chicago in my rearview. Not until she assured me that she was staying by Gemma's side with increased security while they prepared to head home did I agree to drive Gemma's truck back to Montana.

The tenderness in my side paled in comparison to my bruised heart. Gemma's pained words poked at it.

I didn't ask you to do that.

I was getting past it.

I was finally moving on.

Happy.

I had royally fucked up.

Sitting in the cab of her beloved truck, surrounded by her juniper-and-floral scent, was a special kind of hell. My eyes stayed pinned to the road rather than glazing over to the passenger seat. I could still see her, feet propped on the dash, scribbling lyrics in her tattered little notebook as I wound a path down some country road. Her painted toes would bounce to the beat of whatever song came on the radio and, if I was lucky, she'd absently hum along.

Fuck. So much had been left unsaid between us.

I had cracked the window to let in fresh air and give me a break from the all-consuming smell of Gemma when one of her stray blonde hairs was caught in the wind and floated in front of me. I balled my hand into a fist and slammed it against the passenger seat.

"Fuck!" Anger bubbled, and I clenched my fist tighter.

It was all for nothing, and in the end, Gemma bailed.

I had officially failed her.

My foot hammered the accelerator, and I flew down the interstate, pushing the old truck to its limits. I couldn't stand to spend another second in that truck without her, knowing a real shot with her had been *so close* and I'd fallen short.

In a matter of days, I'd also have to face my best friend and tell him I'd failed to do the one thing Evan had asked— see it through to the end and protect his sister.

Feeling helpless and out of control was something that left my stomach uneasy and tight. My entire adult life was a set of controlled decisions that hadn't led me astray. Yet all I could think about were the moments when I gave up that control and willingly submitted to Gemma. Not only our heated moments, but the quiet ones too. When I could let my mind be still and relax into peaceful surrender. With her. Only for her.

Gemma's touch gave me a sense of peace, a lightness that let my stressful thoughts dissolve and melt away. Never in my life had I experienced that relief, and I owed it all to her.

She was a powerhouse.

Nothing could stop her—if only she'd believed that herself.

The trip back to Montana was a blur of shitty motels and fast-food restaurants. I opted to drive as hard and fast as I could in order to leave Chicago behind me. My entire career was up in the air. I wasn't a working federal agent, so instead of pulling into Redemption Ranch, I'd called my sister and headed to the small town of Chikalu Falls, Montana.

She was working at her flower shop when I pulled down the main drag of town, but if I knew my stepsister at all, I was confident she would make the time for me. The soft tinkling of the bell on the door announced my entrance, and Maggie popped her head up from below a large wooden countertop at the back of the shop.

Her eyes lit up when she saw me. "Holy crap! I wasn't expecting you till tomorrow."

I pressed my lips together and offered a sad, defeated wave. Maggie rounded the counter and stepped up to me. "Wow. You look like shit."

I pulled her into a hug. "It's good to see you, too, Sis."

She squeezed me back, and a few of the little jagged bits inside me smoothed over. "Are you kidding me? It's *amazing* to see you. You just surprised me is all." She gave me another squeeze, and I winced.

"What?" Worry creased her brow.

"It's nothing." I gestured to my side. "Just a scratch."

Maggie's mouth dipped into a firm line. She knew better than to believe me but also knew the nature of my job meant I had secrets. Resigned, she wiped the palms of her hands on the front of her jeans and smiled up at me. "God, it's good to see your stupid face."

I smiled at my sister. "Yours too."

Not quite ready to unload all of my shit on her, I looked around her flower shop. She had owned the floral business for a while now, and I was so damn proud of her. My eyes paused on a small table of cacti that looked to be tiny dicks. A tasteful little sign that read *Cock-tus* was neatly folded and propped in front.

I pointed at it. "Nice."

Her grin widened and she shrugged. "They're my best-sellers."

"Of course they are." My eyes rolled.

Maggie propped her hands on her hips. "Don't tell me I haven't seen you in months and you drop into my shop in the middle of the day to talk about phallic succulents. What gives?"

I eyed the door and let go of a deep, resounding sigh. "You got a minute?"

When I raked my hand through my hair, her eyes softened. Maggie set her mouth in a firm line and marched toward the door, flipping the lock and turning the OPEN sign over. "For you? Always."

Sitting at the back of her flower shop, over a can of Diet Coke, I told her everything. Well . . . almost everything. I left out the parts where Gemma was an absolute dynamo in bed and I'd spent my nights eagerly submitting to her every will and whimsy. Sisters didn't need to know that shit. But she got up to speed about our past and that I'd willingly crossed a line with Gemma despite knowing it meant professional suicide.

When I finished, Maggie stared down at her Coke.

"Okay, so let me process this." Her hands rubbed her eyes as she shook her head. "This woman is a federally protected witness."

"Yeah."

"And also kinda young?"

"Yeah."

Her lips pinched. "How young are we talking?"

I gave her a blank stare. "Not *that* young. Twenty-three."

She blew out a breath. "Oh. Okay, well, that's really not *so* bad."

Maggie looked down, seeming to concentrate on how to process all of the information I was throwing at her. "And so you became friends over gin rummy and late-night talks? And you had a little notebook just like your dad keeps?"

I let out a small laugh, a little surprised she remembered that my dad had taught us all to play and kept score in the same way I did. "Yeah."

Maggie's hand fluttered to her heart. "That is so sweet."

I rolled my eyes at my sister. I'd unloaded the whole story, and she, of course, latched onto the romantic bits that made my chest uncomfortable and achy.

"But back then she kissed you and you freaked out."

I let my shoulders sag, admitting defeat. "Pretty much."

"And that's why you left us again? To find who hurt her?"

"Didn't feel like much of a choice."

"But you two can't be together now because . . ." Maggie circled her hand in the air, waiting for me to finish her sentence.

"Jesus, Mag. She's young. She's got her whole life ahead of her. She doesn't need an old man weighing her down. Plus, Evan is one of my best friends. I also very likely don't have a job after this shit show. It just feels like the whole deck is stacked against us." I ticked the reasons off on my fingers as I ranted. "Add to that she's never forgiven me for ghosting her. Hell, would you?"

Maggie offered a gentle, sweet smile. "Cole and I spent *years* circling each other in this town. We held on to disappointments and misplaced anger. But in the end it wasn't worth it—the wasted years not admitting our feelings to ourselves. You love this woman, Scotty."

She leaned over to place her hand on my forearm and gave it a gentle squeeze. "Have the courage to love her out loud."

Her words hit me square in the chest.

Have the courage to love her out loud.

Because I did love her.

I'd loved her four years ago, and I loved her even more today. And when it came down to it, that was what Gemma deserved, wasn't it? To have a man unafraid to stand with her and show the world how she deserved to be loved.

To be worshipped.

My thoughts raced, and I looked at my sister. "This is a lot of shit to wade through. What if she doesn't forgive me or think I'm worth it?"

"Trust me, you're worth it."

I squeezed my sister in a quick hug and dug the keys to Gemma's beat-up truck from my jeans. "I'm going to head out."

Her smile widened. "Don't be such a stranger!" she called out after me. "And next time, bring that girl with you. I can't wait to meet her."

I nodded when my phone buzzed. I paused on my way out and pulled it from the pocket of my jeans.

There was a jumble of missed text messages, and I scanned through them, landing on the most recent thread in a group message.

EVAN

Ma said there was an incident. You were banged up but headed home? Where the fuck are you, bro?

VAL

Turn. On. The. News.

I PAUSED and turned toward Maggie. "Hey, can you flip on the news real quick?"

She walked toward the back of the shop and grabbed a small TV remote. "Sure thing." Maggie clicked on a small television in the back of the shop.

"National news."

It took only a second for her to flip to the correct channel, and after a few minutes of watching, a poised brunette reporter stood in front of a city courthouse.

Maggie turned the volume up.

"In a shocking and dramatic turn of events, the prosecutor in a landmark federal case against accused Mafia kingpin Billy Massaro announced today that a witness—

whose identity was previously undisclosed—made a sensational and altogether incriminating testimony in court.

Reports of money laundering, racketeering, and extortion paled in comparison to the allegations of kidnapping and torture. The witness bravely took the stand and confidently relayed the brutality she'd endured at the hands of Billy Massaro and his men.

This incriminating testimony came right on the heels of a stunning attack in a coffee shop earlier this week. Many believe the witness was the target of that attack."

Maggie's eyes widened as she looked at me and then glanced down at my side. I kept my eyes focused on the television and ignored the sympathetic looks she was giving me.

The newscast then cut to Billy Massaro's defense attorney providing a red-faced and hasty comment as he exited the building, stating the coffee shop attack was unrelated and downplaying the events of his day in court. When it cut back, a clip of Gemma filled the screen.

My heart thundered as she stood tall, chin raised, not a hair out of place as she made confident strides toward the witness stand.

She was dressed in long, cream-colored pants and mile-high heels. Her black top was fitted, sleeveless, and dipped down in a tasteful V in front that tucked into her slacks. Her scars were prominently on display, but she lacked any visible self-consciousness.

Gemma had channeled her inner badass, and I'd never seen her more gorgeous.

Breathtaking.

The reporter talked over the muted clip, but I could clearly see Gemma answering questions, gesturing to the scars running down her neck and arm. She was poised, bold, and altogether stunning.

I was speechless.

Maggie moved to my side as the clip transitioned to more reports from the newscaster. "Holy shit, that was her, wasn't it?"

I nodded.

"Damn. She's tough. And gorgeous." Maggie clicked the television off when the newscast moved on to local weather. "You better get your shit together if you're going to win her back."

A smile pulled at the corners of my mouth. "I gotta run."

Maggie laughed as I sailed out of her flower shop and left Chikalu Falls behind for home.

29

GEMMA

SOPH

HOLY SHIT. I saw you on the news. I want to be you when I grow up.

KATE

Just saw the replay too. Your pretty face is all over the news! So proud of you. BTW, you looked stunning!

Effie called in a favor from one of her former stylists. It felt pretty great in those kickass heels.

SOPH

You looked so bougie. If I didn't love you so much, I'd be jealous.

Are you coming home soon?

Boarding a plane now.

KATE

A plane and everything? Look at you with your big girl panties on! Can't wait to hug you both.

MY FINGERS TREMBLED in my lap, and I clasped my hands together to keep them steady. The first-class seat meant hordes of other fliers would be filing past me any moment. Nerves rattled through my veins, and my skin was clammy. I hated the idea of an airplane hurling through the sky. How they ever managed to take off and fly made zero logical sense to me.

Ma took her seat beside me in the plane and patted the folded hands in my lap. "You did great."

If we die in a fiery plane crash, it would still be for nothing.

I forced another intrusive thought from my mind and smiled at her. I took a breath and shrugged. "Now we wait."

Ma shook her head and buckled the belt across her lap. "With a testimony like yours? No judge and jury in the country would discount that. What you did today was put some very bad men away for a very, very long time."

A moment of peace settled over me. Billy Massaro could no longer hurt me or scared, motherless girls like me again. That specific threat was gone because I had taken a stand—stood up and spoken my truth.

When I allowed myself to acknowledge it, that felt pretty damn good.

My thoughts, as they so often did lately, returned to Scott. We had so much we needed to talk about—him leaving and how he selflessly protected me in the coffee shop even though I'd just yelled at him. I'd been too hard on him. Angry and hurt.

He'd protected me anyway.

I gently cleared the emotion clogging my throat and

tried my best to seem casual. "So . . . my truck should be there when we get back?"

"Your truck is fine." She looked down her nose and tried to hide a small smile. "And so is Scotty."

"Ma, I—" *Shit*.

Finding the words you knew would disappoint the woman who'd become like a mother to you was nearly impossible.

"He saved my life." It was all I could manage.

"It's possible. That attack was likely meant to be more than just a warning. Agent Dunn did his job well."

I hummed and thought about how it was so much more than a job. It always had been with us.

As the plane started lurching down the runway, I gathered the courage to tell Ma the truth. "Things between him and me have . . . shifted. I don't even really know how to explain it. We've always been friends, but the truth is, my feelings for him ran a lot deeper than that—from the very beginning."

Ma smiled. "I am aware. When any person becomes a US marshal, they take an oath—to faithfully execute their duties. He's done that well, but Scott will be also answering for the decisions he's made."

I turned in my seat. "But I want you to know that he never encouraged it. In fact, it was the opposite. He didn't do anything wrong. When I kissed him, he stopped it. Then he left."

Ma softened and brushed her hand over mine. "I have always felt a need to protect you, Gemma. Even in the beginning, you were like a daughter to me. But you're a woman now. A woman who will need to make some difficult decisions about her future. My only advice would be to make those decisions with the heart."

I looked down at my hands. "I'm scared. I'm not like Evan or even Parker. They make a choice and go all in. When they met their soulmates, they just *knew* and trusted that. But what if—what if I can't do that. What if I'm just not enough?"

Ma's eyes grew serious as she looked at me. Her hand covered mine and squeezed. "You, my sweet girl, have always been more than enough. You just need to allow yourself to see it."

Ma settled her head against the seat and closed her eyes as the plane sped down the runway. I gripped the armrests until my knuckles were white. Ma never opened her eyes, but she placed a gentle hand over mine as I struggled to breathe through takeoff.

The engine noise drowned out my tangled thoughts as we took off and headed west.

Home.

MY FEET FALTERED as I took the last step onto the front porch of my cottage. I was overjoyed to be on solid ground, and I used the railing to support me as I climbed the steps. I'd survived the three-hour plane ride home but was in no hurry to fly again anytime soon. Maybe I needed bravery in smaller doses.

I looked up at the tiny space I'd made my home for the last four and a half years. The memory of the kiss I shared with Scott on that very porch still haunted me. It was bourbon-fueled and sloppy. Not at all like the searing kisses I knew Scotty and I were capable of. My fingers grazed my lower lip.

Would they still be the same now that we were back to living our real lives?

The crunch of gravel behind me had my heart jumping to my throat as I spun.

Evan raised both hands and smiled. "Sorry. Didn't mean to startle you."

I exhaled. "It's fine." A staccato laugh mirrored my nerves. "Still a little jumpy, that's all."

Evan's brow furrowed as he took the steps onto the porch in quick strides and bound me in a tight hug. "It's good to have you home in one piece."

"Aw, come on. I'm still as broken as I was before."

He was unamused as I tried to lighten my heavy mood. "It's good to have you home."

Home.

I glanced back up at the small cottage that served as housing for those new to Redemption Ranch and in need of a place to stay. When we'd first arrived, Evan and I had shared a cottage that I could still see from my back windows. I'd stomped and pouted and plotted in order to gain a shred of independence, and with Ma's help, I made an empty cottage my own home.

Now that Evan had Val, they'd moved on to a gorgeous farmhouse on the outskirts of town. Started a family. Had their own lives.

Happiness for them swirled with twinges of jealousy.

Evan loved his life here. He had a good woman, a family, a legitimate job managing the day-to-day operations at Redemption Ranch. He was settled. Complete.

As we entered my small home, I thought about my quiet life and job at the retirement home. Ms. Hannah would shit a brick when I told her about everything that had happened between Scott and me. She was a fellow smut lover and would surely appreciate the sordid details. Outside of my friendship with her, there was little else I was truly looking forward to when my life inevitably went back to normal.

I tossed my keys on the beige laminate counter and hopped up to sit on the countertop. Evan made himself at home and snagged a water bottle out of my fridge.

"Val made sure your place was stocked up before you got here. A few groceries, fresh sheets. That kind of thing."

I smiled. I was lucky to have her as a sister-in-law.

"So," he said, taking a sip of the water and avoiding eye contact. "Eventful trip."

I sighed and leaned my head back against the cabinets. "You have no idea."

"Parker and I were talking and think it's best if you continue to lie low for a while. He's worried about retaliation. I spoke with Ma and—"

"Stop." I closed my eyes and sucked in a breath to calm the fizzing anger that percolated in my gut. "Just . . . please stop."

When I opened my eyes, Evan was looking at me like, *What the hell did I do?* It only made me feel worse.

"I need time, and space, to figure everything out. I feel like my whole world was tossed upside down and nothing fits right."

"We're just trying to help, Gem."

"I know. I *know*. Please don't be mad, but I just need to figure some things out for myself."

Evan took one slow step toward me. "What happened on that trip?"

I shook my head once. "You have no idea. I don't know where to start. I'm not even sure you would understand."

His jaw clenched. "Try me."

I smoothed my fingers across my eyebrows and tried to

collect my thoughts. My whole existence was altered, and being thrown back into the life I had before wasn't working.

I blew out a calm breath and tried to explain it as concisely as I could. "When I was sixteen, you saved me. You gave me everything—protection, a place to stay, a job, *a family*. You rescued me from a life on the streets, or worse. Evan, you are an amazing big brother, but I'm not a little girl anymore."

Evan moved to speak, but I lifted a hand. "I'm not finished."

Surprise passed over his face, and my heart squeezed for my big brother. God love him, he shut his mouth and let me keep ranting.

"I'm different. I don't exactly know how yet, but I feel it. I can't let everyone else make decisions for me. Sure, sometimes it's easier, but those decisions are for other people. Not for me. I need to be the one to live my life. For me."

When I was quiet, he spoke. "What does that mean?"

"I'm leaving the ranch." I hadn't made the decision until that very moment, but as soon as I spoke the words, I knew in my heart they were true.

"Gem, I—" Panic crept into his voice, and I reassured him with a soft smile.

"I'm not *leaving* leaving. But I can't stay here." I gestured around to the tiny cottage. "This isn't a home. It's not somewhere a grown woman makes a life. A scared girl under federal protection? That's not who I am anymore. I'm not afraid."

His cheek twitched with what I thought might be a smile. "Okay, then."

"Okay?" I wasn't sure I quite believed the words, even though I'd given voice to what my heart knew was right.

"Gem, you haven't been that scared little girl for a long time. You know that I fucking hate change. Hate what I can't control. But you're not me."

I smiled up at him. "I'm much cuter."

He rolled his eyes and looped an arm around my shoulders. "You're a bigger pain in the ass. Where do you think you'll go?"

I thought for a minute. "I'm not sure. Maybe somewhere closer to town. Or an apartment in Tipp."

"Oh, thank fuck."

I looked up at him in confusion.

Evan dragged a hand through his dark hair. "Christ, Gemma. I thought you were going to say something like *California* or *Texas*. Even a few towns over I could handle, but I was losing my mind here."

I laughed at my slightly annoying overprotective brother. "I don't want to light my *entire* life on fire. But I am ready for whatever comes next. A fresh chapter."

Satisfied, Evan nodded and moved toward the door. "It's gonna be a good one. I'm glad I'll be here to see it."

I hopped off the counter and bustled him out the door, planting two hands across his wide back and giving him a playful shove onto the porch. "Okay. Enough of the Hallmark moments. I liked you better when you scowled at me and did all my chores."

He laughed and bounded down the stairs toward his truck.

"Don't forget we've got family dinner. Hasn't been the same without you. Oh, and hey. If you happen to see Scotty, tell him I said to keep his hands off my fucking sister." Evan tossed a wink over my shoulder, and my head tipped back as I laughed into the sky.

30

GEMMA

AT THE BACK door of the main lodge, I waited.

Warm laughter and soft conversations floated down the hallway from the main gathering areas. A smile bloomed, and my tummy did a little flip as I worked myself up to finally facing everyone.

Family dinner was familiar. Comfortable.

No doubt people would want to talk about Chicago, but I'd practiced keeping my face calm in the mirror and rehearsing ways to gently steer the conversation in different directions. I'd been gone longer than I ever had since living in Tipp, so it would seem perfectly normal for me to ask about what had been happening on the ranch in my absence.

My fingers were tingly, so I wiggled them a few times and ran my palms down the smooth material of my skirt.

The same floral skirt Scott had appreciated so much on our date.

The same skirt that drove him wild in the botanical gardens.

Memories of Scotty Dunn and his magical tongue

haunted me. His hands were even worse. And that smirk? Kill me.

My whole body shook with anticipation. With Ma's warning about Scott being in trouble, I had waited for him to contact me. So far, nothing.

But he knew better than to miss family dinner. Ma would have his ass.

I clenched my teeth and fought a smile as I took a step toward the brightly lit kitchen.

I caught Val's eye first and she slapped at Evan's shoulder. "There she is. There she is!"

He turned and everyone shouted, "Surprise!"

Val's arms shot up above her head, and Sienna wiped a tear from her eye as Parker wound a protective arm around her shoulder. Josh and Effie stood together, smiling and clapping.

My eyes dropped to the white tagboard sign Evan held. Written in his blocky script was, *Thanks for not ratting us out.*

A laugh burst from me as he let it hang in one hand and pulled me into a hug. Over his bulky shoulder, I looked around and also saw Ma; her husband, Robbie; Sophie; and a few ranch hands.

But no Scott.

I swallowed hard and tried to catch my breath. "What is all this?"

Evan released me, but I was quickly captured in another hug.

"The sign was Effie's smart-ass idea," Evan said.

Ma *tsked* and swatted away the group that encircled me. She pulled me into a warm, motherly embrace. "Tonight's family dinner is in honor of you, dear. We are so proud and elated to have you back."

Emotion heated my cheeks. "Thank you," I whispered as I squeezed her back. Overwhelmed and a little shell-shocked, I let myself get passed around the group and hugged. Finally, they relented.

Robbie Brown looped his arm around Ma's shoulders and gestured toward the large kitchen island, littered with dishes of food. "We've got beef tenderloin, twice-baked potatoes, green beans . . . all fixed up, just like you like it."

A meal my own mother would never have considered making, and now the hodgepodge family that had truly saved me was gathered to share a meal and honor *me*.

I beamed up at Ma and Robbie—the type of strong woman I wanted to become and the man at her side who never wavered. I knew in my heart I'd never meet anyone with as much grace and acceptance in their hearts as those two.

"I made mini chocolate molten lava cakes for dessert," Effie proudly stated, and the room politely smiled and looked around.

Effie was a lot of things, but a good cook was *not* one of her talents. I forced a smile to keep from laughing at the awkward silence. "Can't wait, Eff."

Evan clapped his hands together and gestured for me to take a plate. "Well, let's eat."

As I made my way around the island, piling food on my plate and letting the chitter of casual conversation roll over me, I paused to whisper to Ma.

"I, uh . . ." I cleared my throat and hoped to sound casual. "I thought maybe Scott might be here."

I glanced over her shoulder to see Parker's signature scowl deepen as his wife's hand fluttered to her chest.

Ma lowered her voice, but the conversation was far from private. I schooled my face into a passive nonchalance, but her words rattled my insides. "Scott is on administrative leave. There will be a formal review of his conduct. He no longer has access to Redemption Ranch."

She glanced around again, lifting her chin at curious eyes. The ranch hand eavesdropping on the conversation immediately looked down as she continued: "It would also be best for him for you to keep your distance. Any indication that he made any missteps could cost him dearly."

Any missteps. Oh, like sleeping with a witness eleven years his junior that he was assigned to protect?

I pinched my lips in a flat smile and whispered gently, "I understand."

A hot coal in my stomach fizzled and burned through me.

No contact.

My appetite shriveled and my throat went dusty. I spent the rest of the evening pushing food around my plate and smiled politely as Evan made a toast and my family celebrated what they called bravery and strength.

I was hollow.

The small talk I'd rehearsed was wooden and awkward. I recognized the questioning glances from Sophie and Effie, but I ignored them.

As I looked around the table, nearly everyone was living the life they wanted. A life of love and happiness and babies and contentment.

Everyone but me.

31

SCOTT

FUCK THIS SHIT.

I was stuck in limbo, waiting while some douchebag in the Employee Relations Division sat behind a desk, reading a case file and deciding whether or not my actions in the line of duty went against some purely subjective oath. I busted my ass in the name of serving my country and my superiors.

Part of that oath was to *faithfully execute the duties of that office*.

Had I not done that? Gemma was secured. She'd arrived in Chicago unharmed, had been protected when a threat was presented, and had provided her testimony to fulfill her obligations as a federal witness.

I even got *stabbed* for it.

Sure, I'd also fallen madly in love with her and used federal resources to extend our little road trip and morph it into something else entirely, but, c'mon. I just called that being resourceful.

I wasn't sure the suit and tie reviewing my case would feel quite the same way.

It had been days since I'd seen Gemma in Chicago. I agonized over calling her every day. Knowing she was so close but off-limits was physically painful.

I should have taken Maggie up on her offer to stay with her in Chikalu Falls. Maybe even stayed with one of my brothers, instead of convincing Al to let me rent out the shitty apartment above the Rasa.

The two windows that overlooked Main Street were streaked with dust and grime, and the entire place stank like stale beer, probably wafting up from the bar itself. But without work, I was left to stare out the windows and hope to see a streak of blonde hair.

Just a glimpse.

I was a fucking mess over that girl.

I turned my back on the windows to survey the studio apartment. On the small table that served as a separation between a love seat and the kitchen sat the floppy pink piglet from the Wild Bronc Festival.

His askew eyes and lopsided grin mocked me. I pointed an accusatory finger in his direction. "You shut the fuck up about it."

I couldn't do it.

Gemma would stay away.

If I knew anything about her feelings, I knew she wouldn't risk hurting my chances of getting back my badge.

Which meant, if I was going to see her, let her know my feelings hadn't wavered, I needed help.

I swiped my keys off the table and stalked toward the door. Two steps away, I shook my head and turned around.

Swiping the polyester piglet off the table, I held it at eye level as its eyes pointed in different directions.

"This better fucking work."

"I DON'T KNOW, kid. You sure this is a good idea?" Al stroked a hand down his long, braided goatee and eyed me.

"It's all I got, Al. The only way."

He sighed and shook his head. "You damn kids sure need a lot of help figuring your shit out."

I raked a hand through my hair. "Yeah, I know it." I sighed. "So you'll do it?"

His grin widened. "Course I will. Now get outa here before I put you to work in the back."

I slapped a hand on the marred oak bar top before turning and heading for the door and my next stop. "Thanks Al," I called over my shoulder. "Couldn't do it without you!"

"Yeah, yeah," he called to my back as I sailed out of the Rasa with renewed energy.

Time to get my girl.

32

GEMMA

HE LEFT. For me. There was no way my naive nineteen-year-old heart could have understood it back then. Hell, it would be difficult to understand even now, but knowing Scott the way I did, it made sense.

Scott's need for order and control meant that he made decisions based on duty. Honor. And a sense of rightness.

It had been three long days since family dinner, and I still hadn't heard from him. A skittering sense of panic had weaseled its way into my brain, whispering dark and dangerous thoughts.

He left again.

He'll be gone for good this time.

My not-so-subtle poking around town revealed little. It was as if I had suddenly been cast as a Tipp outsider and treated with the polite yet cold shoulder the everyday passers-through received.

It was maddening.

Finally, when Wednesday evening rolled around, I couldn't take it. Sophie had taken me up on my offer to meet downtown. I had to get out from under the pity smiles I got on the ranch and the confines of my cottage. The four tiny walls were closing in on me.

"You look perfectly miserable."

I looked up from scowling at my own hands and saw Sophie's kind eyes. They held the same pity as the rest of this damn place. "Hey, Soph."

She hung her purse on the back of her chair and sat across from me.

"Still nothing, huh?"

"Nope."

She toyed with her lip, concern flooding her eyes. "I just don't get it. When you told me everything that happened— how things changed so much between you two, I thought . . . I don't know. I thought it was all gonna be different for you."

I lifted my shoulder and let it drop. "I don't know what to think anymore."

"Once his review or whatever is done, then you can be together, right?"

My eyes burned and hope bloomed in my chest, as it always did whenever I thought about the tiniest sliver of a possibility that we could end up together. No one but Ma really knew the extent of our relationship, and even then, all she knew was that things had *developed* between us.

No one had any idea I was over the moon for him.

Heartbreakingly in love.

"I'm not sure," I said, defeated. "If he keeps his job, he could get reassigned. If he's fired, he'll be crushed. His career is everything to him. His sense of purpose."

Sophie went to speak when we were interrupted.

"What can I get y'all?"

I forced my best smile up at our server and rattled off my order. "Vanilla latte with nonfat milk, please. Extra shot of espresso and extra hot." My chest pinched at the memory of Scott rattling off my coffee order with ease.

How long would these memories haunt me?

Sophie ordered, opting for an iced chai latte.

As we waited, she looked out onto Main Street and squinted against the dying sun. "I don't really want to talk about it. Is that okay? Maybe we get our coffees and just walk for a little bit?"

Ever the steadfast friend, she smiled. "Of course. Let's go for a walk."

A few minutes later, the server came back with our drinks.

"We actually changed our minds and are taking these to go. Can we get the check, please?"

A sly smile crept over her face as she clasped her hands in front of her black apron. "No need. Your bill has been taken care of."

Sophie and I exchanged a curious glance. "Taken care of? I don't understand."

I reached for my wallet and tried to dig out a few bills to pay for my coffee. The server smiled and spoke up again. "Your money is no good at Brewed Awakening. I'm supposed to let you know that your coffee is paid for. Indefinitely."

Sophie's eyes went wide. She gathered her purse and moved to my side. "Well, then. Thank you." She nodded at the server, who stood smiling beside our café table.

"Have a good evening, Ms. Walker."

My head whipped around at the server's farewell.

Ms. Walker. Could it—no.

"What the hell was that?" Sophie bent her head and whispered conspiratorially, barely stifling a giggle.

Still a little shell-shocked, I allowed her to move me down the sidewalk. "I have absolutely no idea."

"Well I, for one, am not about to look a gift coffee in the mouth." She grinned again and took a hearty sip of her warm chai.

I rolled my hot coffee between my hands. Something weird was definitely up.

I continued walking arm in arm with Sophie down the sidewalk. Being evening, it was littered with people popping in and out of the various shops and businesses. Those who recognized me offered kind smiles and friendly waves.

I couldn't help but search each face for Scott.

Lost in my thoughts, my coffee sloshed out of the little hole in the top of the cup after Sophie stopped short.

"What the hell?" I flicked the spilled coffee from my hand and looked at her.

Sophie's face was tipped up, her eyes wide.

"Dude. Look."

I followed her gaze to the two large windows above the Rasa. As long as I'd lived in Tipp, no one had rented the cramped studio above the bar. It was loud and busy, and Al's bristly personality didn't lend itself to a harmonious rental relationship.

"I don't know, Soph. I don't really think living above the Rasa is much of a step up."

She bumped my shoulder. "No." Her nose scrunched and her mouth twisted. "No one would rent that place. It's disgusting." Her hand lifted. "Look in the window."

I followed the invisible path her manicured finger drew across Main Street until it stopped at a large, white poster board nestled in the right corner of one of the twin windows.

Written in black marker, in blocky handwriting, were the words *Whatever you ask of me.*

Butterflies erupted in my belly. My throat pinched closed.

I swiveled my head and turned my body in a circle, scanning the people meandering down the town's sidewalks.

There was no sign of him, but there was absolutely no denying they were Scott's words openly displayed across the busiest street in town.

"What do you think it means?"

I couldn't fight my grin. "I know exactly what it means."

Her eyes lit up and she practically squealed. "Is it him?"

I nodded and fought the swell of tears. Relief.

He hadn't left me.

It was his way of showing me that although we couldn't be together right now, he was still here.

"Last night I had a guy from Hinge text me a picture of his dick. When he asked if I wanted to 'see his dong,' I thought maybe he'd just misspelled *dog*." She'd used air quotes to emphasize and then threw her hand toward the sign in the window as she shouted, "Is this too much to ask for?"

When an elderly woman gasped in shock at Sophie's outburst, I laughed and pulled her in for a hug.

Though there was still no sign of Scott, we finished our walk, and the smile never left my face.

SOPH

It was a freaking billboard, right there in the middle of town.

> Not a billboard. A sign.

KATE

Close enough. But you still haven't actually seen him?

> No. He's like a ghost.

SOPH

A hot, swoony, romantic ghost. But what about you, Kate? Find any help for the house rehab?

KATE

Well . . .

Aunt Tootie hired someone, but it's not going to work out. It's Declan's brother.

> Wait. As in your ex-boyfriend Declan? As in his hot as hell older brother?

KATE

That would be the one.

SOPH

This requires video chat.

And wine.

IT WAS the truth that Scotty Dunn had been like a ghost in Tipp, Montana. No wonder he was so good at his job—fitting in, not standing out, being there but going completely unnoticed.

It was a little unnerving, to be honest.

Around every corner I looked for another sign of him, but so far today, nothing. I made it a point to make an extra trip in town on Thursday. As I drove past the Rasa, I peered into the window.

Another white sign.

Finally see what it means to be living.

Of course.

Of course he'd choose Tracy Chapman lyrics that sliced right to my core. I practically had "Fast Car" on repeat along with a hundred other sad songs that reminded me of him.

I lifted my phone and snapped a picture of the sign and kept walking with a soaring heart, humming the lyrics as I went.

The tinkling bell mirrored my hopeful mood as I opened the door to the Rebellious Rose.

"Oh, Johnny? Dah-ling! I need you!" I called in my poshest voice and broke out in a fit of laughter.

My ridiculousness turned a few heads, but I gave them a small smile and worked my way toward the back of the store, where my friend abandoned his merchandise.

"About freaking time. I see you *once* in a week?" He turned his nose up in disgust. "Uncalled for."

We hugged, and I squeezed him an extra-long second.

"Have you seen the commotion above the Rasa? Someone finally rented out the old apartment." He smiled over his shoulder as he went back to folding merchandise for the table.

A fresh blush heated my cheeks. "I did see them."

"There is all kinds of chatter over those messages in the window. Who they're from. Who they're *for*." Johnny ran a finger across his lips. "But I'm not saying a word."

I lowered my voice as curious ears wandered closer. "He's under some kind of investigation. I haven't even been able to talk to him, but I know the notes are from him. They have to be, right?"

"Your boy is causing quite a stir around here."

I sighed in frustration. "I just want it to be over."

"I hate to be the downer here, but what happens if the investigation doesn't go well? What happens then?"

I shrugged, the wind leaving my sails just a bit. "I'm not sure. If he gets fired, it'll be really tough on him. If he gets reassigned somewhere? I don't know. We never really talked about any of this." I worried the nail on my thumb.

Shit. Had I gotten ahead of myself? If he got reassigned, would I go with him? Would he want that? Would I?

"Hey." Johnny put his hand on my shoulder. "I can see you freaking out. Just breathe. I'm not trying to upset you, but I don't want to see you get hurt either."

"I know." There was nothing else to say.

Johnny gently clapped his hands in front of him. "Perfect. Now that I got my best-friend duties out of the way . . . I have something for you."

I lifted my eyebrows at him.

He hurried away and then quickly returned carrying a black box with an ornate floral design on the top. The box was thick and luxurious, with a magnet securing the top flap.

Johnny placed the box in my hands. "Special delivery."

I rolled my lips together and fought the grin that was completely involuntary.

With one last knowing smile, Johnny called over his shoulder. "I'll just leave you to it."

I lifted the flap and pulled back the top of the box. Delicate white tissue paper covered its contents. A small note was folded in half. With my free hand, I opened the note and read: *Whatever you ask of me.*

I peeled back the tissue. A blush heated my cheeks. Inside the box was a wine-red velvet bodysuit. The straps were black with intricate lace. Down the bodice were leather details that led to a black belt that would nip in my waist. My favorite feature was the bottom edge of black lace that would run over my hips and back along the lines of my ass.

It was sexy.

Powerful.

My thighs clenched and my pussy tightened as I thought of wearing such a badass bodysuit while Scott willingly followed my every order.

My temperature rose just thinking about it. I swallowed hard and snapped the lid down. I hurried out of the shop, barely able to wave goodbye to Johnny as I tucked the box under my arm and made my way to where I had parked my truck.

This was ridiculous. We were circling each other in the same small town. Fuck it if it went against the rules. I needed to see Scotty.

Now.

GEMMA

APPARENTLY, a federal investigation into one of their own US marshals is a bigger deal than I thought. Despite my desperate attempts to get information from Ma, she was a vault. All she would tell me was that the investigation was ongoing, and any involvement I had could be disastrous for Scott's outcome.

Well shit.

The only good that came from our conversation was a date. Two weeks.

Two weeks and a decision about Scott and his future as a US marshal would be decided. Two weeks and no matter what that outcome was, I'd finally see him.

It ended up being the longest two weeks of my life.

Every single day, there was a new note on the poster. It had become a point of curiosity in town, people taking pictures, posting on social media, and speculating whom the messages were for.

But I knew.

And now those two weeks were whittled down to a few days. In that time, an officer from the Employee Relations

Division would be making the decision on whether Scott violated his ethical obligations as a marshal by our actions on the road trip to Chicago.

My nerves were at an all-time high as I obsessed over the various outcomes. Some days I was flying high—confident that he would be absolved and we'd be free to finally be together. Some days I felt nothing but hopelessness that he'd be reassigned and it would be the end of whatever it was that had blossomed between us. Other days, like today, I felt . . . uneasy.

The uncertainty was a roller coaster of emotions, and I fucking hated it. So I buried myself in work and family dinners and workouts at the gym with Val.

Anything to keep my mind off the man I had desperately fallen in love with.

Again.

Today, as I'd done every single day since the first poster showed up in the window, I walked downtown with my free coffee and anticipated what he would write to me.

I glanced up at the window, shading my eyes from the afternoon sun.

She's still not yours, but she was lonely without you.

I read the sign again.

What the fuck?

I glanced around as others stopped on the sidewalk to snap a photo of the sign that had captured the town's curiosity. For the first time, I had no clue what it meant.

Who isn't yours? Who is lonely?

I took my own picture, tucked my phone into my back pocket, and frowned down at my latte as I walked toward the gym. Val and I were planning a midday sparring session, and then I was due for an afternoon shift at the retirement home.

I was lost in my thoughts. And then it happened.

I felt him before I ever saw him.

My head lifted, and standing across the street was Scott Dunn.

A few people walked around him as he stood, rooted to the ground.

My breath hitched, and my heart hammered wildly against my ribs.

Scott appeared as handsome as ever, though his hair looked like his hands had permanently raked through it and his stubble was a little longer, from what I could tell. He looked tired but devastatingly handsome. The only thing that separated us was a two-lane road.

I took one step forward but stopped.

No.

I couldn't.

We were so close and had made it this far. I couldn't risk it now.

I wouldn't.

I could see his throat bob as he swallowed. I did the same. The corner of his mouth lifted in a smirk as he tucked his hands into the front pockets of his jeans.

Scott lifted his chin and, with a wink, disappeared into the hardware store behind him.

"HE JUST WALKED AWAY?" Ms. Hannah's voice was incredulous as I replayed the scene from earlier.

"He did."

Worry deepened the crepe-paper lines in her face. "Doesn't make much sense to me. In all the best romances, he would have stomped across the street and kissed the crap out of you!"

I laughed as I tucked a blanket around the frail body of my sweet friend. "Yeah, that would have been pretty awesome, I'm not gonna lie."

"Boys these days, no sense of romance," she muttered.

Ms. Hannah was from a different time. I wasn't sure she'd understand that a single smirk and a wink was balm to my heart.

We knew the stakes. If we had a real chance, neither of us could fuck it all up by being reckless. We had to see it through until the end of his internal investigation no matter how much my heart warred with my head.

Changing the subject, I glanced at the pretty spray of flowers by her bedside.

"Secret admirer?" I asked.

She offered a shy smile. "I had a visitor today. He was quite handsome."

"Oh, really? A new suitor. How scandalous, Ms. Hannah."

"No, dear. His heart belongs to someone else. He just came by for a chat and to ask a favor of me."

My brows creased. Tipp was small, but senior fraud wasn't completely unheard of. If some strange person was targeting Ms. Hannah for money or benefits, it could be dangerous. "A favor?" I probed.

"For you, dear."

I blinked at her. Ms. Hannah often got confused and her timelines blurred. While some memories were crystal clear, others were fuzzy and disjointed.

"I'm a silly woman." Her wrinkled hand swatted the air between us. "I should have told you earlier. He left something for you. Such a sweet boy."

My heart raced.

"Open the drawer. I kept it safe, like I promised."

I sat on the side of Ms. Hannah's bed, as I'd done a thousand times, listening to her stories or reading a book to her to pass the time. When I slowly opened the bedside table, pale-pink polyester came into view.

I reached in to pull the soft fabric out of the drawer and came eye to eye with a droopy, cockeyed stuffed piglet.

She's still not yours, but was lonely without you.

A laugh bubbled up in my throat as I held the stuffed piglet to my chest. After all this time, he'd held on to the stuffed animal he'd won at the Wild Bronc Festival. The same one he'd refused to give to me and had spent the evening cradling in the nook of his arm as we'd walked through the festival.

I buried my nose in its soft material and could swear the faintest scent of Scott's cologne clung to the fabric like a lifeline.

Tears stung my eyes.

It was then I knew. Within a few days, Scott would find out what his future held—and if I might fit into that future of his somehow.

But I was done. Done waiting for someone else to tell me how the rest of my life would play out.

It was time to take control and grab onto my future with the man I was in love with.

MA

I have news. Let's meet.

Your office?

MA

I'll come to you.

THE FACT that we weren't meeting in Ma's office at the ranch stirred the sludge that had settled in my gut.

Something was off. Wrong.

When the knock came at the apartment door, I looked around. It was a sad, pathetic state my life was in, and the woman behind the door held the news as to whether I could dig myself out of this shithole.

I held my hand on the door handle and took a deep breath.

Time to face it.

When I opened the door, Ma was standing tall and

proud in her work boots and had a blue flannel tucked into her faded denim jeans. Back in Montana, she was more herself than dressed in the tailored suit she'd worn in Chicago.

I knew the feeling well.

Ma's face gave nothing away as I scanned her features to see if I could read what was behind her calm, assessing green eyes.

I stepped aside and gestured toward the interior of my temporary living space. "Come on in."

Ma stayed silent, but her glance swept around the apartment. "This place is disgusting."

Truth was, in all the spare time I had waiting around for the Employee Relations Division to make its decision, I'd scrubbed the windows, washed down the floors, rearranged the three mismatched pieces of furniture seven times, and completely disinfected the refrigerator.

Musk still clung to its interior.

"Home sweet home."

At my wisecrack, Ma softened. Her hands reached up to grip my shoulders. "How are you, son? Really?"

I lifted my chin. "Fine."

Her lips pressed together. I figured she'd call me on my obvious bullshit, but instead, she moved to dump her purse on the cracked laminate countertop and leaned against it.

"The Employee Relations Division has made a decision. After an additional review by the Human Relations Department, it's official."

I squared my stance, ready to take the news that would alter the course of my life.

Ma clasped her hands in front of her and glanced around the apartment once more, avoiding my eyes.

"Fired, then, is it?" I beat her to the punch. No reason to draw this out when she was clearly stalling.

Ma smoothed her hands over her hips. "Deputy Director Walsh made a call."

My jaw clenched. "Fucking great. That guy hates me." My arms crossed, and I balled my hand into a fist to keep it from flying into the already cracked drywall.

"He vouched for you." My head whipped up as she nodded to confirm I'd heard her right.

"Why would he do that?"

Ma offered a small smile. "Walsh and I have a history. An understanding. I can't stand his by-the-book stance on most issues, and he doesn't understand why I love what we do here, but when shit hits the fan, we trust each other."

My hands dropped to my sides. "Thank you, Ma. Truly."

"The agreement is that you can keep your position as a US marshal, but it will go in your file that you were found guilty of improper association with a witness protection program participant, failure to follow supervisory instructions, carelessness in the line of duty, failure to follow security measures, unprofessional conduct, failure to report possible conflicts of interest, and violations of the Code of Professional Responsibility."

"Jesus, anything else?"

"A thirty-day suspension. He wasn't willing to count this administrative leave toward those suspension days either. But as it stands, your position as a US marshal is intact. Shockingly."

Relief swept over me, cool and swift. My stomach dropped to my boots as I exhaled the breath I'd been holding. I could have knelt at her feet and wept with relief. A smile cracked across my face, and I took a step toward her, ready to sweep that stubborn, stoic woman into a hug.

As I moved, she cut in, her hand raised. "Transferred, Scott." I'd never heard her so quiet.

My boots paused, stuck and rooted to the matted brown carpeting. My eyes focused on the unidentified stain next to the couch.

I couldn't breathe.

"Transferred?" I repeated—the word like acid on my tongue.

"Reassigned," she clarified. "If you fail to report to your duty station as assigned, you'll be removed and no longer be an officer for the United States Marshals Service."

"Where?"

Sadness laced through her voice. "Northern Mariana Islands."

I met her eyes and my nostrils flared. Seething anger simmered just beneath my skin.

Across the fucking planet. An ocean apart from any chance of making a life with Gemma.

"There is also an additional stipulation."

I shook my head in disbelief and released an angered breath out of my nose.

"To keep your position, you are not to return to the Montana branch."

That was it—the final nail. I was being punished, and she damn well knew it.

Ma paused, a wariness moving over her features. "I'm sorry, Scotty. I really did everything I could."

"Yeah," I croaked out. "I know you did."

"I know you've formed . . . attachments." Her eyes flicked to the white poster board taped into the large apartment window. "This was the only way."

I had no words for her. I was hollowed out.

Empty.

Ma left in silence and offered a hand on my shoulder as she passed. "I hope you come see me one last time before you leave."

With her back to me, she swiped a finger under her eye, and the fist around my heart gripped tighter.

My thoughts spiraled.

Reassigned.

Banished.

My time with the United States Marshals Service had defined my entire adult existence—but my friends, my family, Gemma. My entire world was in Montana. Despite the miles and months between us, I'd always known Montana was my home.

And that was gone.

I DIDN'T HAVE the balls to call or text Gemma. I couldn't face her.

Not yet. But soon. Once I figured out what the fuck I was going to do about the mess I'd made of my entire goddamned life.

Instead, I walked downstairs to the Rasa, stepped behind the bar, grabbed a bottle of Mortlach, and flipped Al the bird over my shoulder as he grumbled at my back.

I'd eventually pay for the top-shelf whiskey—in both cash and Tylenol, but I couldn't stand the rotting ache in my chest.

I stood at the threshold of the upstairs apartment, sucking its stale stink into my nostrils. The hazy windows glowered back at me, daring me to enter and be devoured by grief and apathy.

"Fuck this."

Without a second thought, I turned on my heels, slammed the door, and didn't look back as it rattled on its hinges behind me.

GEMMA

"WHAT DO YOU MEAN, GONE?" I pinned my brother with a stare as he had the audacity to look at me with pity.

"I'm telling you, Gem, he's not at the apartment. Al hasn't seen him in a few days." Whispers that Scott had been delivered the decisions from the Employee Relations Division had been circulating around the ranch, and I was crawling out of my skin. After two days, I hauled ass in my truck to Evan and Val's place to see if they knew anything. Even when Scott had disappeared for years, he had been sure to check in with his best friend.

Evan had to know something.

"Well?" I forced my palms open and gestured toward Evan.

"I haven't heard from him, Gem."

My anger was boiling over, sizzling and frothing beneath the surface. "You know, it's really hard to step up and grab life by the balls when the person you're trying to do that for is fucking *gone*."

Evan opened his mouth once, then blinked, and snapped it shut. "Oh. Um . . . well, I—oh."

I lifted my eyebrows. "Yeah. *Oh.*" I pulled both hands through my hair and held it back. I tipped my chin up and shouted to the roof of the covered porch. "Damn it!"

"So you and Scotty . . ." His brows drew together again.

I looked at him. His large frame was folded in a chair, but he was hunched forward, resting his elbows on his knees as he stared at me.

I rolled my eyes. "Oh, please. Like you didn't know."

He only harrumphed and added, "Isn't he kind of . . . old?"

An unintentional laugh bubbled from me. "He's the same age as *you*."

The furrow deepened. "Exactly."

"Look. I love you, but I can't deal with this whole protective big brother thing right now. I am a grown woman, and whether you choose to accept that or not is on you. I make my own choices, and my choice is him. It always has been."

"I think it's sweet." Val joined us on the porch and dropped a kiss on the top of Evan's head before she took a seat right on his lap. His hands wrapped around her hips and held her close. My stomach pitched at how comfortable and obviously in love they were.

I have to find him so we can figure this out.

"There have been whispers," Val said. "Most likely gossip, but some of the other agents are saying he's been blacklisted."

Evan shook his head. "Damn."

"Blacklisted? Like, fired?" I asked.

"Not fired, but not welcomed either. For a marshal, it's career exile. If there's any truth to it, it's not good. I'm so sorry, Gem."

My jaw tightened.

No. This couldn't be it. This isn't how this was supposed to end.

Val looked at me. "Where would you go if the life you thought you knew suddenly blew up in your face?"

Realization dawned on me. "I know where he is."

And I knew exactly what I had to do.

❀

"PLEASE BE NORMAL, PLEASE BE NORMAL." I whispered the prayer to myself as I waited for someone to answer my knock.

I looked around the busy sidewalk. I tried to return the friendly smiles, but my nerves likely made me look like a deranged serial killer. Tiny electric sparks jumped on my insides. Next to the bar was a brightly lit bakery, and my stomach groaned in protest. I wanted to stuff my face with whatever pastries lined the window display, but at the thought of actual food, my stomach rolled again.

I knocked on the thick wooden door a third time and noted the sign that indicated the bar wouldn't officially be open for several more hours.

I closed my eyes and sent up a prayer. "Please, *please* open up."

When the door moved, light from the outside spilled onto a polished wooden floor. The smells of leather and saddle soap were a surprise. The Rasa, beloved as it was, smelled more like Cheetos and old beer.

My gaze moved up the impressive frame of a man whose curious eyes looked at me. "Can I help you?"

The man held a pastry, and I ignored another stabbing pang of hunger. My hand shot up and across my body in a single awkward wave. "Hi. Um, I'm looking for a man named Colin McCoy. Is that you?"

A cocky smirk painted his face. "Yes, ma'am. How can I help you?"

I steadied my breathing.

This has to work.

"I'm going to preface this with the fact that I am not, in fact, unhinged. But to get through this, I am going to need five minutes of your time"—I pointed at the uneaten pastry in his hand—"a bite of that cruller, and a shot of tequila."

For a heavy moment, he stared at me while my heart beat wildly against my ribs. Then, with a shake of his head, he stepped aside to hold open the door. "Well, by all means, come on in."

THE ABSOLUTE LAST place I wanted to be on a Friday night was sitting in some dingy honky-tonk. Though *dingy* was an unfair assessment. The Dirty Pigeon was anything but. Everyone in western Montana knew it was the place to go for good food, incredible music, and a night of dancing.

The happy din of the growing crowd drove tension between my shoulder blades. I would have been back in my truck and headed toward Tipp had it not been for a text from my sister, asking me to move our lunch plans to tonight.

I should have left already.

It felt shitty leaving without saying goodbye. Maggie and my brothers would have understood—probably wouldn't have even been all that surprised—but I didn't want to be that kind of brother anymore.

So despite my back to the wall and one eye out the door, I sat in the Pidge and nursed a beer next to my older brother, Hayes. We sat in companionable silence as he watched the gathering crowd.

"Sizing up the competition?" I asked.

Hayes's dark eyes crinkled as he smiled at me. I'd been shocked when he decided to open his own brewery, but the business had been thriving.

"Nah. Different vibe. People come here to dance and meet women. Besides, the Pidge has Pronghorn on draft, so it's a win-win." He took a deep gulp of his own signature IPA.

A band was nearly done setting up on the large stage. Dancers eagerly lined the perimeter, ready to two-step or line dance to some of the county's best country music. I glanced at my watch again, and Hayes caught it.

"Got somewhere to be?" he asked.

I swiveled my back to the crowd and swirled the bottom of my glass on the dark oak bar top. "Kinda. I wanted to see you and Mag before I head back out."

He clamped a hand down on my shoulder. "Well, we appreciate that, little brother. It's nice having you around."

I'd kept myself buried in work for four years of self-imposed hell, but change was coming—that was for damn sure.

When Maggie texted that she was still running late, I drained the last of my beer. My hand dug into my back pocket to pull out some cash. "Look, man, I gotta run. I'll let Maggie know, but if you see her first, tell her I'm sorry. She'll understand."

He barely shook his head but stood to shake my hand. "Take care of yourself." He patted my back as I shook his hand and turned to leave. "And don't be such a stranger, all right?" he added.

A sharp pang pierced my insides. It was then I realized that I'd hurt more than just Gemma when I left. My family had been the collateral damage when I'd set out to avenge her.

Changes definitely needed to happen. At least I had that figured out. I only hoped the rest could fall into place.

I sighed and dragged my palm over my face.

I started to move toward the door.

Seven steps.

I was seven steps from the exit when the lights dimmed and a voice came over the speakers.

"Um . . . hi."

The hairs on my neck stood on end. I'd know that throaty, feminine husk anywhere. Mainly because it haunted me in my sleep.

I turned on my heels. The crowd gave an encouraging clap as Gemma stood on stage, under the spotlight.

My heart stopped in my chest.

The band settled in behind her as someone crossed the stage and handed her a guitar. She looped the strap over her head and adjusted herself atop the worn stool.

Gemma looked out onto the crowd and ran her palms down the sides of her jeans. I could feel her nerves from across the room, but she kept her elegant smile in place.

"I'm Gemma. Colin's giving me one song up here, so I've got to make the best of it."

Encouraging whoops and hollers shot up from the floor, and she smiled down at the acoustic guitar across her lap.

She gently cleared her throat, and the strums of the guitar floated over the crowd, directly to me.

I couldn't take my eyes off her.

Couldn't fucking breathe.

Only a few chords in, Gemma's voice burrowed into my soul and wound around every tender part of myself. It was an unfamiliar song, but the crowd was completely enamored. You could have heard a pin drop as conversations died down, and they were all focused on her words.

On stage, Gemma was flawless. Vulnerable but strong. Unlike that night at a random dive bar singing karaoke with a crowd, she was owning it. Alone. It was all her, and her presence on stage was arresting.

I couldn't take my eyes off her.

Fucking perfect.

By the third verse, the band behind her had joined in, and any nerves she had shown melted away.

Gemma *belonged* on stage.

And if I could possibly believe the words she sang, she hadn't given up on me yet. Better yet, she still wanted me.

My feet pounded the wooden floor as I made my way through the crowd and toward the stage. Gemma's gaze moved over the dance floor, and my movement through the crowd caught her attention. As she finished the song, her eyes found mine. She held me there, singing *her song*.

Just for me.

When the final notes of her song faded, the crowd erupted. A huge smile stretched across Gemma's face as she looked down and gave a quick little wave to the crowd. She stood, removing the guitar strap from her shoulders and handing it over to Colin.

He looped it over his head and stepped up to the mic. "Well, damn. That's a tough act to follow." Laughter rolled through the crowd as he settled behind the mic. "Let's hear it one more time for Miss Gemma Walker!"

The crowd erupted in applause and shouts of approval. Colin introduced the real opening singer as the band transitioned to a new song and more people filled the dance floor.

I tracked Gemma's movements, my eyes never leaving her as she hurried to the side of the stage. A bouncer helped her down. A small crowd of people waited for her. They clapped and shook her hand and asked to take selfies with her. She was polite, if not a little surprised, but she acknowledged each of her newfound fans. Then, in an instant, I was face-to-face with the woman who held my heart.

Her breaths were quick, and her chest moved with each heavy exhale. "Scotty, I—"

I reached forward, gripping the back of her neck, and hauled her toward me. Our mouths fused. A soft, surprised moan pushed out of her, and I swallowed it down as I devoured her. My tongue moved over hers, and every jumbled piece of me clicked back into place.

Four weeks. It had been thirty days too long since I'd had my lips on hers, since I'd held her in my arms. She moved forward, melting into me and fitting against my body in the most perfect way.

We were made for each other. That much was fact.

When we finally broke apart, breathless and thrumming with desire, I did my best to steady my breathing.

"How? How did you know I'd be here?"

A shy blush moved onto her cheeks, evident even in the dim lighting. "Maggie."

"My sister?"

"You mentioned she lived here. I just started driving, but on the way here, the idea hit me. I remembered you mentioned she has a good friend who was some big deal in the music scene. Five minutes of googling gave me everything I needed to know. After getting here, I stole his doughnut, pleaded my case, and convinced him to let me sing. She helped make sure you would be here."

I studied the incredible woman in front of me, my hands still tangled in her hair and my thumbs brushing across her cheekbones. A thought made my brow furrow. "Did you pull the truck over to google that?"

She rolled her eyes and my heart ticked faster.

Damn it, I love that eye roll.

She smiled up at Colin, who had made his way off the stage and toward us. Gemma tipped her head toward him, pulling him into our conversation. "He didn't even make me sing for him before he agreed to help me. I could have been *atrocious*."

Colin stepped forward and smiled. "Hey, who was I to stand in your way? You're a very convincing woman when you're hungry."

I reached out my hand. "Scott Dunn."

Colin shook it. "Colin McCoy. It was my pleasure. Maggie talks about you a lot. Glad I could step in and help. Though I gotta be honest"—he directed his attention back to Gemma—"I'm floored. If you're in town for a bit, stop by tomorrow. I'd like to talk to you about an opening we've got in the band."

Gemma's eyes went wide. "Um, yeah. Absolutely. Thanks!"

He smiled and nodded a quick farewell as he moved through the crowd. Gemma turned slowly, her eyes round as a deer in headlights. She silently screamed into the air, *Oh my god!*

I laughed and pulled her in for another hug.

There was so much to say.

"There you are!" My sister bumped into my back as she pushed through the crowd.

"You're late," I teased.

Maggie grinned wider and pulled Gemma into a hug. "I had to stall you somehow."

"I almost left."

Maggie swatted the air between us. "Nah. I had Hayes in on it. He wasn't going to let you get too far."

I looked across the bar at my brother, who lifted his beer bottle in salute.

Fucking hell. The entire family was in on it.

"Well," Maggie said. "Let's celebrate! Drinks on me!" She spun toward the bar and dance-walked her way toward Hayes.

Gemma laughed and I grabbed her hand. "Before we join them, can I have a minute?"

Worry flickered over Gemma's sweet face.

"Just a few minutes," I reassured.

Her hand gripped mine as I pulled her to the side of the bar and out a side exit to the back alley. The small alleyway was lit and added a soft glow to Gemma's gleaming skin.

With the music from the bar muffled behind the door, I sighed and pulled her in close. My forehead rested against hers as I exhaled. "Goddamn, I missed you."

"I hated being apart. Knowing we were so close and I couldn't even talk to you."

"It was hell," I agreed.

"And then you were just *gone*. I thought maybe you left again. For good this time."

I looked up at her to see worry and unease flicker through her gorgeous blue eyes. Leaving town was a mistake and had left her feeling insecure.

"I fucked up. A lot." Shame washed over me. I always wanted to be in control, to handle everything perfectly for her, but I couldn't manage to not trip over myself. The only thing left to do was hand over that control to the one person I could trust with it.

"Listen," I started. "The Employee Relations Division made their decision. In the end, I got to keep my job, but they want to transfer me. Overseas to some hole-in-the-wall duty station. It's a punishment—for the decisions and choices I have made."

Gemma lifted her chin. She was trying hard not to cry.

So brave.

Before she could interrupt, I barreled on. "I never should have left. Four years ago, I thought I was doing the right thing, the honorable thing. I thought you needed saving."

Gemma squeezed my hand. "I know now that your heart was in the right place."

I shook my head. "I didn't realize at the time that you didn't need saving. But I see that now. You never needed me to step in and save you—you were busy saving yourself."

Her sad smile nearly broke my heart as she looked at the asphalt ground between us.

"I never left you." I cleared my throat to keep from choking on my words. "Just like you never left me." I lifted her chin with my fingers. "The gin rummy notebook, the two-of-hearts tattoo. They were all just little ways of keeping you with me."

Unshed tears shimmered in her eyes as uncertainty wedged its way between us. "So what's next?"

A knowing smirk teased my lips. "Whatever you ask of me, Ms. Walker."

Her eyes searched mine. "But—with work? I mean, we can do the long-distance thing, but . . ."

"But what?"

"Maybe it's all too much for you?"

I clenched my jaw to stop a full-on grin. She had no clue how completely in love with her I was, and it was going to be my absolute pleasure to show her just how much she meant to me. "Too much? You're emotional and impulsive, and sometimes you're a little flighty. You talk too much when you get nervous, and you can't drive for shit. You eat nachos like a linebacker and you're too damn young."

I held her and smoothed a hair behind her ear. "But, Gemma, you are *everything*. Why would I ever go find less?"

A tear finally spilled over her lower lashes, and I stepped closer to press my lips and catch the drop as it fell. "It's you and me."

"What about your job? You'll be so far away. How are we going to make that work?" she whispered into the darkness.

"I've got a solution for that too, Ms. Walker."

Gemma leaned back to look me in the eyes. Uncertainty was replaced with curiosity.

I brushed her blonde hair from her face and tucked a strand behind her ear. "You one-upped me with that song," I teased.

A sexy little pout pushed out her lower lip. "What do you mean?"

"After I met with Ma and she gave me the news, I came here to sort a few things out with my brother. Ask him for a job."

"A job?"

"After Ma told me about the Employee Relations Division's decision, I thanked her for everything she'd done for me. Then I told her she could keep my badge and the division officer could shove my new assignment up his ass."

Her eyes grew wide as I dropped to one knee, then

lowered the other. Kneeling in front of her, I stared up at the most gorgeous woman I'd ever laid eyes on.

"I am on my knees for you, Ms. Walker. I am yours. Every minute of every hour, my heart will be in your hands. It always has been. I will love you with every breath I take. Whatever you ask of me, I will do. But right now, I have a question of my own. Gemma, epic pain in my ass and goddess of my life, will you marry me?"

GEMMA

SOPH

I KNEW THE SONG WOULD WORK! I wish
I could have been there to see it.

KATE

Seriously. So so happy for you!

> My heart is still racing. I still can't believe it
> happened!

SOPH

Also . . . you are going to be Mrs. Dunn!

KATE

I'm driving in to celebrate. Just say when!
Also, send a pic of the ring already!

"I STILL CAN'T BELIEVE you asked her in a dirty alley
behind a bar." Scott's stepsister still held my left hand in
hers as she glared at him. "Did I teach you nothing?"

Scott only smirked and shook his head. We both knew

that his proposal was absolutely perfect, and I wouldn't have wanted it any other way.

When he'd dropped to his knees, both of them, and not only asked me to be his wife, but promised me a life I never thought possible, the only answer was an emphatic *yes*. I screamed it so loudly someone burst out of the exit door to see what all the excitement was about.

It didn't matter that he didn't have a ring on him or that it wasn't done on some overtly romantic hot-air-balloon ride with cello music and doves. I hated heights anyway.

He was mine and I was his.

The engagement party my friends and family threw for us was bringing in quite a crowd. When Effie insisted that it be the "party of the season," I joked that her Hollywood was showing again. She only rolled her eyes and powered forward with managing every opulent detail.

Somehow, her charm and tenacity paid off because she'd gotten the entire town of Tipp together to celebrate Scotty and me. The whole strip of downtown Main Street was closed off to have an outdoor celebration in our honor.

I worried that passers-through or people we didn't know would be angry that Main Street was closed off, but Al assured me that all of Tipp would be there, and anyone who was upset about it could "eat shit."

I found our grumpy resident bartender through the crowd. His long white beard looked freshly braided, and he was even wearing a shirt that was ironed. Affection bloomed in my chest for that cantankerous old man. Most people found him gruff and abrasive, but I knew his particular brand of standoffish customer service was meant to keep our town, and those in it, safe. To provide a second chance without our pasts lurking in the shadows.

Al and his cool demeanor at the Tabula Rasa kept us protected.

Scott's arm wound around my shoulders as he unapologetically took flak from his sister. "Had to do it, Mag. I couldn't risk her walking away."

"That's right," Maggie's husband, whom everyone called Deck, answered. "Gotta lock that shit down." He tipped his head to me. "No offense."

I laughed, happy that my tiny family was finally expanding. "None taken." Scotty squeezed my shoulders and I leaned into him. "He didn't have much to worry about. I'd been secretly scribbling *Gemma Dunn* in my notebook for years, so all he had to do was ask."

"I didn't know that." Scott looked surprised but amused.

"You don't get to know *all* my secrets." I raised an eyebrow at him, and he leaned forward to plant a kiss near my ear.

His soft growl sent a tingle racing down my spine.

"Come on, babe. Let's let them do their rounds." Maggie corralled her husband away as we looked over the impressive crowd that had gathered for us.

Evening had settled over Tipp, and the mountains in the distance were backlit by the fading sun. Their silhouette was outlined by a riot of indigo and plum. Splashes of tangerine disappeared into the horizon. Strands of Edison-bulb twinkle lights crisscrossed overhead, illuminating the street in a soft glow. There was food and music and laughter.

It was there I felt it, tucked under Scott's arm, watching my friends and family mingle and laugh and dance.

Home.

I looked down at my left hand, still not fully believing it wasn't a fever dream.

"You're sure you like it?"

I watched the light dance and refract in the ring Scott had picked for me. An obscenely huge indigo-blue oval sapphire, sourced from Montana itself, was surrounded by asymmetrical round and oval clusters of the most sparkly white diamonds I'd ever seen. It was unique. Imperfect. Breathtaking.

It was absolute perfection.

I shrugged a shoulder. "It's okay."

Worry etched in deep lines across his forehead. "I knew I should have gone bigger," he grumbled.

A laugh burst from my chest. "You're ridiculous." I turned to hold his face in my hands. "I am in love with it. Almost as much as I'm in love with you."

He softened, as he always did when he looked at me, and my heartbeat bounced. "Gemma, you've had my heart since the minute I laid eyes on you. I will spend the rest of my days making up for how I left things."

I shook my head. It didn't matter how many times I'd told Scott I had forgiven him. He was hell-bent on making amends for walking away all those years ago. My heart had forgiven him a long time ago, and once my head caught up, I knew there was nothing that could break the bond we'd made during midnight conversations over a game of cards.

Nothing.

Kate and Sophie were dancing in the distance, smiling and getting twirled in a two-step by a duo of very handsome cowboys.

Val and Evan were wrangling the kids. Evan had Mateo perched on his shoulders, and Val looked up at him with love and affection clear as day in her eyes.

Parker was looming, as he tended to do, on the outskirts of the crowd, a protective arm wrapped around Sienna. She had finally finished her semester at school, and her very large pregnant belly was on full display. His arms wound around his wife and cradled her belly like it was the most precious thing in the world.

Because it was.

Across the crowd, Effie was on the dance floor. She was stunning as ever, her auburn hair floating around her shoulders as Josh held her and danced. It looked like he was whispering something, probably something dirty—Effie had let it slip that Josh was a closet dirty talker—and she beamed at him.

When she looked up, our eyes locked, and I placed my hand over my heart.

Thank you, I mouthed. Tears pricked beneath my eyelids.

I love you, she mouthed back.

"Is it my turn to congratulate the happy couple?" Johnny stepped into view with a bright smile across his handsome face.

He pulled me into an embrace, and we rocked back and forth as he squeezed the breath out of me. When he let me go, his eyes shot to the darkening sky as he fought tears. "Stop. You stop it right now. You'll ruin the whole look if I mess this up." He gestured to his unfairly chiseled, flawless face. I swear the man never had a zit in his whole life.

"Thank you." Scott stepped between us and held out his hand. When Johnny took it, Scott pulled him into a quick embrace. "Thank you for everything."

Johnny smiled. "I don't have a clue what you're talking about."

When I looked between the two men, Johnny just winked at me and sauntered away with a smile.

I looked at Scotty. "What was that about?"

We both watched Johnny mingle with a small crowd outside of the Rebellious Rose. "Do you really think I could have pulled it all off without his help and connections? That man will be mayor of Tipp one day. Mark my words."

Affection and comfort warmed my soul. I loved being part of a tight-knit town and not only knowing its residents as family, but being known. Being seen. Being *me* and still being loved for it.

I breathed in the cool night air and leaned my head against my fiancé's muscular shoulder.

Scotty pulled me closer, his warm breath tickling the shell of my ear. "So about that gift Johnny helped me procure . . ."

A slow grin spread as a tight coil wound through my belly. I tipped my face toward Scott. I hummed as I tried to keep my smile in check. "Well, I have a secret." His hand fisted the back fabric of my dress. My whisper was heady and thick. "I'm wearing it right now."

He groaned and buried his nose in my hair.

"Get the truck. Now."

"Yes, ma'am."

TANGLED IN HIM, my legs squeezed his hips as he tried to open the front door. One hand palmed my ass as he fumbled with the keys. It hadn't taken us long to decide on a piece of property on the outskirts of town, not too far from Evan and Val, to build our forever home. In the meantime, my tiny cottage on the ranch was perfect for us.

Scott dragged his tongue up the column of my neck. "Door, Scotty."

"Working on it."

He finally—finally—managed to muscle open the door, but as soon as it was closed at my back, he continued his assault. Wet, open-mouthed kisses sent sparks flying down my spine and out my toes. We were frantic. Needy.

I wanted this to last, to be memorable, so I lowered my legs and planted my palm against Scott's chest to pause him. "Stop."

His body went rigid.

"Such a good boy." I smirked as heat flushed his cheeks. "Do you like it when I tell you what to do?"

He huffed a breath. "You know I fucking love it."

Excitement tingled my belly. I loved this man so much. "Get comfortable."

Scott moved with ease through the small cottage, backing away from me as he peeled his shirt off his back. My eyes snagged on his firm pecs, and his abs flexed with every breath. When he got to the entrance of our bedroom, Scott lowered his slacks and the tight black boxer briefs underneath them.

My breath hitched in a quick uptake, still impressed with his length and anticipating its thickness. I went slick knowing exactly how it felt to have him notched between my thighs.

I slowly slipped the buttons from the front of my gauzy teal dress. His eyes tracked my fingers as they moved lower and lower until I reached the hemline. I cocked a hip and planted my hands at my waist, spreading the dress open and revealing the bodysuit hidden beneath my seemingly demure outfit.

"Holy fuck." His breath was ragged.

My throaty laugh filled the air. His obvious approval and appreciation made me feel desired.

In control.

Cherished.

I stepped forward. His hands immediately met my hips and squeezed before sliding back over the curve of my ass. His thick fingers teased at the black lace that edged the bodysuit.

"On the bed."

Instead of moving, Scott continued his assault on my senses and pulled me closer to him. His hard cock thrust between us, and my body moved, up and down, feeling his steely warmth as I ached to feel him inside me.

"Don't make me tell you twice." My warning had him chuckling and moving us both toward the bed.

As he sat on the edge of the mattress, I turned, facing away from him. With a dangerous slowness, I peeled off the bodysuit. Starting at my shoulders, I trailed my fingertips over my arms. My thumbs hooked into the waistband of the lingerie and pulled it down over my hips as I bent forward, thrusting my ass toward his face.

"Tell me I can taste it. Please, Gem. Please."

My toes tingled as he practically begged to feast on me. I turned to face him. My fingers sent sparks across my skin as I explored my own body for his viewing pleasure. My scars weren't even an afterthought. The way Scott looked at me held nothing but lust, adoration, and pure, deeply rooted love.

I had never felt more beautiful than when I was stripped bare in front of him.

"Lie back."

Scott pushed himself back as I moved forward, flattening him against the mattress. My legs straddled his hips, but I continued forward, my knees moving toward his face.

His grin widened.

I shook my head. "What are you smiling at?"

"Just you, Mrs. Dunn."

My heartbeat ticked faster. "I'm not Mrs. Dunn yet."

"The fuck you are. You're mine. Now sit on my face and let me show you how much I love you."

On a moan, I sank lower, feeling his searing mouth move across my pussy. His fingers dug into the flesh of my ass as he devoured me. My hands tangled in his hair, and I was lost to him.

Sure, I was the one in control, but the truth was he owned me just as well—our control fused and unable to separate.

We owned each other.

Body, heart, and soul.

Minutes passed. Hours. Days. A blur of limbs and mouths and pants.

When we were spent, Scott's hearty chuckle filled the darkened room. A satisfied huff of his breath as I curled into his side.

His hand ran up my arms, glancing over my scars, and I tucked one leg over his hip.

I hummed in utter satisfaction.

"Thank you for loving me," he whispered into my hair. "And for never giving up on us."

I pulled him closer. Nothing and no one could ever take this man from me again, and we would spend the rest of our lives sharing the power of an all-consuming love.

EPILOGUE
SCOTT

MY KNEE BOUNCED. My heart hammered against my ribs. I'd never been so nervous in my goddamned life—not even when I'd asked Gemma to be my wife.

Evan clamped a hand on my shoulder and squeezed. "Relax, man. She's gonna be great."

I nodded. I knew he was right, but I wiped my slick palms across my jeans anyway.

When the house lights dimmed, a loud whistle floated above the crowd, and I watched as our makeshift family clapped encouragement. Parker and Sienna. Effie and Josh. Evan and Val. The entire staff at Redemption Ranch was corralled in the corner as we stood together to watch Gemma perform on one of the biggest stages in the county. As her set ended and she exited, everyone was on their feet cheering and hollering. Begging for an encore.

All eyes were trained on the wooden stool at the center of the stage, a spotlight illuminating where Gemma had been.

The opening chords to a familiar song—her song— flowed from the speakers, and the entire place went wild.

With an acoustic guitar hanging from her neck, Gemma strode toward center stage with a mile-wide grin stretched across her face. She walked with confidence, her tight, high-waisted jeans flaring out and a large belt buckle—mine—sparkling under the bright lights. Her top was a cropped, fitted tank, and while she wore a western-style cardigan, it hung casually at her elbows. Her white cowboy hat shielded her crystal-blue eyes from the harsh stage lights.

She gripped the mic and smiled again. "I heard you might want one more."

The crowd erupted. I cupped my hands around my mouth and shouted encouragement to my gorgeous wife.

Gemma settled on the wooden stool, adjusted her guitar, and slipped arms from the sweater, letting it drape at her sides.

When her long fingers danced over the strings of the guitar, she leaned toward the microphone again. "I wrote this song about a man. A man that I loved for a long time. We were both afraid, and kind of dumb." She chuckled softly when a gentle *aww* rose up from the crowd. My chest ached for her. "Lucky for me," she continued, "I wore that man down and got him to marry me."

The cheers were deafening. Parker leaned over and tipped his chin at me. "Dumbass."

I grinned back at him. Everyone knew the truth—I was head over heels for that woman, and there was nothing and no one that could ever change that.

Gemma was charming, owning the crowd. They couldn't look away. She was the sun and her gravity was immense. "So I wrote this song for him," she continued. "I hope you like it."

As Gemma launched into the song I would forever think of as "our song," goose bumps rose on my forearms.

They'd added background instrumentals and remastered it a bit, but at its core, it was Gemma's song.

When the crowd started singing along, a rock lodged in my throat.

She'd done it.

Colin walked up and reached out his hand. We stood shoulder to shoulder and watched Gemma's encore performance in silent awe.

"She is a force, that one," he finally said.

I nodded in agreement.

That she is.

"My old manager would like to have a talk with her."

My eyes whipped to Colin. Back in the day, he'd been on the fast track to country superstardom himself before family ties had put an untimely halt to his career. He'd found his stride in the outskirts of the music business and prided himself in scouting local talent. The last act he'd vouched for blew up so fast you couldn't find a country station that wasn't blasting their songs on the radio.

"It's big." He nodded at me, the weight of his words settling between us. "If she wants it, there's a hell of a deal waiting for her."

Pride swelled in my chest, and the oxygen sucked from my lungs. I shook his hand again. "That'll be her choice to make."

As Gemma finished, the crowd erupted and she stood. Waving to her adoring fans, happiness radiating from every inch of her.

I couldn't wait to see what she said when she found out about the music deal. In quiet moments, she'd admitted to wanting it all—a successful music career, more songwriting, a life of adventure with me by her side.

Gemma's star was about to rocket into space, and I couldn't wait to be the one to see her shine.

NEED MORE GEMMA AND SCOTTY? Read an exclusive Bonus Scene at: https://www.lenahendrix.com/get-gemma-and-scott-bonus-scene/

GEMMA'S SONG

WORDS AND MUSIC BY ALYSSA BRIGIOTTA

I hate that I miss him when he's not around
Hate that I haven't quite found my own sound
Hate that I want him when I've never wanted
    anything else
He's everything I've stayed away from
So why do I hope he will stay long

I want him in the mornings
In the afternoons
At sunrise
When the sun sets too
Wanna know his mom
And his favorite songs
Wanna know what makes him blue
Honey, I want you

He kisses like heaven
He plays like a sin
He tells me I'm pretty
Nobody else did

I laugh 'cause it's something that I can't resist
When he smiles, I always win
My heart skips when he walks through the door
I hate that I can't ignore

That I want him in the mornings
In the afternoons
At sunrise
When the sun sets too
Wanna know his mom
And his favorite songs
Wanna know what makes him blue
Honey, I want you
Oh, oh oh, honey, I want you

Girls look at him while he looks at me
Do I deserve to be this happy?
I want you in the mornings
In the afternoons
At sunrise
When the sun sets too
Wanna see your smile
And hear your voice
I swear I hate this, I do
But, honey, I want you

Watch and listen to the video that brought Gemma's song to
life! Written and performed by Alyssa Brigiotta on TikTok
at: https://www.tiktok.com/t/ZTR4gnvo2/
(Coming to Spotify soon!)

EXCLUSIVE BONUS SCENE
GEMMA

"Mom! Mom, he came! He *actually* came!"

Bleary-eyed I registered the excited, bouncing energy of my four-year-old son JR. His hot, stinky morning breath wafted across my face and I groaned as I peeled my eyes open. "I'm up. Baby, I'm up."

As I wiped the sleep from my eyes, JR's hazel stare peered up at me, hopeful and barely containing his excitement. He was nearly vibrating out of his own skin. As I looked down at him, I couldn't help but smile. It was a good thing we'd named him Scott Dunn, Jr. He was the spitting image of his father, but early on we'd taken to calling him by the initials JR for short.

"Where's Daddy, baby?"

JR's grin widened. "He's making coffee." He leaned closer to whisper, despite the fact we were the only two in the room. "He also sneaked me a cookie."

My eyes widened in feigned shock. "Oh. A cookie for breakfast? That is sneaky."

JR giggled and warm, affectionate love spread through me. I sat up in our bed, swinging my legs to the side while

JR bounced wildly beside me. His silliness and infectious laughter almost made my 5am wakeup call worth it.

Almost.

"Mom, there are *millions* of presents downstairs."

I stood, stretching my arms above my head, knowing full-well Scott probably went overboard and added even more presents after I went to sleep. Despite the December chill in the air, I knew Scotty would have a fire started in the living room, so I only swiped a hair tie off my nightstand and opened my arms for JR.

He stood on the bed and wound his little body around me. "Merry Christmas, Mom."

My hands raked through his soft, blonde hair. "Merry Christmas, my love."

JR's face was buried at my chest, and my scarred arm wrapped around him. They never fazed him. In fact, they rarely fazed me anymore. A child's love never hinges on things like scars or hair or perfection. In their innocent eyes, mothers are perfect.

It was a gift I never knew I needed until a few nights of tempting fate without protection resulted in my pregnancy. We'd been married and had briefly talked about the *possibility* of children, but my hesitancy with my life on tour and past trauma with my own mother never allowed me to embrace the beautiful possibility of creating life.

Once we found out we were expecting JR, Scott admitted to me he'd secretly hoped we would have a family sooner rather than later and was overjoyed with the prospect of being a father.

Little did he know, I had a secret of my own. My hand swept over my lower belly, sending love and tenderness to the baby growing there. I couldn't wait to tell them both today.

"All right, kiddo. Let's check out these *millions* of presents."

Like a shot, JR bounded out my bedroom door and down the stairs.

I followed him down and the scent of freshly brewed coffee greeted me at the bottom of the stairs, along with a bare-chested Scott with a devilish look in his eye. If he wasn't careful with that look, we'd end up with a lot more babies than he'd bargained for.

"Mrs. Dunn."

After a long day celebrating Christmas at Redemption Ranch, we were all beat. I glanced into the backseat and, sure enough, JR was lightly snoring with his head tilted at a wildly uncomfortable angle.

"It was the perfect day." Scott lifted our twinged fingers and brushed a kiss along my knuckles.

I smiled at him and looked out into the inky black night as we made the short drive to our home.

Despite the tours, the long stretches of time on the road, this was home. Tipp, Montana, a tiny town in the middle of nowhere, was the center of my universe. Halfway between Tipp and Chikalu Falls, the location was the best of both worlds.

Scott pulled his truck into our driveway. I often missed my beat up old piece of shit truck. When it had finally given out, I didn't have the heart to sell it, so instead, Scotty had a new engine put in and the truck is still living its best life on Redemption Ranch. Whenever I extend my visit, I climb inside and drive around, remembering all the memories piled inside its dusty cab.

I walked up our front porch steps as JR hung limply in Scott's arms. As he walked past, I placed my hand on his shoulder and whispered. "Why don't you get him to bed and come back downstairs. Let's have a nightcap before we head to bed."

Scott leaned toward me, placing a kiss on my cheek. "Yes, ma'am."

Heat blazed in my eyes as his smirk lifted the corner of his mouth.

As Scott tucked JR into bed, I busied myself with fixing two hot cocoas, only one with a shot of Irish liqueur, and a healthy swirl of whipped cream on top. When I heard Scott's footfalls on the stairs, a zippy shot of adrenaline coursed through me. I couldn't wait to tell him.

Best. Present. Ever. Top that, hotshot.

For years now, Scott and I had tried to one-up each other with "the perfect gift." Much to my annoyance, usually, he won.

"Mmm. Smells good. Cocoa?"

I handed him a mug and tried to contain the fit of giggles I could feel rising in my belly. "Yep."

Scott sniffed his mug and took a tentative sip. "Spiked." He smiled and sipped again. "It's delicious."

I leaned against the expansive marble of our kitchen island and watched him as he took another clueless sip. "Only yours is spiked," I said with a shrug. "You know, because of the baby."

I did my best to look innocent as I sipped my own cocoa. A choking snort escaped his throat and the puff of air sent whipped cream flying off the top of his mug. He set his cocoa down with a snap.

"The what? Are you—? Are we—?" The words

tumbled out of his mouth. His thoughts tripped over one another as he took a step forward and crowded my space.

I finally let my laughter free. "Yes!"

Scott scooped me in his arms with a delighted laugh. The rumble in his chest vibrated against mine as he held me.

"I knew your boobs looked bigger today."

A barking laugh escaped me as I swatted at his arm. "You are unbelievable!"

Scott set me on my toes and lowered his mouth to mine. "No. You are unbelievable, Mrs. Dunn." His mouth on mine was warm and sweet. Hints of cocoa mingled with his masculine scent. Warmth pooled in my limbs as I went pliant in his arms.

Every swipe of his tongue sent sparkles simmering down my arms. When his mouth moved down to nip at my jawline, a switch flipped.

I planted my hands at his chest to give myself some distance. I tipped one eyebrow at him. "So you agree I won this year? Best present of the year?"

His knowing eyes smoldered. "Yes, ma'am." His hands spread open at his sides. "How may I be of service?"

The thrill, as it always did when Scott relinquished control, and I eagerly gathered the reins, raced through me. I perched myself on the edge of the kitchen island, leaning back and capturing his hips between my feet.

I dragged him forward. One step. Then two. I already knew the answer before I even asked the question, but after all these years, I still loved to hear it. "Anything I want?"

Scott's eager, devilish grin sparked with an intensity that told me it would only be a matter of moments before we both surrendered control. I had loved that man since I was nineteen years old, and the years in between only added to the deep and comforting love we shared. In each other, we'd found ourselves.

The deep rumble of his voice skated across my skin. "Whatever you ask, Mrs. Dunn, I'll do it."

When he closed the gap between us, I was lost to him.

SNEAK PEAK OF ONE LOOK
THE SULLIVANS, BOOK 1

Chapter One: Wyatt

"Do you think I'll get to see a dead body?"

I stared at my seven-year-old daughter, Penny, unsure about how to navigate this particularly morbid topic. I adjusted the sleeves on the white button-up I'd pulled on. "Get to or have to?"

Penny picked at the hem of her blue dress as she sat with the rest of the skirt rumpled beneath her. She didn't make eye contact, only shrugged.

I slipped a tie around my neck and worked to get the knot right. "It's a funeral, so there will be a memorial before we go to the cemetery. You won't have to go up there if you don't want to, but people will come to pay their respects to Uncle Bowlegs."

An unladylike snort came from her little body as her face scrunched up. "Uncle Bowlegs? That's his name?"

"Just a nickname."

"What's his real name?"

I paused and laughed a bit to myself. I had no fucking clue.

"I'm not sure. I only ever knew him as Uncle Bowlegs. Usually just Bowlegs for short."

Penny's lips twisted. "Why did people call him that?"

Her hearty giggle was infectious, and I tried to embrace the lightness of her mood. Maybe it would ease the dread pooling in my stomach. "Well, I guess because he was bowlegged."

Penny turned on the bed so she was lying on her back, her head dangling upside down off the edge. "Does everyone in your hometown have a nickname?"

I took a deep breath and shook my head. Ridiculous nicknames were only one of the utterly asinine aspects of Outtatowner, Michigan. Even the town name itself —Outtatowner.

What a joke.

I pulled the knot loose from my crooked tie and tried again. Penny waited for me to answer. Stubborn, that girl. She could outwait a monk if she put her mind to it.

"Not everyone," I conceded. "But a lot of people."

"Why?"

I shrugged. "Just something that started a long time ago. I think it's a small-town thing."

"Why?"

I realized we were on the brink of playing the *why* game and I'd walked right into it.

Not today, Daughter.

"I don't know. The town's just weird, okay?"

"You said it's not nice to call people weird."

It was annoying as fuck when your child threw your parenting back in your face. I looked over my reflection one last time and turned toward her. "You're right. They're just a little different. You ready to go, Pickle?"

She righted herself and bounced on the edge of the bed with a smile. "Is that why you call me Pickle?"

I stepped toward my precocious, pain-in-the-ass spawn. I tapped my knuckle on the end of her little upturned nose. "I call you Pickle because sometimes you're sweet and sometimes you're sour."

Penny pretended to chomp at my hand.

"My point exactly." I pulled her from the bed. "Let's go, kiddo. We have a drive ahead of us, and I don't want to be late."

Thankfully, Penny was feeling agreeable, and we left the cramped apartment without losing a shoe or misplacing her beloved Blue Teddy. Once she was securely buckled in the back, I laid my suit jacket across the passenger seat and got behind the wheel.

On the outskirts of downtown Kalamazoo, I drove through the college town. Penny kept her nose to the window, watching the buildings flicker past as we drove, Blue Teddy getting strangled by the crook of her arm. Last Christmas she'd asked for a blue teddy bear—two days before Christmas. I had scoured the internet and the best I could do was a baby-blue hippopotamus with a dark-blue ribbon around its neck. There was no fooling anyone, because it was definitely *not* a teddy bear, but Penny loved him, and though it was barely a win, I was taking it. Some days it felt like I needed all the wins I could get.

Her ponytail was lopsided, but despite the late-night YouTube tutorials between game film playbacks, I still hadn't come close to mastering a french braid. That shit was pure witchcraft.

I swallowed a sigh. It would be our third city in three

years, and I didn't miss the sadness that crept into her eyes as I watched her from the rearview mirror.

"You'll like it here, I promise." A lump formed in my throat. I really hoped I wasn't lying to her.

"There's the church."

When I glanced up again, her index finger was pressed to the glass. I tracked her stare and, sure enough, in the distance was Waldo Stadium and the Athletic Center. It wasn't the biggest stadium I'd coached at— certainly not the biggest I'd played at, but for now it was home.

"Sure is, baby."

As the stadium whirred past us, Penny settled into her seat, squeezing Blue Teddy's neck a little tighter. "How long is the drive?"

I glanced at the clock. "Only about an hour."

The tiny sound of disgust told me I didn't have more than twenty minutes or so until she was bored out of her mind and the *why* game would start back up. Flipping through the radio stations, I found some toe-tapping garbage I knew she liked and turned it up a bit.

Then we headed west toward the coast. Toward the hometown I'd hadn't seen in years.

"Well, holy shit. The prodigal son returns!" A grin split across my little brother Lee's face as he stomped across the parking lot of the funeral home. Even a few miles from the coast, the fresh, coastal air stirred around us.

It had been a long time since I'd seen my little brother. He'd always been the reckless one, a bit of a wild card. A charmer. So it was no wonder after his time in the service,

Lee had found his groove as a local firefighter and had never left our hometown.

His hand swooped to mine and gave it a hearty squeeze. Lee had bulked up too. His scrawny arms had filled out, and he'd gained a few inches in the years I'd gone without seeing him in person.

Before I could introduce him, Lee crouched down to Penny, who was tucked behind my leg. "Who's this rat? It's definitely not the Pickle I saw on FaceTime last month."

Penny rolled her eyes and stepped out from behind my frame. "Hi, Uncle Lee." Her voice was laced with boredom and annoyance, but it simmered with shy delight. Some days I swear she was seven going on seventeen.

Lee reached out to her and captured her around the waist, hoisting her high in the air. Her delighted squeals only egged him on as he bounced and jostled her.

"Who. Are. You. And. Where. Is. Penelope?"

A hot lance of regret speared my side as she giggled and horsed around with my little brother. I'd denied her this simple joy.

That was on me.

After Dad got sick, our family was scattered, broken. I hadn't made it back to Outtatowner in years, and that meant Penny knew my family only through sporadic video chats and presents mailed at holidays and birthdays.

I cleared my throat to dislodge the hot coal that had taken up residence there. "Is Katie coming?"

Our youngest sister had a wanderer's soul, not unlike my own. Once she'd graduated from high school, she'd found some random college in Montana and never looked back.

Lee's smile didn't falter, but I heard a bit of sadness creep into his voice. "Nah. She couldn't make it in."

I pressed my lips together and nodded. "Duke?"

Lee set Penny on the ground and she beamed up at him. "Getting Dad."

I nodded. Dad's early-onset dementia had deteriorated so rapidly that he lived in the local memory care ward in town. It was difficult, but with the four of us as broken as we were and Aunt Tootie unable to care for her brother herself, we'd made the choice to provide him the nursing care he needed.

The thought of a fifty-eight-year-old man requiring full-time nursing care ate at me, especially when I thought about all the times he was lucid. Himself. Until I thought about how upsetting it was when he wasn't. Confused. Angry. Scared.

His sister loved him fiercely, but Aunt Tootie couldn't do it on her own, and we weren't equipped to help him. The thought of seeing him today, not knowing the kind of day he was having, stacked a slimy layer of unease on top of my already-churning stomach.

Let's get this over with.

I glanced around the nearly empty parking lot. "Figured the King boys would be here." My fingers clenched into a fist just speaking their name aloud.

"Aunt Tootie and Bug worked it out. Sullivans have the first hour, and then the Kings can pay their respects after."

I nodded. The long-standing feud between the Sullivan family and the Kings was a thing of legends, going back longer than I could remember. Though Outtatowner was a coastal tourist town, those who were from there, us townies, knew the line was drawn. You were either with us or with them, no two ways about it.

The only two who'd managed to find some peace were Aunt Tootie and the Kings' aunt Bug. Even though they didn't like each other, they took it upon themselves to make sure we didn't tear down the town around us when we got to arguing with each other. For the tourists' sake, we kept outward appearances, but it wasn't unheard of to have a throwdown at the pub on a Saturday night.

I reached out to Penny, and she tucked her little hand in mine. Together we walked with Lee toward the funeral home. The warm air inside whooshed out as I pulled the heavy door open. The familiar smell of roses and musk turned my stomach.

The foyer was nearly empty. Hushed voices floated through the air, and small handfuls of people huddled in groups.

"Why is no one here?" Penny whispered.

My heart sank. I remembered Uncle Bowlegs as a kind and soft-spoken man. A little odd, even for a townie. Neither a Sullivan nor a King, he was a staple in our community. Every day he'd walk the town in his Moon Boots, collecting cans or feeding the wildlife.

My eyes swept through the sparse crowd and recognized every single person in the room.

Except her.

I hastily signed the guestbook as Penny asked Lee a thousand questions about Uncle Bowlegs, my eyes tracking the unknown brunette weeping in the corner.

Outfitted in a formfitting black dress that swept just past her knees, an air of elegance swirled around her. The short sleeves fluttered around her slim biceps. The woman dabbed a tissue under her pert nose, and a soft sob escaped her again. I watched her take a shuddering breath before fresh tears leaked out from thick, dark lashes.

I leaned into Lee. "Who the hell is that?"

His gaze fell onto the stranger and he shrugged. "No clue."

"Daddy, I'm hungry." Penny pulled at my hand, and I looked down at her. Her eyes sliced toward the open casket.

Lee leaned down to her. "Are you starving . . . to *death*?" Mischief laced his tone as a cackle erupted from Penny. Heads turned in our direction.

I shot them each a warning glance as a hand clamped over her mouth, and Lee pulled his lips in to stifle his own laughter.

"I already paid my respects. I'll find Pickle a snack. You go ahead."

I looked at Penny to make sure she was okay with the plan, and when she laced her hand into Lee's, I knew she was relieved to not be going with me toward the casket. I nodded, and Lee brought Penny down the hallway toward the small room that would undoubtedly be filled with coffee and pastries.

As I made my way toward the front of the room, I couldn't help but watch the mysterious woman. I noticed others had started watching her too.

Deeply upset, the woman wept, silent sobs racking her body.

Did Bowlegs have a daughter?

Clearly a stunner like her wasn't some unidentified widow. Sure there were rumors he was secretly wealthy, but Bowlegs was an elderly man, and this woman was a knock-out. Surely she had her pick of any man.

With a sad shake of her head, the woman looked long-ingly at the casket a final time before turning. As she swept past me, our eyes locked.

My breath seized.

My heart hammered.

What the hell?

Time moved in slow motion as her mossy hazel eyes swept down, her wet lashes nearly touching the apples of her cheeks.

The wind was knocked straight out of me. My head spun. My blood was thick, and all she'd done was walk past me.

I watched her leave, and despite the alarm bells clanging in my skull, I silently followed. Down the darkened hallway, the woman stood across from Tootie and Bug. The aunties nodded as the mystery woman smiled.

Just like that, the weeping probably-not-a-widow was clear eyed and smiling kindly at the women. I hung toward the wall, feeling like a creeping asshole watching the three women talking in the dark hallway, but then it happened.

Tootie reached into her purse and placed a stack of bills into the woman's hand.

What. The. Actual. Fuck.

Pre-order One Look, book 1 of the Sullivan family series, on Amazon!

ACKNOWLEDGMENTS

To my readers, I felt compelled to make sure that I give a HUGE shout out to you first. Without you, none of this would be possible. Who knew Mafia cowboys could be so much FUN to write?! I am thrilled that you came on this journey with me. We're all busy and the fact that you take precious time out of your day to spend it with my characters means more to me than you will ever know. I love you all.

To my husband, thank you for always being the loudest cheerleader. You encourage me to chase down my dreams while also reminding me when to slow down. I couldn't do any of this without your love and support.

To my parents, I hope I make you proud. I never should have been afraid to tell you about my writing because in the time you've known, you both have been incredible supporters and champions of my work. Because of you, I dream fearlessly. I love you!

To my friend and assistant Leanne, thank you for knowing when I need you to reassure me and also when I need a swift kick. I trust you and your judgement. Thank you for sharing your time and always being a shoulder to lean on. I am so grateful to have you in my life.

To Elsie, I wouldn't want anyone else as my ride-or-die. Not only are you an amazing sprint partner, but you are an incredible human. I also get to tell everyone how hot my work wife is. So, you know, that's a plus.

To Kandi, I am grateful for your friendship every single

day. You are a breath of fresh air and a true light of goodness. I don't know what I ever did to deserve you, but I will always be glad we found each other! Thank you for always listening and being an incredible wealth of compassion and knowledge.

To Melanie, no words can express my gratitude for how much of yourselves you give to lifting others up. I would be lost in the sea of indie publishing had it not been for your guidance and encouragement.

To Nicole, you are a dream come true! Your eye for story is unrivaled and I love that we can talk books, home decor, and general procrastination. I look forward to our video chats and love that my hair and makeup can be a mess, but you love me anyway. I can't wait for us to be together in Seattle!

To Alyssa, thank you for being an incredible reader and supporter of indie authors. I love that we connected over books and when you posted your original song on Tiktok, I knew in my heart, it was Gemma's words coming to life! Your music gave Gemma a voice that is strong, beautiful, and powerful. Thank you for allowing me to use your music and to share it with my readers!

To Dani at Wildfire, thank you for your patience, knowledge, and attention. I'm beyond grateful to have you on my team!

To my editor James and proofreader Laetitia, my stories would be lost without you. Thank you for helping give them the polish they need to shine. You both push me to be a better writer and I am so grateful to have worked on Redemption Ranch with you.

Finally, to my ARC readers and street team, the Vixens will forever be a special and sacred place! Some of you have been on this journey from the beginning and I am so blessed you've been by my side. As we grow, we are only getting stronger and I am so glad it's a place where we support each other. Every post, shout out, and recommendation makes a huge difference and I am so thankful for each and every one of you!

HENDRIX HEARTTHROBS

Want to connect? Come hang out with the Hendrix Heartthrobs on Facebook to laugh & chat with Lena! Special sneak peeks, announcements, exclusive content, & general shenanigans all happen there.

Come join us at:
https://www.facebook.com/groups/lenahendrixread-ergroup!

ALSO BY LENA HENDRIX

Chikalu Falls

Finding You

Keeping You

Protecting You

Choosing You (origin novella)

Redemption Ranch

The Badge

The Alias

The Rebel

The Target

The Sullivans

One Taste (charity novella - early 2023)

One Look (Coming March 2023!)

ABOUT THE AUTHOR

Lena Hendrix is an Amazon Top 20 bestselling contemporary romance author living in the Midwest. Her love for romance stared with sneaking racy Harlequin paperbacks and now she writes her own hot-as-sin small town romance novels. Lena has a soft spot for strong alphas with marshmallow insides, heroines who clap back, and sizzling tension. Her novels pack in small town heart with a whole lotta heat.

When she's not writing or devouring new novels, you can find her hiking, camping, fishing, and sipping a spicy margarita!

Want to hang out? Find Lena on Tiktok or IG!

Printed in Great Britain
by Amazon

44486380R00219